The Legs Collector

Ted Tillotson

Evil often wears
many faces.

The Legs Collector

Published by Dragon Lair Books

Avenal, California

http://www.tedtillotsondragonlairbooks.com

First Edition: January/February 2014

Book design by Dragon Lair Books

ISBN 978-0615582443

Printed in the United States of America

Also By Ted Tillotson

Available on Amazon.com and other retail outlets

Deathmaker
A dark psychological thriller

Published by G&J Publishing
Palm Springs, CA

* * * *

The Magic Meadow
Kayla's fantasy

Published by
Dragon Lair Books

Avenal, California

* * * *

Thorns of the Rose
A contemporary love story

* * * *

Darkness – Demons and Light
Short story collection

* * * *

Time Gate Crossing
A Breach in the fabric of time

For

Barbara

My late wife
1949 to 2008

* * * *

Many thanks to my proof readers:

Marcia K. Feese

* * * *

James Callahan

* * * *

Norma Howell

* * * *
&

Gayle Farmer

Their collective input has been priceless.

~ ~ ~ ~ ~ ~

The black dragon is fully awake.

He stretches his huge wings.

The beast is hungry. It is now

time to feed again.

The Book of Dark Shadows

Chapter One

The First Mutilation

𝕳𝖆𝖗𝖉 𝖗𝖆𝖎𝖓 spattered against Michael's bedroom window with wind-driven fury.

Lightning flashed in the distance.

A few seconds later a clap of thunder rattled the glass.

Each flare of white-hot electricity revealed Mickey's image in the dresser's mirror. He hated the nickname, but his mother would never call him Michael. She taunted him. *Mickey, Mickey, Mickey Mouse—that's who you are, and will always be! Stupid, Mickey Mouse.*

Another jagged strike reflected an image of his mother standing behind him. *You've been worthless since you were born!*

Her scolding voice echoed in His head.

"Shut up, Mother! You're dead twelve years—leave me alone."

The next rolling thunder covered Michael's painful scream, "Stay dead!"

He fell back on the bed and covered his eyes.

* * * *

When Mrs. Elizabeth Moran passed on, Michael inherited the fourteen room Victorian and a substantial family fortune. The old house was in good repair and Michael kept it up. He worked at home.

He had just turned thirty-six, was in excellent health, and independent.

* * * *

At the far end of the, hospital-clean, basement. Michael had built a medium sized operating room. He hadn't gone to the expense required for an EKG monitor, Resuscitator, or the services of an anesthetist. There was no need, his patients would never feel a thing when he started cutting.

* * * *

"It'll all be over soon, Mary Jane." He tied on a surgical mask, as if it mattered, scrubbed his hands, air-dried, and snapped on a pair of latex gloves.

"Ready?" The would be, Dr. Michael Moran smiled. "I assure you, Ms. Ott, I've spared no expense on top of the line instruments." The information didn't matter to the woman, she was already dead.

* * * *

CRYSTAL PIER
4500 OCEAN BLVD.
SAN DIEGO, CA
MONDAY - 7:30 AM:

Special Victims Detective Matt Kellogg, an athletic looking, sixteen-year veteran homicide cop, squatted beside the body.

At six foot two, and rugged in appearance, he seemed younger than his thirty-nine years.

"This looks like a shark attack."

"If it is, the fish had training in surgical procedures." Medical Examiner Judy Wake, an attractive, thirty-something, African American, stood, waved at the two men from the coroner's office and made a note on her clipboard. "I called you guys because the vic has ligature marks on her neck and wrists."

SVU Detective Ken Black, slightly overweight, and acting irritated, joined them. He had ten years with the San Diego PD, and looked older than his thirty-five years. He opened his notebook. "Any sign of sexual assault, Doc?"

"I won't know until I get her on the table. The woman's been in the water for about four hours." She bent down and zipped up the black bag. "That young couple over there, with the patrol officers, saw the body in the surf and called it in. Then I got word from downtown saying they had a floater. The minute I saw the vic, I notified CSI. Two techs from the lab showed up and took pictures all around."

Kellogg looked at his partner. "The vic had her legs cut off and was dumped under the pier. The crime scene is somewhere else. Sexual violation or not, It's our case."

Ken looked at the ME. "Anything official on cause of death?"

Dr. Wake stepped aside to let the body bag crew have the corpse. "Strangulation is a good call. I can't be sure until I get inside."

Matt lit a cigarette. "Give us a call."

* * * *

MONDAY– 8:30 AM
GROSSMONT
SHOPPING CENTER
LA MESA, CA
STARBUCKS:

The counter girl smiled and handed Sally
Patterson her usual Cappuccino and said,
"How was your special weekend behind the
scenes at the zoo?"
"It was the most fantastic experience with
animals I've ever had."
"Great! We'll have lunch and you can tell
me all about it."
"I have pictures—I got to pet a cheetah!"
"Oh my God! Can we do lunch today?"
"Yes, let's meet at Hooleys." Sally
beamed with pride. "I have more news."
"You met a new hunk?"
"I wish. My promotion came through at
PETCO. I'll tell you about it at lunch."
"That's great, I want to hear all the details."

Michael had gone to the center hunting for
another victim. He sat at a small table near
the front of the coffee shop and heard every

word of Sally's conversation. She turned him on. He smiled and sipped his latté. *Sally, deciding to wear a short skirt this Monday morning was your fatal mistake.* He admired the shape, form and tone of the young woman's beautiful tanned legs. *I believe you and I are going to get to know each other.*

* * * *

SDPD–SQUADROOM–11:30 AM
SPECIAL VICTIMS UNIT:

Matt's desk phone rang, he picked up on the second ring. "Kellogg. What've you got?" He made a note. "Thanks, we'll be right there."

Ken got up from his desk and pulled his jacket off the back of the chair. "That was Judy, right?"

"She has a COD on our vic and an ID."

"I guess we're going to the morgue."

"That's where they keep the cold ones."

"Including those without legs."

"Ken, sometimes your humor sucks."

* * * *

Michael browsed around the *PETCO* store and then waited out front until he saw Sally leave. He followed her to *Hooleys* where she met up with her friend. The eatery was just a short walk away. *Such great legs.*

* * * *

GROSSMONT CENTER 12:45 PM:
HOOLEYS RESTRAUNT:

Sally and Lauren, were having a good time enjoying lunch. Their animated conversation was not difficult to hear.

"You wouldn't believe what it's like behind the scenes at the zoo."

Lauren bubbled with excitement. "The cheetah—weren't you afraid?"

"Not for a second. The handler was right there. I scratched the cat's neck and he purred like a kitten, only a lot louder."

"I'm so happy for you. Does your promotion change anything?"

"Nope, I'm in at the same time, out at five thirty and off on weekends."

Michael smiled and took a bite of his *calamari* taco. *I'm happy for you too, Sally. It will be so nice to have your legs.*

* * * *

KEARNEY MESA– SAN DIEGO
CITY/COUNTY MORGUE
SAME TIME:

Dr. Wake pulled the sheet down. "Your vic is Mary Jane Ott, twenty-eight."

"COD?" Ken studied the face of the dead woman.

"It was death by strangulation. The perp used some kind of rubber tubing, or a pair of pantyhose."

Matt bent down to get a closer look. "Why do you say that?"

Judy drew her finger across the vic's throat. "The ligature marks are consistent with a material that would stretch or give as it was pulled around the neck. Ordinary rope wouldn't do that, and it would've left burn marks."

"Were her wrists bound the same way?"

"No, he used some type of rope." She raised Mary Jane's left arm from under the sheet so Ken could see the difference. "The abrasions are slightly smaller and the burns are obvious."

"You sure CSI got pictures of all this?"

"They did, and I shot close ups here. They're all bagged as evidence."

Matt said, "Evidence of a murder without a clue regarding who did the killing." He thought a moment. "What'd you find on defensive wounds?"

"There aren't any." Judy exposed the vic's right hand. "She has long, acrylic nails. If she had fought the killer, or scratched him, there would be some tissue under her nails. I found nothing, or any bruising on her knuckles. Whoever killed her had complete control."

Ken said, "You mean like, drugged?"

"That's exactly what I mean. The lab ran a tox-screen on the vic's blood. It came back positive for traces of *Rohypnol."*

Matt opened his notebook and wrote the chemical name. "That's a date rape drug."

Wake re-covered the vic's body. "It caught me by surprise. Date rape drugs are usually ingested and take time to work." She removed her latex gloves. "I found nothing in the vic's stomach revealing any drugs, so I ordered the blood work. Your vic was *injected* with the drug and it would've knocked her out almost instantly."

Matt said, "May I?"

"Go ahead."

He lifted the sheet off the woman's right arm and studied her wrist. "I'm wondering, which was done first?"

"Does it matter?"

"It helps give me a little insight into the killer."

"Judging from the forensics, I'd have to say he tied the hands first. The bruising would be less otherwise."

Ken jotted a note. "How so, Doc?"

"It would take time to complete the strangulation and remove the tubing, or pantyhose. The Vic's heart would've stopped pumping blood when he got to the hands and ankles. I'm guessing he tied those too."

Matt covered the woman's right arm and said, "You've called the perp *he* several times, why?"

"I saved the worst for last. There's vaginal and anal tearing and the acts were performed post mortem. He used a condom. There are no fluids."

Ken made another note. "This maniac is a necrophile."

"And he's medically savvy. I said so at the scene. Your perp removed Ms. Ott's legs with a surgeon's skill."

"As I said earlier, the pier was the dump spot. Not the crime scene." Matt took a last look at Mary Jane. "Thanks, Doc."

"Anytime, gentlemen. Tony has all the paperwork at the lab."

"You're a peach."

"So I've been told."

* * * *

HOOLEYS
GROSSMONT CENTER
1:30 PM:

Sally picked up the lunch check. "It's my treat to celebrate my promotion."

Lauren finished her green tea. "I'm so proud of you. It's been tough, but you did it, girl."

"Yeah … I guess, but I lost Nick in the process."

"True, but wasn't he more about *Nick* than he was about you?"

Sally nodded.

"It turned out that way."

"I don't want to be an alarmist, but there's a man two tables behind you who's been watching us."

"Is he good looking?"

"Yes."

"Then there's hope yet."

"Don't turn around. There's something I don't like."

"What?"

"He's the same dude who was eyeing you at the coffee shop this morning. I didn't say anything then because I wasn't sure. Now, I am."

"You sure it's the same guy?"

"Positive—I don't like the feel of this."

"I'm going to look."

"Don't."

She turned around anyway.

Michael smiled.

The ladies got up and left the table.

Michael enjoyed every move of Sally's legs as she and Lauren walked toward the cashier.

* * * *

SDPD - CRIME LAB:

Chief Technician, Tony Gonzales got up from his work station to greet Matt. He handed Kellogg a file folder. "Everything you need is in there. I ran her through DMV. Ms. Ott's address is, 5924 Severin Drive, La Mesa."

Matt sat on the edge of a work table. "Anything else?"

"Insurance information says Mary Jane owns a late model Honda Civic. Cal vanity plate, MJ Ott 97, and She's a donor, but that's moot, the four-hour window is closed."

Ken grinned. "I believe the vic has already donated the only pair of legs she had."

The other two men stared at him.

Matt closed the folder. "Black, you're a sick puppy." He held up the file. "Thanks, Tony." To Ken he said, "C'mon, numb nuts.

We're on our way to La Mesa PD."

THE OLD VICTORIAN
AT THAT SAME TIME:

Michael came up from the cellar and saw Samantha standing in the doorway. "You startled me." He nearly dropped the basket of women's clothes with Mary Jane's purse riding on top. "How many times have I told you not to ever, ever sneak up on me?"

Sam's blue eyes did not smile.

"I know, you want supper and I'm running late." He carried the basket down the hallway and into a large bedroom. His father spent the last six months of his life dying there. Finally, colon cancer claimed him.

When Michael stepped into the hall, Samantha was waiting.

"You're starting to make me angry and you don't want to do that." He hesitated. "All right, c'mon, I'll fix dinner before you faint from hunger. Fat chance of that happening."

The cat swished her tail and trotted along behind.

Michael looked down at the animal. "If you're good tonight, I'll bring home treats."

Sam went right to her food dish.
Michael grinned. "I believe Sally will be sweeter than Mary Jane."

The gray and white cat licked her chops.

Chapter Two

Return from La Mesa

SDPD - SQUADROOM - 4:30 PM
SPECIAL VICTIMS UNIT:

Captain Roy Sawyer walked into the room from his office the second the detectives came in. "How did it go over in the East County?"

Matt went straight to his desk. He held up his notebook. "I need to make a few calls."

Detective Black opened his notepad, gestured toward his desk and walked in that direction. "Well, to start with, it's a brutal killing." He sat at his desk. "Cause of death was strangulation. The vic had been sodomized and there is evidence of vaginal and anal tearing."

"What the hell are we dealing with?"

"I'd have to say, your basic, home-grown, necrophile, Captain."

"Just what we need. You two know the drill."

"Add to it, the perp must have a thing for women's legs." He hesitated. "Our vic had both of hers surgically removed."

Sawyer checked his watch. "Okay, this is going over the top. What do we have on the perp?"

Ken leaned back in his chair. "At the moment, we're in limbo and have nothing, nada, zip."

"Not so." Matt looked up from his desk. "The beach patrol found Ms. Ott's Honda in a parking lot near the pier. I ordered a tow."

Sawyer said, "Maybe we'll catch a break." He looked at the detectives. "Are we going to have a problem with the La Mesa PD?"

"I doubt it." Ken pushed his chair up to his desk. "Lieutenant Howard made it clear that unless the crime had been committed in his jurisdiction, he doesn't want any part of it."

Matt slipped into his sports coat. "We sealed the vic's apartment after the crime team did their job. Everything was in perfect order; no sign of foul play. The complex manager told us the woman lived alone and he never saw her with anyone, male or female."

Ken put his notebook away. "Maybe it's nothing, but it struck me as odd that there are no family pictures of any kind and no next of kin. I found that out at the manager's office. The rental agreement requires a list of relatives. Ms. Ott checked none."

Captain Sawyer looked at his watch again. "I'm not going to authorize overtime on this for now. It's past five anyway. Maybe we'll get lucky with the Honda." He paused and tapped his chin. "You two start a murder book on this case and be damn sure all the details are accurate. Pack it in for the night. We'll start fresh tomorrow at eight sharp. Things always look better in the morning."

THE VICTORIAN CELLAR
THIRTY MINUTES EARLIER:

Michael stepped out of the walk-in freezer, closed the door and checked the wall clock. "Just an hour and half, my lovely Sally, then we meet face-to-face." He took off his white lab coat and hung it in a closet just outside the custom built operating room.

Mickey, what you're going to do is bad, very bad!

An image of his dead mother sat on the stainless steel operating table.

The room became ice cold.

"Shut up, Mother."

You've killed innocent women, Mickey, you'll have to answer for that.

He ran into the room and grabbed for the apparition. It vanished. "Stay out of my life, you old bitch."

Michael leaned on the edge of the table and shuddered.

Old images played across his troubled mind.

* * * *

Two days after his father's funeral, he sat in the living room with his mother. Mrs. Moran shook her head. "I knew you'd fail the moment you were accepted in the medical program."

"I never wanted to be a doctor from the day dad decided that I should follow in his footsteps."

"Your father was good to you, Mickey. He died believing you were studying medicine. The poor man was proud of you without knowing that you had quit, given up."

"I didn't want to disappoint him, and he was nowhere near poor in the least."

"No, he wasn't. Your father's surgical practice flourished. He wanted the best for you and you let him down, Mickey."

"Stop it. You know I hate that name."

"You're a failure, Mickey, a complete flop."

* * * *

Michael shook off the memory and looked at the clock again. "Four thirty. I have an hour, that shouldn't be much of a problem."

He crossed the basement and climbed the stairs rather than take the lift to the kitchen.

Samantha greeted him when he opened the door. "Hi, Sam." He reached down and petted the cat. "I have a date with Sally tonight. She doesn't know it yet, but she'll have the best time of her life."

Without response, the feline followed her master down the hall and into his bedroom.

* * * *

BREE MANOR
EL CAJON, CA
APT 124 5:45 PM:

Detective Kellogg studied the entries he had made in the murder book. He lit a smoke and sat back from his desk. "Ann, could you fix us a really stiff drink? I'm ready"

"I've read your mind, my love, and here we are." Sergeant Ann Beck brought two gin and tonics to Matt's home work station. "I guess you and Ken caught a good one."

"We did, I'm going to ask the captain to put you and your partner on the case to help with the investigation."

"Fine by me, I'm sure Jack will be delighted."

* * * *

GROSSMONT CENTER
AT THE SAME TIME:

Michael waited patiently in his Mercedes. He got lucky finding a spot facing the *PETCO* storefront. "Don't keep me waiting, Sally."

A moment later, Ms. Patterson appeared at one of the checkout counters and talked with the young woman on duty.

"Cut the chatter," whispered Michael. "You're wasting time." He started the car and checked all three mirrors for possible shoppers who might bear witness.

Ms. Patterson came out of the store and headed straight for a nearby row of parked cars.

Naughty girl. Employees are supposed to

*park farther away and save the choice spots
for the daily throng of paying customers.*

Michael backed out and kept Sally in sight.
She approached a blue Toyota. He pulled up
behind the small car and got out.

"Excuse me, I'm a little lost. Can you direct
me to the *Sears* store?"

Sally unlocked her car and opened the
driver's door. "You're in the wrong center.
Sears is in *Westfield Plaza* in El Cajon." She
took a quick breath. "You're the guy who was
at *Hooleys.*"

"Very observant." He was on her before
she could get into her vehicle.

"What do you want?"

He pulled the syringe from the pocket of his
leather jacket, jerked the cap off the needle,
and plunged it into Sally's neck. "I want your
legs, those beautiful, long legs."

She struggled in his arms. "Let me go!" She
began to get limp. "I'm falling!"

"I got you, you're safe now."

Images of co-workers and animals from
the zoo slipped across Sally's clouded mind.
Lauren's face appeared, wavered and faded
into total darkness.

Michael held her up, put her in the front
seat of his Mercedes and latched the seatbelt.
"Okay, Ms. Sally, enjoy your nap."

He went back to the Toyota, took the keys

out of the door, grabbed Sally's purse and dropped them into it. He pushed down on the door lock and closed it. "I bet it'll be forty-eight to seventy-two hours before your car is found."

* * * *

BREE MANOR
APT 124 6:30 PM:

Matt closed the murder book and finished bringing Ann up to speed on the Mary Jane Ott case. "I believe this crime sets a precedent for SVU."

She sipped her drink. "For the unit, yes it does, but not for the department."

"How So?"

"Eighteen months ago, before SVU was set up, I worked out of robbery-homicide in the North County Division. Jack and I had just become partners and we caught the first of four gross mutilation type of killings."

"Right, I do remember a case like that up in Rancho Bernardo. I think they called it the golf course murders or something like that."

"You're close. We labeled it, *The Oaks North File.* The victims legs were dumped in bushes near the maintenance building on the back nine. There were four murders in all. Every vic was female and the perp had skillfully removed their feet and left the legs."

"If memory serves, the perp is still in the wind."

"Exactly and the killings stopped. We had several possible suspects, including the greens keepers, but no one had any medical training. "Not one, but the footless legs tell me that the same killer is back."

"Didn't it seem strange that all the victims' legs were dumped in the same place?"

Ann went to the kitchen to refresh her drink. "The first two had me going nuts. Then I realized what the perp was up to."

"He hated something about the golf course or maybe owners and management."

"Actually, you're pretty close. You want another drink?"

"I'm good, thanks."

She came back from the kitchen and joined Matt at his desk. "It took a while to get a handle on it. The perp knew something about a crime scene." She stirred the drink with her index finger. "The immediate area was, of course, ground zero, but the killer knew that we'd shut down the back nine for the duration, which turned out to be ten days." She took a sip of her drink. "The thing is, like the case you just caught, it was a dump site."

Matt pushed away from the keyboard. "That's a lot of lost revenue for Oaks North."

"Several thousand bucks a day. I believe it was the perp's intent. Two days after we closed the site another footless, female leg turned up in the same place. That's the way it played out with each of the victims."

"I'd bet we're dealing with the same perp and a change in MO."

"You may be right. I'll pull the cold case files in the morning and we'll go from there."

"Sounds like a plan. That's tomorrow. Right now, I'm taking you to *Red Lobster* for a huge glutton's seafood feast."

"I think that's a great idea, Mr. Kellogg."

* * * *

THE VICTORIAN CELLAR
AT THAT SAME TIME:

The elevator doors opened into Michael's spotless basement. "Just a few minutes more, Sally and you'll be at peace forever." He pushed the wheelchair into the operating room and locked the wheels. "Relax, Ms. Patterson you have nothing to fear."

Sally's struggle was fruitless. "What are you going to do to me?"

"For starters, I'll be enjoying your legs."

"Please don't hurt me. I've done nothing to you."

"Be still, you're not going to feel a thing." He lifted Sally out of the wheelchair and laid her on the stainless steel table. "Can you move your arms or those lovely legs?"

"No, I can't."

"That's a good sign. You're an excellent patient. Now I can prep you for surgery."

"Oh my God!" Sally tried to move her arms and legs, but they wouldn't budge. "Please don't cut me."

"You made the mistake of wearing a short skirt and exposing your great, long legs. You wanted them seen. You were showing off and once I saw them I had to have both all to myself."

Sally started to cry and the tears blurred her vision. "Who are you?" She managed to raise her head and see the fuzzy image of a man wearing a surgical mask. "Are you a doctor?"

"Surgeon, Sally. You might say a real specialist. My expertise is amputating pretty legs from young women who can't resist putting theirs on display."

"I'm sorry. I didn't mean to offend you."

"No offense. Actually, your legs aroused me quite a bit. That's why you flaunt them isn't it?"

"Please, let me go, I promise not to tell anyone."

"That's a nice gesture, but unnecessary. I know you won't tattle on me."

"No, I never will. Please let me go."

"I believe you." Michael picked up a three foot length of rubber tubing from a tray of instruments near the operating table. "It's time for you to go to sleep."

"What are you doing?"

"Easy, in just a moment or two you'll be in heaven or hell. Of course that depends on the life you've been leading. My guess is, there's a place for you in heaven."

"Please, I don't want to die!"

"That doesn't matter." He put the tubing around her neck, tied a simple knot and pulled it tight. "Goodbye, Sally ... rest well."

Her arms and legs moved in random spasms. The woman's open eyes bulged and hemorrhaged internally.

"Good girl. Rest in peace." He left the ligature in place and closed Sally's eyelids.

"Now, those shapely legs."

* * * *

BALBOA PARK
SAN DIEGO, CA
Tuesday 3:30 AM:

Security officer, Andy Walker came around the fountain in his golf cart and spotted someone sitting in a wheelchair in front of the Aero Space Museum. When he got closer he could see it was a woman.

"Excuse me, Miss. The park is closed. The exhibits open at 10:00 AM."

No response.

Andy stopped near the wheelchair. "Did you hear me, Ma'am?"

A gust of wind blew strands of long, dark hair away from the woman's face.

"Holy Mary, Mother of Christ!"

He got out of the cart and approached the chair.

The woman's head had been tied to a make-shift support to appear as though she were sitting upright.

"I can't believe this." He shined his light over the corpse. The dead woman had a blanket across her lap. Andy pulled the cover away and threw it off the body. "Oh my God." He went back to the golf cart and called it in.

"Three-six to base, over."

Go ahead, Andy.

"Get SDPD here, ASAP!"

What's the problem?

"I have a dead woman in a wheelchair in front of the Space Center."

What?

"You heard me. And her legs have been cut off."

* * * *

THIRTY MINUTES LATER
BALBOA PARK
THE DROP SITE:

Detectives Kellogg and Black joined *ME* Judy Wake at the entrance to the Aero Space Museum. Ken said, "I wish this perp kept normal hours." He called to one of the two CSI lab techs who were folding up the wheelchair. "Ray, did you lift any good prints?"

"A few latent thumb and palm prints, but they've been compromised. I'm sure the perp wore latex. Most of the prints are smudged."

"That's no surprise. Nor is the fact that this isn't the crime scene."

"I can't argue with that. We have two body drops in two days and I hope it isn't what it looks like. There's an identical MO, and this time with a prop." Ray spoke to his assistant. "Put the chair in the van, we're done here."

Ken said, "Hang on, Bill, we'll take it."

"It has to go to the lab, Detective."

"Not so." Kellogg stepped toward the young man. "Leave it; we'll bring it back later. Did you get enough pictures?"

"Yes sir, plenty of the vic and the chair."

"Good. That's all you need for right now. We'll be responsible for the chair."

The assistant shrugged. "Is that okay?"

Ray said, "Fine with me."

Flashing blue and red lights from two black and white cop cars bathed the immediate area in alternating, erratic shadows and color.

Kellogg watched the CSI van drive away and shuddered. *This is just the beginning of a full blown nightmare.*

Dr. Wake zipped up the body bag. "The killer is on a roll and he has an agenda." She waved at the two coroner's assistants. "Take her to my lab and drop the paperwork on the desk."

"You want it in the fridge?"

"Yes, and leave her in the bag."

"You got it, Doc."

She looked at the two men. "Dave."

"Yes?"

"Neither you nor your partner know anything beyond a routine body pick up. Are we clear with that?"

"Absolutely. Mum's the word."

"Great, I'll be back in my office in about two

hours. Do I need to remind you that what you have in the bag cannot be leaked to the media?"

"No, Ma'am, not a single whisper."

"Good. Get her out of here."

Detective Kellogg stood by the empty wheelchair. "Judy, did you get a load of this?" He patted the right arm of the chair.

"What is it?" She shined her flashlight where Matt was pointing. "It's a rental."

"Exactly, and it has a La Mesa address. Are we catching a break on this case or what?"

Ken approached the uniformed officers. "Who's in charge here?"

The Lieutenant stepped away from his radio car. "I am, Karl Margolis, supervisor."

"Pleased to meet you." They shook hands. "Thanks for your quick response. You and your guys got here before we did. I'll put in a word with your watch commander."

"We don't usually get a call like this."

"Understood. I'm sure you're aware of what we have here."

"Absolutely, and I know what you're going to tell me."

"And that is?"

Margolis grinned. "We file our reports at the end of shift, and none of it needs to go on the overnight blotter."

"Good man. The last thing we need is the media getting onto this mayhem before we can sort out the details."

"I agree, and my officers will be so instructed."

Kellogg came up to the lieutenant. "It's imperative that we keep a lid on what we have here and your watch commander needs to be advised."

"Consider it done. If we're through here, we need to get back on patrol."

Kellogg shook the lieutenant's hand. "We're on the same page, thank you."

Margolis hesitated. "Are we looking at a serial killer here?"

"As of this morning's incident, I'd say that's exactly what we have on our hands."

"I was afraid of that. Okay, Detectives, we're going back on the street."

Ken said, "Thanks again, and take care." The patrol units cut their flashing lights and left the scene.

Kellogg scribbled a few notes and looked at Judy and Ken. "Let's get some breakfast and hit *East County Medical Equipment Rentals* when they open."

Judy put her case and clipboard in her car. "You're on. Sausage and pancakes."

Matt closed her driver's door. "Your breakfast is on me."

Chapter Three

Speculation

DENNY'S RESTRAUNT
KEARNEY MESA–5:30 AM:

𝕸𝖊𝖉𝖎𝖈𝖆𝖑 𝕰𝖝𝖆𝖒𝖎𝖓𝖊𝖗 Judy Wake finished
the last of her scrambled eggs and took a sip
of coffee. "I didn't expect to be having
breakfast so early, but then, I'll be done with
the autopsy before lunch."

Detective Black buttered a second slice of
his whole wheat toast. "The number of prints
Ray got off that wheelchair surprised me."

Matt pushed his empty plate away and
opened his notebook. "What's your estimate
of prints?"

Ken bit off a piece of toast and nodded.
"Ray lifted twelve index and six palms off the
chair's arms. Most of them were smudged."

Detective Kellogg made a note. "The best thing from the chair is the location of the rental place."

"Chances are, we'll find out its stolen." Ken waved at the waitress for more coffee.

Matt pointed to his cup and smiled at the young girl. "Judy, you want a refill?"

"I'm fine, thanks." She hesitated. "How does someone steal a wheelchair? I don't recall seeing one sitting out in the open where it could be snatched."

The young woman said, "Judy, you sure on the coffee?"

"Yeah, I'm done."

Christy smiled. "Let's see, we have the ME and two detectives having breakfast before daybreak. You guys come here a lot, but not this early. Do we have breaking news in the making?"

Matt grinned. "We're just getting an early start on the day."

"I'll bet. You want anything else?"

Ken said, "No thanks, just the check."

"Okay, you all have a great day."

Matt waited until Christy got out of earshot.

"We're dealing with a perp who has an inflated ego. He's playing us." He put a packet of powdered creamer in his brew. "To answer Judy's question, our killer is crafty. It's obvious he wants attention. He may have rented the chair himself, or was in the right place to grab it."

Ken took a sip of coffee. "I put my money on theft."

Judy slipped out of the booth. "Gentlemen, I'm off. There's a Jane Doe waiting for me in the lab. You two have a productive morning."

Matt said, "I got the check. We'll probably see you late this afternoon."

She said, "By then, I'm sure Tony will have an ID on the victim."

Ken slid over in the booth. "I didn't catch it when you bagged the vic's hands. Anything stand out?"

"I'll know more in about two hours, but there were no defensive wounds. I'll see what I get from a closer look."

"You're nothing but the best."

"And you are trying for points."

"You got that right." He waved and smiled, then turned to Matt. "You were saying the perp is playing us."

"The wheelchair and the body, what's left of it, were meant to be found."

Ken bit into another piece of toast. "He dumped the first body under the pier. It may *not* have been found."

"That was an attempt to throw us off. This psycho is sharp, he wants our attention. Planting the wheelchair in front of the Space

Center was risky, and took some guts. He only had a short window between the security guard's rounds to get there and get out without being seen."

"Then he had to be aware of the security routine."

"In and out, and he knew he could pull it off."

Ken thought a moment and put more butter on his last slice of toast. "If you're right, I believe we have another problem."

"Because?"

"Our, Mr. Nut case is seeking more attention than just ours."

"Exactly. How many people outside of our team know about the killings?"

"Okay, we have the young couple who found the first vic. There's the coroner's body-bag guys, they've seen two bodies within forty-eight hours."

"Right, I don't trust them on any level. Now we have the security guard who found the wheelchair."

Ken added, "Our waitress, who picked up on us being here at an unusual early hour."

Matt finished his coffee. "We'll be lucky if both murders aren't leaked before the six o'clock news."

"It's not really our concern, is it?"

Matt made a note in his pad. "If these

killings get media attention now, it will launch a panic. We'll have women all over San Diego County fearing for their lives."

"Not so, Matthew, it may be a deterrent to another abduction."

"I'm not following you."

"Young women with great legs will be frightened into wearing slacks and keeping them covered. The perp can't see their legs, so the ladies become safer. The killer will be frustrated."

Matt picked up the check and climbed out of the booth. "You may actually have a valid point."

"Thank you, I believe I do, but we need to bait the nut."

"And, we do that how?"

"Put undercover women on the street. Let them flaunt their great legs and draw the guy into the trap."

They walked to the cashier and Matt paid. On the way out he said, "You're talking *street walkers?*"

"Of course not." He held the door. "We use female cops with good legs to work a mall and public places."

"Sometimes, Ken, I'm sure you've lost most of your marbles. The chances of nailing the perp with your suggestion is as possible as winning the lottery tomorrow."

"It was just a thought."

"Pure investigation and good police work, Ken, that's how we nail his ass."

"You may be right, but the story will get leaked to the media—count on it."

Matt held the door for two men coming in from the rapidly filling parking lot. He nodded. To Ken he said, "Let's get over to the East County and check that rental place."

"It's ten after six. We got close to four hours before it opens."

"I'll bet there's an emergency number on the front door or in the Window and we'll use it."

Ken grinned. "You intend to roust the owner?"

"He or she needs to get an early start this morning, we did."

* * * *

THE VICTORIAN
TWO HOURS LATER:

Michael read through the local section of the San Diego Union Tribune for the third time. He folded the paper and slapped it on the kitchen table next to his breakfast plate.

"Damn!"

Samantha looked up from her place

setting at the other end of the table.

"Dammit to hell!" He shook his head and spread strawberry jam on the bottom half of a toasted English muffin. "It's the second day, Sam, and there's nothing in the paper about the lovely Ms. Ott, or the PETCO Queen, Sally Patterson. But then, the press wouldn't have that story in time for this morning's edition."

The cat continued eating a chunk of rare meat.

"I was there when that young couple found the body and called the police." He took a bite of muffin. "I saw them, Sam." Michael poured fresh coffee into his china cup. "The cops are not releasing the stories to the media and that's pissing me off!"

Sam pulled a piece of meat off her plate and started chomping into it on the place mat.

"Don't eat like that, keep your food on your plate or I won't let you dine at the table."

The feline paid no attention and kept munching her breakfast on the mat.

"Did I get that too rare for you? I fixed it the same as mine. I believe it should taste better than your canned beef and gravy." He forked a slice of meat from his plate and chewed it. "It's perfect, Sam, I don't want to hear any complaints."

She finished eating and lapped some

cream from a bowl with her name on it.

"Good girl." He ate another bite. "As soon as I finish the dishes, I'm calling the Tribune." Michael tapped the folded paper. "I'll light a fire under their asses about two hot stories they're not getting." He sipped coffee "I might even give them a hint as to what's yet to come."

Samantha jumped down from the table and went out to the cat box on the back porch.

* * * *

EAST COUNTY MEDICAL
EQUIPMENT RENTALS
7:30 AM:

Owner, Mrs. Alice Foster, put Matt's business card in a small accordion-type folder near the register. "Like I said, Detective, there's no rush to get my chair back."

"We appreciate your cooperation, Mrs. Foster." He handed her a receipt. "I'm sorry for dragging you in so early."

"That's not a problem, young man. I'm pleased to know the police are doing their job."

Ken studied the name on the rental papers. "How do you pronounce the renter's last name?"

"It has a ring to it. ELLIS – TAN – NOVICK. Not VICH as in ITCH. Fred Elistanovick."

"Thank you, I'll be sure to say it right."

"Please tell him I didn't send you."

Matt put one of her cards in his notebook and closed it. "Just a couple of routine questions. Somebody stole the wheelchair and we need to look into it."

"You boys have a nice day."

"Thank you for your help." Matt nodded and followed Ken out the door. When they reached the parking lot he pulled out his cell. "I'll bring the captain up to speed."

Ken said, "This Elistano—whoever, is a dead lead."

"You never know, Partner. Yeah, hi Ann, put me through to the boss."

"He just came in." She hesitated. "Is there another Jane Doe?"

"Are you clairvoyant?" He tossed the keys to Ken and climbed into the black Crown Vic. "We caught it this morning at about 3:30. Judy called us out."

"Same MO?"

"To the letter. Our perp's on a roll. He parked the vic in a wheelchair in front of the Space Center in Balboa Park. A security guard found her. Wake's doing an autopsy now."

"A wheelchair? Where are you?"

"La Mesa. We tracked the chair to a medical equipment rental place. CSI took a set of prints to the lab and we have the name and address of the person who rented the chair. We're going to have a chat with him now."

"You gotta get me and Jack on this. I promise you, it's connected to the unsolved *Oaks North* murders and we have all the evidence you need."

"I want you involved and I'm positive the captain will agree."

"Excellent. Sawyer's at his desk now. Hang on, I'll buzz him."

"Thanks, I'm sure he'll love the news."

"Matt?"

"What?"

"We're going to nail this sonofabitch to the shit house wall!"

"That's a colorful thought."

"The captain's picking up."

"We'll do lunch."

"Got it."

"Sawyer."

"Morning, Cap. It's Matt."

"Don't tell me."

"We caught another one. Same MO, dropped off in a wheelchair at the Space Center. She was found by a security guard."

"Jesus H. Christ!"

"Judy has her and we have prints."

"Where the hell are you?"

"On the way to interview the wheelchair renter."

"I want a tight lid on this."

"Tight as we can keep it." Matt cleared his throat. "I'm requesting Sergeants Towne and Beck to be assigned to the case. They have evidence and information from similar unsolved murders in the North County. We believe they're connected."

"You have something going with Beck?"

"Not so's you'd notice."

"Okay, Kellogg, it's all in your lap. You'd better have all your ducks in a row. When the Chief of Detectives gets wind of this, and that will be soon, he'll be on my ass with boots and spurs."

"I understand, sir."

"Do you? Shit rolls downhill."

"We'll nail this asshole."

"You better hope that happens real soon."

"Thank you, Captain."

"For what? I just authorized you to hang yourself."

"Copy that. We're due for a break."

"Get to work, Detective."

"We're on it, sir."

Chapter Four

Michael Contacts the Press

Ken pulled onto the 125 connector and headed toward Lemon Grove. "Matt, you're a case."

"What?"

"You shovel more shit than my dear departed uncle did when he worked his ass off on his dairy farm."

* * * *

THE OLD VICTORIAN
AT THAT SAME TIME:

Michael finished loading the dishwasher, rinsed his hands under warm water and dried them on a fresh kitchen towel. He folded it and hung it over the chrome handle.

Samantha came in from the back porch and jumped up on the counter

"Know what, Sam? I'm tired of not getting noticed for my excellent work."

The cat purred and rubbed her face against Michael's arm.

"Thank you for understanding. It's time I let this world know just who I am and what I can and will do."

Sam nuzzled his arm again.

"Treats, you want treats? Well, my lovely, you shall have them." He went to a nearby cupboard and brought down a package of dried morsels sealed in a plastic baggie. "These have been preserved from my foot removals in the North County." He opened the baggie and gave Sam a few crispy pieces.

"Is that tasty?"

She crunched away at her treats and swished her tail with delighted approval.

"Very soon, Detective Matthew Kellogg and his lame team will know who they're dealing with. Yes, I know who Matt is and his

SPECIAL VICTIM'S UNIT. What a crock they are."

Samantha ate the rest of her treats and jumped down off the counter. She scurried off to her kitty bed near Michael's recliner.

He went to his den and set out the electronic device that would alter his voice. He hooked it up to an untraceable cell phone and dialed the San Diego Union newsroom.

"Tribune, City-Desk, How may I direct your call?"

"I wish to speak with one of your crime reporters."

"Just a moment, sir. Will you hold please."

"Yes, I will."

The switchboard operator buzzed Hal Marks.

"Yeah, what is it?"

"I have a nut with a weird voice who wants a crime reporter."

"Are you serious?"

"Yes, I am."

"Put him through."

"This is Hal Marks, how can I be of service?"

"Want a great murder story?"

"Okay, right off, you're losing me with the electronic voice. I talk to people not machines."

"Watch your smart mouth, Hal, I have the

details on two brutal murder stories you're not getting because the cops are keeping them under wraps."

"Are you for real?"

"Keep fucking with me and I'll dump the mother load on radio and TV and you'll be sucking hind tit!"

"Okay. I'm going to record this call. You'll hear a beep."

"I love beeps, Marks, but you can't trace the call, so don't bother."

"No trace … what've you got?"

"Remember the OAKS NORTH case about eighteen months ago?"

"Yeah, so what?"

"That was me—and I still have feet that were never found."

"I remember the case. Why are you bringing it up now, a little guilt on your part?"

"You *are* a smart-ass … you trying to play me?"

"Look, your call is a bit strange, I have to question you."

"I wouldn't advise you to do that."

"You said you have something new."

"Early Monday Morning, I left a woman's body under the Crystal Pier." Michael laughed. "Her legs had been cut off."

"I think I would've heard about that."

"Your cop buddies haven't told you."

"You know I'll check this out."

"Of course you will, and while you're at it, look into a legless, female body found in a wheelchair and left at the entrance to the Space Museum in Balboa Park at about 3:00 AM."

"You're not serious?"

"Serious as a heart attack. Detective Matthew Kellogg has all the details on both murders, and he's not sharing with the press. I'm afraid I have to add, there's more to come."

"More what?"

"Now what do you think, Hal?" Michael laughed again. "I have a young girl in my sights as we speak. She'll be found within forty-eight hours. I've enjoyed sharing with you."

"Wait—what do I call you?"

"The legs collector, yes, that's appropriate. *The Legs Collector*, I like the sound of it. Be sure you run the story under a banner headline on the front page. Have a nice day." Michael hung up.

Hal stopped his recorder. "Son of a bitch."

He speed-dialed SDPD.

Chapter Five

A Person of Interest

FRED ELISTANOVICK
RESIDENCE-2234-KENWOOD DRIVE
LEMON GROVE, CA- 11:30 AM:

𝕶𝖊𝖓 𝖕𝖆𝖗𝖐𝖊𝖉 in front of the house. "Nice middle class neighborhood."

"Should that make any difference?"

"Well, yeah, to my way of thinking."

"Which is?"

"Check it out. That's a late model Buick Park Avenue in the driveway. It's expensive."

"And that means what?"

"Why rent a wheelchair? It would cost more than buying one."

"Maybe the need is temporary."

"Look closer, Matthew. The front entrance has a permanent access ramp."

"So the cost of a rental could be an insurance deal or a tax write off. You're trying to make something out of nothing."

"Just being observant."

"I have a hunch Elistanovick is not our perp, but he's connected to the stolen chair. It'd be pretty stupid to rent it and then use the thing in a crime and leave it to be found. Let's find out what the renter knows."

* * * *

The door opened on the second bell. A tall, thin man with silver hair stood in the entrance.

"Yes?"

"Sorry to bother you." Matt flashed his gold shield. "I'm Detective Matt Kellogg, this is my partner, Detective Ken Black. We need to ask you a few questions about your stolen wheelchair."

"Two plain clothes detectives are chasing down a lost wheel chair?"

Ken smiled. "May we come in, sir?"

"Of course." He stepped back. "That was a month ago and we have a new one."

Matt entered the living room first. "We're aware of that, Mr. Elistanovick, but it's important we get more information."

"It's Fred. What's all the fuss about an old wheelchair?"

"Who's here, Honey?"

"Two detectives. They're asking about the missing chair."

"Oh, my stars … did they catch that sneaky thief?"

Fred's expression brightened.

"Gentlemen, allow me to introduce my wife, Alexandra. She believes she saw the culprit."

"Pleased to meet real detectives. I watch all the crime shows on TV." She pushed the wheels of her chair forward with arthritic hands and her pale blue eyes sparkled. "My, my, such a pleasure." She reached out to Matt. "Call me Alex."

"I'm, Matt Kellogg." His voice cracked. "We're sorry to interrupt your day." A thousand aches crept across his heart.

Alex turned to Ken. "And you are?" She shook his hand.

"Ken Black, Ma'am. Nice to meet you."

"Well for heaven's sake, detectives, please sit down and welcome to our home."

Kellogg took out his notepad. "We don't want to be any trouble. Your husband said you may have seen who stole the chair."

She's barely a hundred pounds and frail.

"Excuse me, but how was it that you weren't in the chair?"

"You're not troubling us, Detective ... I love this, being involved in a real police investigation. It was just a few weeks ago."

She wheeled herself closer to her husband. "Do I have that right, honey?"

"You do, dear. It was four Saturdays ago."

Alex thought a moment and grinned.

"Actually, it's funny." She curled her crippled hands in her lap and continued. "We decided to have a garage sale and sell a few things that were just collecting dust."

"I don't think they need chapter and verse."

"Yes, they do. They're investigating a crime and they want details."

Matt smiled. "Alex is right, Fred ... we need the facts, Ma'am."

She laughed and shook her head in delight. "Do you remember that TV show years ago, *Dragnet?*"

Ken grinned. "I never missed an episode."

Alex leaned forward and tapped Ken's knee. "Sergeant Friday would always say, '*Just the facts, Ma'am, just the facts.*'"

Matt opened his notebook to a new page and smiled. "Let's have those facts, Ma'am."

"We started the sale about eight in the morning and I wanted to be right there with Fred and all the excitement. I couldn't sit in the wheelchair all day so we had my nephew, Harold, bring my recliner out from the house. He and Fred plopped me in it with a blanket so I'd be comfortable." She winked at Matt. "It's a pain in the ass to be old—mark my word."

Fred gripped his wife's thin wrist. "Go on, mother, these detectives have other things to do."

"Sorry for rambling. Anyway, the wheelchair was folded and set near the side door of the garage. Fred put a sign on it 'NOT FOR SALE.' About noon, I noticed a tall, good looking, well dressed young man checking some pieces of milk glass we were selling. He asked me if they were from the forties and I told him they were. He smiled and bought a bud vase and a candy dish."

Fred said, "I remember him well. He paid and I gave him change. He asked if he could go out the side door. I said sure."

Alex added, "My nephew put the man's purchase in a plastic bag. I remember saying, *'Be careful with those'.* The stranger thanked me and left."

Ken wrote a note. "Was that man the only one to go out through the side door?"

She nodded. "So far as I can remember."

"When did you miss the wheelchair?" Matt asked.

"It wasn't until well after we closed the sale." Fred sat on the arm of a recliner. I went out in the hall and it was gone."

Matt stood. "We're sorry you had to go through all of this, but you did get a new chair."

Alex looked up at Matt. "Why is all this important enough to have two detectives doing an investigation?"

"There have been several robberies and burglaries involving medical equipment in the East County. We're clamping down on them."

"Go get 'em and book 'em, Detective."

Matt smiled. "It's been a pleasure to meet you."

"Young man, you have given this old lady the joy of a lifetime." She took his hand. "Find him, he's doing the devil's work."

Ken shook Fred's hand. "Thanks, you've been a big help."

"I hope we gave you something you can use."

"I assure you, you have." He hesitated. "Alex, would you be willing to describe the man you saw to a sketch artist?"

"I would be more than delighted, yes, of course."

Matt said, "We'll have an officer call and set up a day and time."

"Will we need to go downtown?"

"That won't be necessary. One of our people will come here. By the way, they don't do much sketching anymore."

Alex grinned. "I've seen it on TV. They'll bring a laptop and create a face right on the screen."

"That's how it works." Kellogg chuckled.

Fred shook his head. "Alexandra, for Pete's sake."

"Again, we appreciate your help."

"You're welcome. It's been fun for me."

Ken put his notebook away. "Someone from the department will call tomorrow and set up the ID appointment." He glanced at Matt. "We done here?"

"I believe so." He shook Fred's hand. "You folks have been more than helpful."

"Would you let us know when you catch the crook?"

"I sure will, sir. You take care now."

* * * *

The detectives walked to their car and climbed in. Ken said, "It's after twelve, we need to get lunch."

"Head up to the Wendy's in Kearney Mesa. We'll grab a burger there and then go see Judy."

"Are you okay?"

"Sometimes this job crawls up inside you and chews on your guts. I thought I'd lost my sensitivity." He lit a cigarette. "Alex brought it all back."

"She got to you as soon as you laid eyes on her. She touched me a bit too."

"The second I saw her shining blue eyes, and heard her laugh. She was a perfect picture of my late mother. I'll hang on to Alex's graces as long as I can."

"It's what, two years now?"

"Two years ago last Friday ... before we caught this case."

"The human swill that took your mother is dead. We saw him get the needle."

"Yeah, and I'll never forget the fact that I had no feelings watching a man die."

"He was a piece of shit, Matt. Don't let all that back in your head."

"It already is."

Chapter Six

Michael Buys Three Books

CARMEL MOUNTAIN PLAZA
NORTH COUNTY–SAN DIEGO
BARNES & NOBLE–1:00 PM:

𝔥𝔢 𝔥𝔞𝔡𝔫'𝔱 𝔟𝔢𝔢𝔫 𝔦𝔫 the store for more than ten minutes when a matronly woman approached. "May I help you find something?"

Michael noticed red lipstick on her teeth when she smiled. "Perhaps you can." *Christ, she reminds me of my mother.* "I'm looking for a new novel by Angela Tipton." *Lady, you need to cut back on your cheap perfume.*

The woman's smile turned upside down.

"That would be, *The Legs of Hillary Long.*
You'll find it in fiction, one aisle to your left,
under thriller."

"Thank you. Your expression tells me you
don't approve of Angela's writing. She is a
bestseller."

"Frankly, I don't, but if you like murder and
mayhem, you'll love it."

"That's exactly what I do enjoy." *If only you
knew, bitch.* "I can't wait to get right into it with
a glass of good wine."

"I'm sure you will. Have a nice afternoon."

"Thanks, you too." D*amn old hen.*

Michael found his way to the fiction section
and met up with another B&N employee.

"Sir, follow me, I'll show you right where
Angela's book is displayed."

He turned and saw the delight of his
afternoon trawl. "Hello."

"Hi, I couldn't help but overhear your
conversation with Marge."

The tall, young, woman smiled. There
wasn't any lipstick on her teeth and her scent
reminded him of fresh roses. Her long, curly
brown hair danced on her slender shoulders.

"It wasn't much of a conversation." He
grinned.

"That's Marge, she's a retired librarian,
and would like to censure a lot of the books
we have here." She gestured toward the

thriller shelf. "I'm Robin."

"Hi, Robin, I'm Michael."

"Pleased to meet you." She pointed to a shelf at eye-level. "There's Angela. We've had to reorder to keep her in stock."

"Face out, I could've guessed that from all I've heard about her new novel" *Robin, you have no idea how pleased I am to meet you.* "Have you read it?"

"I'm halfway through it. This is her third and I love the way she writes. Some of her chapters are frightening, but I can't stop reading every word."

"You've sold me. Are the first two books available?"

"They're right there on the next shelf."

"I'll buy them all."

"Excellent, let me check you out when you're ready."

"I like you a lot more than Marge."

"Thank you." She smiled and held his eyes.

Not often was such a connection possible. This time everything clicked and fell into place. "Listen, Robin. I was planning on a late lunch at TGI Fridays. Excuse me for being so bold, but would you consider joining me? It would be my pleasure and my treat."

"I've had my lunch break, but I get off at four."

"How about an early dinner then?" *She's lonely and there's no resistance. Don't blow it.* "I'm sorry, Robin, I should never have come on to you like this. I apologize." *Work her, she's there.* "I'm embarrassed. I need a slap in the face."

"Yes—I mean, no." She hesitated. "Yes I'll have dinner with you."

You have her, now play it. "I'm really flattered. We'll have a nice dinner and talk about Angela's work. I promise you a special evening."

"It'll be great to share our interest in good books. Thank you."

"Excellent. You want to meet me there at about five or five-thirty?"

"Perfect, I'll spruce up here and drive over."

"You're just fine as you are. I'll have a table ready for us. Just ask for Michael."

"I'm glad you came here today."

"So am I. Let's get me checked out and then, I'll see you at dinner."

"I warn you, I can't stop rattling on about novels."

"Neither can I. Especially the *Legs* series."

Chapter Seven

Victim Two

SAN DIEGO CITY/COUNTY
MORGUE – ME LAB 2:00 PM:

𝔐𝔢𝔡𝔦𝔠𝔞𝔩 𝔈𝔵𝔞𝔪𝔦𝔫𝔢𝔯, Judy Wake pulled the
sheet up over the vic's face. "It's the same
MO, Matt, to the letter."

"Sexual evidence the same?"

"All post mortem. Vaginal and anal tearing,
and no fluids. He used the same type of
ligature. Cause of death, strangulation, and
the rope burns on her wrists are identical to
the first victim." Judy crossed the room and
put a *Healthy Choice* selection in the

microwave. "Late lunch."

Matt looked at the paperwork. "Sally Patterson, twenty-seven, and she also had a La Mesa address."

Doctor Wake took a knife and fork from the center drawer of her desk. "The thing that puzzles me, and this is more in your area, there's no crime scene for either vic."

"That's the missing piece and we'll find it."

Ken came into the lab. "I turned the wheelchair over to the crime guys and left it with Tony." He walked to the stainless steel table and glanced at Judy. "May I?"

"Knock yourself out." She removed her lunch from the oven.

Ken pulled the sheet back and shook his head. "She's just a kid for Christ's sake."

Matt stood and folded the paperwork. "You didn't notice that at the park?"

"It was dark, Kellogg, no, I didn't."

Judy opened the lid on her hot food. "As I said when we were at the scene, there were no defensive wounds, and I didn't get any DNA from under her nails."

Ken gently covered Sally's face. "Tony pulled Aaron Brunswick in from the CSI lab and he'll be taking the wheelchair to his team. Tell you what, that caused sparks. Brunswick is pissed. There's no crime scene and he's not a happy camper."

Matt slipped the folded paperwork into his sports coat pocket. "Aaron's a good man. If there's anything more we need off the chair, he'll find it."

His cell rang.

"Kellogg … are you serious? Shit—we'll be right there."

"What've we got?"

"That was Beck. We're sitting on a ticking bomb!"

"On what?"

"The media—Hal Marks, from the Tribune is in the captain's office with a tape from the perp."

"I don't believe this crap."

"Neither do I."

Judy said, "I hope it's a break, Matt."

"Yeah, right. If Marks leaks this, I'll break his neck."

Chapter Eight

The Tape and Michael's Date

SPECIAL VICTIMS UNIT
SDPD – 3:00 PM:

𝕿𝖍𝖊 𝖋𝖔𝖚𝖗 𝖒𝖊𝖒𝖇𝖊𝖗𝖘 of the SVU team,
Captain Sawyer and Hal Marks, gathered in
the main conference room. It was recently
added to the new east wing of the sprawling
SDPD complex.

   Hal pressed stop on his tape recorder. "I'm
sorry ladies and gentlemen. I can't sit on this.
You heard the nut. If I don't have something
in the morning Trib, he'll give it to radio, TV,
and all the county-wide rags."

Matt leaned on the table. "How did you verify the alleged crimes?"

"Give me a break, Kellogg. You know damn well I won't tell you that. But you can be assured, I know the murders were committed."

"I'll bet you a steak dinner I know who your sources are."

"That's between me and them."

Captain Sawyer held up his hand. "Okay people, we're not here to debate the first amendment. Hal came to us instead of running the story. Let's give him credit for that." He grinned at the reporter. "If he had done otherwise he'd never get anything from the squad again."

Sergeant Ann Beck turned away from the east facing window. "Sir?"

"Go ahead."

"The man on the tape is the killer. Hal, rewind back to his comments about the North County case."

"Sure." Marks pressed rewind and then play.

Remember the oaks north case about eighteen months ago?

Yeah, so what?

That was me—and I still have feet that were never found.

Ann said, "Stop there."

Ken shuddered. "Jesus H Christ!" He got up. "What the hell are we dealing with?"

Beck continued. "Jack and I caught that case when we were in Robbery Homicide out of the North County Division." She nudged her partner, Sergeant Towne, who was seated at the table.

"Exactly, there were four murders in all and nothing about the severed feet was ever released." He took a sip of water. "The dude on the tape is our Perp."

Hal pressed fast forward. "You guys need to hear this part again." He hit stop and pressed play.

"You're serious?"

"Serious as a heart attack. Detective Matthew Kellogg has all the details on both murders and he's not sharing with the press. I'm afraid I have to add, there are more to come."

More killings?

Now what do you think? I have a young girl in my sights as we speak. She'll be found within forty-eight hours. I enjoyed sharing with you.

Hal pressed stop. "I have to publish this story and you all know it. I'll do my best job on it, and San Diego will count on you to do yours."

Sawyer said, "I want that tape." He struck

the table. "I don't need to see one word in your piece regarding the feet—clear?"

"Not a word, Captain, that's out." He ejected the small cassette and handed it to the captain. "I have another copy." Hal stood and picked up his machine. "You all need to know, I respect you and I'll be true to the letter on these killings." To Ann he said, "I'll need to link all this to the Oaks North case."

Ann smiled. "I know you will. Jack and I have no problem with that."

Towne responded. "I doubt you'll screw it up."

The captain slipped the tape into his shirt pocket. "Does your editor know about this little gem?"

"Not a word. He'll kick my ass for not telling him."

"Have him give me a call, I'll smooze it over a bit."

"Thanks." Hal was about to release one of the most explosive crime stories of his career. "I'm well aware of how a story like this can stir up the public. You have my word, I'll do it right."

* * * *

Ann stared out through the east window of the conference room into the afternoon sun. She watched a bright red San Diego Trolley glide into downtown from the East County. *I wonder how many young women are riding that train and being watched by our perp?*

Matt came up behind her. "Hey, you okay?"

"Yeah, just trying to get a grip on all this." She turned to face him. "The case is a bitch from the get-go, and the one thing I can't get out of my head is the fact that our perp is on the move now. I fear for an unknown vic who's going to turn up tomorrow." She hesitated. "I'd like to forget all that for now and have a nice dinner with you."

"It's been a long day, but that's the best way I could ever imagine ending it."

"You're on, detective … someplace expensive?"

"Would the Hotel Del suit you?"

"You mean that?"

"Absolutely. Go home, slip into something sexy and I'll pick you up at seven straight up."

"There's no man on earth like you."

* * * *

CARMEL MOUNTAIN PLAZA
TGI FRIDAYS – 6:45 PM:

As usual, Fridays bustled with young people even though it was a Tuesday evening. Laughter and voices came from the bar area where groups of men and women enjoyed their favorite fancy drinks.

Michael and Robin shared a corner booth while they finished their early dinner.

Robin took a sip of a smooth California merlot and tapped the hardcover of Angela Tipton's first novel. "You have to read all three in order so you can get an understanding for the main character."

"I feel I already know her after hearing your glowing review of the trilogy." He drank the rest of his scotch.

"Did I sound like a giddy college girl?" She put the books back in the B&N shopping bag.

"No, not at all, I enjoyed your excitement. You're delightful."

"Thank you." She sipped more red. "This has been the best part of my day—hell, the best part of my whole month!"

"I'm flattered." He flashed his best boyish smile.

"And I'm serious." Robin flushed and finished the rest of her wine.

Michael reached across the table and

patted her hand. "I'd love to have dinner with you again sometime."

"I agree. I'm at the store five days a week." The thought of another date brightened her smile and glowed in her dark eyes.

The waitress stopped by their booth. "Are we okay here?"

Michael said, "We're great. Could I have the check please?"

"Coming up." The young lady left.

He glanced at his *Rolex.* "I'd love to continue this perfect evening, but I have a procedure early tomorrow and I need to be rock solid for that."

"Procedure? Are you a doctor?

"Actually, I'm a surgeon."

"I'm one hundred percent impressed."

"That's exactly the reason I didn't mention it earlier. I'm not in the habit of flaunting my profession. A few of my younger colleagues get a kick out of impressing people."

"My mother would go nuts if she knew I'd met a doctor—a surgeon no less."

"I'm sure you'll tell her." He smiled and glanced at his watch again.

"She'll hear about you before breakfast."

"I'm flattered."

The waitress returned with the check.

"Here we are."

"Thank you." Michael put his American Express card in the little wallet and handed it to the woman.

"I'll be right back."

Robin smiled. "My last name is Anderson. I came out here from Wisconsin six months ago."

"An attractive young woman from the Dairy State comes to Southern California to find a new life. I'm pleased to meet you, Ms. Anderson."

She laughed. "And you are?"

"Dr. Michael Moran, your friendly surgeon."

"I'm pleased to meet you, Doc—very pleased." A chill of nervous excitement skittered up the back of her neck and bit her behind the ears.

The waitress came back with his credit card. "Thank you."

"My pleasure." He signed the authorization slip and added a nice tip. "You have a good night."

"Thanks to you, I shall."

Michael looked at Robin and shook his head.

She sat back. "What?"

"I shouldn't tell you this, but the young woman I have to operate on, in the morning, is about your age, and she's the mother of two sweet little girls." He took a short breath, just for effect. "Becky is five and her sister, Cindy, just turned four. It's really troubling for me, but there's no choice."

Robin leaned forward and took his hand. "It's not routine surgery is it?"

He blinked back forced tears and swallowed hard. "No, it isn't." His voice cracked with the skill of a trained actor and fell to a whisper. "The woman was in a severe car crash early last Saturday morning." He hesitated. "I'm sorry."

Robin squeezed his hand. "No, please, Michael … let it out."

He swallowed again, this time he managed to make a clicking sound in his throat. "Her legs were badly shattered. The best bone specialists from Los Angeles teamed up with our guys at University Hospital."

Michael actually made a tear spill down his right cheek. It was a stunning performance. "I got the call yesterday." He wiped his eyes with a napkin. "I'll be amputating both legs in the morning." He choked and looked down at the table. "I apologize. I should not have dumped my grief on you."

Robin wiped away real tears. "It's okay, I understand. You're a very sensitive person, I felt that about you right away. Dear God, I feel so sorry for the woman."

"There's no alternative." He took a long drink of water. "I'm okay." He smiled. "Thank you for listening, I needed to get it out."

"I'm glad you did." She patted his hand. "You can share anything with me, Michael. I'm happy we met."

"Me too. Let's put all this sad negativity behind us."

"I agree." She handed him the bag of books.

"Where are you parked?"

"I walked from the store. My car is on the far end of the lot near the building."

"That's too far. It's getting dark. I got a spot right out front. I'll drive you to your car."

"Okay let's do it."

* * * *

When they approached Michael's Mercedes he hit the remote, the car lit up and sounded the horn.

Robin Laughed. "My old Chevy can't do any of that."

"Like I said earlier, you're a delight." He held the passenger door for her while she slid in.

"Thank you."

"My pleasure." Michael went around to the driver's side, climbed in and tossed the bag of books onto the backseat. He started the engine, put the vehicle in reverse and the four doors locked. "Buckle up."

Robin chuckled. "My place or yours?"

"You're kidding, right?"

"Yeah, just teasing."

"I'm not—we're going to my place."

"Really? I don't think we should."

"Yes, we really have to."

Michael's moves were so swift all Robin saw was a blur. The sting of the needle pricked her neck.

He backed the Mercedes out of the parking spot. "Relax, we're going home."

Whatever mumbles came from Robin were unintelligible. Michael had increased the strength of the drug.

"Don't try to fight it. Just go with the flow."

Chapter Nine

After Dinner Drinks

HOTEL DEL CORONADO
OUTDOOR LOUNGE – 9:15 PM:

𝕬𝖓𝖓 𝖘𝖎𝖕𝖕𝖊𝖉 her pina colada and smiled at Matt. "I'm glad we did this."

"So am I." He enjoyed the way the sea breeze played with locks of her auburn hair. "We both needed a break, this week hasn't started out as a walk in the park." He moved the flickering candle to Ann's left.

"Do you like fooling with fire, Mr. Kellogg?"

"Yes, especially when it glows on your face and sparkles in your eyes."

"Wow, how am I supposed to react to that?"

"Just be you, there's nothing better." He

sat back and took a drink of his tall gin and tonic. "I'm glad you're on the team. Now we can work together on this *Legs* case."

Ann adjusted her white shawl around her bare shoulders. "There's a storm brewing right now, and nobody knows it but us."

"That'll change when Hal's story hits the street in about nine hours." Matt finished his drink. "You want another?"

"Why not, it's still early." She drank the rest of hers. "By six the morning news will be leading with all the details of the two killings."

Matt flagged the waiter and pointed to their empty glasses. "I wouldn't want to be in the captain's shoes on any level."

"Sawyer's going to be forced into a press conference by noon. Count on it."

"Yeah, and I'll have to come up with a statement at that, not so distant, event." He lit a Pall Mall. "Shit … we don't have anything worth telling."

"Reality, Matt, just tell it like it is. The media can't expect anything more."

"I'm not concerned about the press as much as I am regarding the brass. Crap rolls down from the top. When Hal's story hits, the pressure is on."

Ann bit into one of the last two shrimp from her cocktail order. "I feel sorry for Sawyer, the Chief of Detectives will be on him before the conference."

"True, but the chief has got to know what we're up against."

"Don't count on it. Jack and I took major flack on the Oaks North case."

Kellogg raised his glass. "Here's to whatever tomorrow brings."

She lifted hers. "How would you like to chuck all this and move to a desert hideaway?"

"As long as you come along, I'm all for it."

* * * *

THE OLD VICTORIAN, LA MESA-1:30 AM
THE BASEMENT OPERATING ROOM:

Michael adjusted Robin's severed legs on the stainless steel table with her black high heels intact.

"Excellent. Kellogg will go crazy when he sees these." He held his *Canon* digital camera steady and used auto-focus. He snapped two shots.

"Perfect." He took three more pictures and set the camera aside, then picked up the legs and carried them to the walk-in freezer.

A few moments later, Michael adjusted Robin's hair around her shoulders. Through the lens he framed a nice head-shot. "You're as beautiful in death as you were in life." The shutter clicked three times more.

"Matt, you'll love these pictures." He switched off the camera and carried it to his desk, then checked his watch. "Plenty of time." Michael went back to the table and studied Robin's face. "Sorry, you were in the wrong place at the wrong time. I got to know you a little, it made the surgery more personal. I won't let that happen again."

After zipping up the black body-bag, he lifted Robin Anderson's remains and put them on a flatbed dolly and pushed it into his home elevator.

Michael looked around the basement. "We're good to go." He switched off the lights, entered the lift and went up.

When the door opened Samantha was waiting. "Yes, I brought a fresh snack for you. I didn't mean to be so late, but time just got away from me."

He pushed the dolly to the kitchen entrance of the garage.

Sam got in front of him. "Okay. You know, sometimes you can be a royal pain in the ass." He pulled a plastic baggie out of his lab coat pocket. "C'mon."

The cat jumped up to her place on the kitchen table.

"Here, enjoy." He shook out several

chunks of raw meat into a clear glass bowl. "There, that should hold you until I get back."

Sam chewed away on her tasty treats.

"You're not the least bit grateful are you?"

No response from the purring feline.

"I have to run an errand. I'll be home in plenty of time to have a nice breakfast with you, and share my story, which had better be in the morning paper."

Chapter Ten

Union Tribune/Metro Edition

ONE AMERICAN PLAZA
SAN DIEGO, CA-4:15 AM:

Henry Gerlinger stopped his battered *Toyota* pickup in front of the thirty-four story building. He whistled one of his favorite tunes while climbing out of the cab. He grabbed two heavy bundles of the Metro Edition out of the bed of the small truck and dropped the tied newspapers by the dispenser.

It was the prime city route and his papers were the first to hit the street. Henry took pride in that responsibility.

"Morning, Henry." Paul Carpenter, one of the building security guards approached. "What's the news today?"

"Just wait till you get a load of this." He cut the twine on one bundle and used three quarters to open the dispenser. "We got a nut loose in the county." He snatched the first copy off the stack and shoved it into the display window. "All those pretty ladies who work in your building got somethin' scary to be worried about." He handed Paul a copy and stacked the rest of the first bundle in the machine.

Carpenter stepped back and read the banner headline. "Holy shit!"

"Open the door for me an' I'll carry the rest inside." Henry emptied the coin box and closed the lid.

Carol Foley saw the two men heading toward the entrance and opened the glass door from the inside. She worked as a morning news reporter for the FM radio station on the thirty-third floor. "You're late, Henry."

"Longer press run, sweetheart. Let me set this down an' you can have your paper." He dropped the bundle on the imported Italian marble floor near the security desk and cut the twine. "Have at it."

She pulled the top copy off the stack and took a short breath. "Sonofabitch!" Carol looked at Paul.

He shook his head. "I can't believe it."

"I gotta get this on the air—now!"

Henry said, "Nobody else knows about it yet."

"They will, real soon." She ran to the express elevators.

The old man grinned. "Lovely girl."

By 5:30 AM every radio, TV station, and local independent newspaper was on the story. Carol got the brass ring. She had it first.

The SDPD switchboard became overwhelmed with incoming calls. The media demanded a press conference and they would get it.

* * * *

CARMEL MOUNTAIN PLAZA
BARNES & NOBLE PARKING LOT
NORTH EAST OF THE STORE – 8:30 AM:

Marge Harrison and the store's manager, Chuck Baker, drove into the lot. They car pooled from Rancho Bernardo. Today Marge did the driving.

Chuck spotted Ms. Anderson's Chevy in its usual spot. "Robin's in early. Good girl."

Marge said, "I like her, but she tends to get into too much *book-talk* with the customers."

"Actually, Marge, you should try a little

more of that yourself."

"After what we've been hearing on the news this morning, I don't think I really want to get too friendly with strangers."

"Those are most likely isolated incidents and probably involved people who knew each other. That's usually the case." Baker leaned forward. "Robin's sitting in her car."

"That's odd." Marge parked alongside the Chevy. "Something's wrong."

"Maybe not, let me check." He got out and approached the car. He tapped on the driver's window. "Robin, are you okay?" He shaded his eyes and looked in. "Oh my God." Chuck could see that Robin had no legs. "Oh my dear God." He turned to face Marge in her vehicle. He waved at her. "Stay in the car!" He took out his cell phone and dialed 911.

Marge lowered the passenger window. "What is it?"

"Don't get out—oh my dear God."

* * * *

SDPD SVU SQUADROOM
FIFTEEN MINUTES LATER:

Matt Kellogg hung his suit coat over the back of his chair, studied the front page of the paper again, and said, "Marks did a good job

All right … I could wring his neck for the graphic details."

Ken sat back at his desk and sipped on a French Roast he picked up at *Seven/Eleven.* "Hey, he had to tell the whole story. I think Hal did a fair job of writing it up. If he watered it down it wouldn't be right."

"Okay, I'll give him the benefit of the doubt, but the piece now has every young woman in San Diego County scared out of her wits and afraid to show her Legs."

An image of Sally Patterson chilled him.

"Good, the chicks will wear slacks and the perp will become frustrated."

"*The Legs Collector.* Hal came up with one hell of headline?"

"It'll be a movie title inside of six months."

"You and I and the team are in for the long haul on this case, and we better start getting some answers soon."

"And we don't have squat to go on."

"Sawyer's going to be under the gun real quick, and I smell a press conference before noon."

Matt's desk phone rang. "Yeah, Kellogg." His face went pale. "What?" He pulled out his notepad and pen. "North County? When?" He started writing. "We'll be there in thirty-forty minutes, depending on traffic." He finished his note. "Got it, Judy, we're on the way."

Ken sat up straight. "What've we got?"

"Another legless body. The vic was found in her car."

Captain Sawyer came out of his office in a hurry. "Matt, is this one another drop?"

"Yeah, female. Civilian called it in. Wake and two uniforms are on the scene now. The CSI guys just got there."

"As you well know, the lid's blown off. Keep a tight lip on this one as long as you can. I want both of you back here by eleven thirty. The press conference is at noon and we need to show some strength."

"You want me there, Cap?"

"Yes, Ken. Isn't that what I just said?"

"Just asking."

"I want all four of you there. The public and press need to know we're on this mess. Towne and Beck are at the Patterson apartment and have been notified. The chief has just requested my presence in his office."

Matt said, "Chief of Detectives?"

"No. The big one. He called the house before I finished breakfast and he's boiling over."

Kellogg grinned, "We might catch a break on today's case."

"Which would be?"

"Judy said there's a change in the perp's MO."

"Let's hope it's in our favor. Get up there ASAP—code three if you have to."

"Thanks, Cap … good luck with the old man."

"Yeah, I'll be on my best behavior. Now, get a move on."

* * * *

THE OLD VICTORIAN - 9:00 AM:

Michael chuckled and enjoyed another fork full of scrambled eggs and a slice of crisp homemade bacon. He had prepared the strips of meat especially for himself and Samantha. "Really tasty. Did you enjoy your breakfast, Sam?"

The cat flicked her tail and lapped up cream from her bowl.

"You know, Kitty, most cats just get water and dry food, not the kind of *Royal* meals I serve you. There will be a lot more enjoyable morsels from Robin. She was *special*, but I let myself get too close to her. It's an ache in my heart. I can't let that happen again … no I won't." He thought a moment.

"Okay, Detective Matt Kellogg, you have a lot on your plate for one week. Do your best cop-work. Maybe I'll take time off and let you have a respite."

He started reading the paper for the fifth time. "I love it. You did a great job, Hal. You could be nominated for the Pulitzer." Michael laughed. "How about it Samantha, your daddy has a title … *THE LEGS COLLECTOR*". He folded the newspaper and drank the rest of his coffee. "Don't you think it has a nice ring to it?"

His mother's voice seemed to come from the cat. *You're sick, Mickey—terribly ill. You should be in an asylum for the criminally insane.*

"Shut up, mother, you can't spoil my big day."

Mickey, Mickey … so sick you are.

"Go away—back to the dead, you witch." He slammed the paper on the table hard enough to rattle the dishes and topple the pepper mill.

Samantha jumped down and scooted into the living room.

His mother's voice ceased.

Michael sat still and stared into space for several moments. He looked down at his trembling hands and fought an urge to vomit.

Chapter Eleven

A Change in MO

CARMEL MOUNTAIN PLAZA
BARNES AND NOBLE
NORTHEAST PARKING LOT – 9:15 AM:

𝕿𝖜𝖔 𝖇𝖑𝖆𝖈𝖐 𝖆𝖓𝖉 𝖜𝖍𝖎𝖙𝖊 𝖈𝖗𝖚𝖎𝖘𝖊𝖗𝖘, the coroner's van, and the ME's blue Crown Vic had successfully blocked Robin's Chevy from the crowd of onlookers.

The CSI team loaded equipment into the back of their white van. The leader, Ray Conner hefted his investigation kit to the rear deck of the vehicle and motioned to Kellogg as he held up a plastic evidence bag. "We're done with the car. The only prints we got are the vic's."

"That's no surprise."

"Bill took prints off the body and I compared them to what I got from the interior of the vehicle and they're a match."

"Anything else stand out?"

"Other than the change in MO, nothing jumped out at us. Judy has the best part. The perp left the vic's handbag and complete ID, right down to address and phone number." He closed the back door of the van. "The absence of a crime scene with three killings has my team uptight."

"Understood. My crew shares the frustration."

"Yeah … we're outta here. See me at the lab later, maybe I can find something we can get a hold on."

"We'll be stuck here for a while and probably miss the press conference."

"That's an event I'm happy to be left out of."

"Okay, Ray, take care."

Matt spoke to one of the uniformed officers. "Call for a tow. The sooner we get this scene cleared, the better."

"You want it to go downtown?"

"I need the vehicle locked up in the evidence impound. Order the truck from the North County Police Garage. We don't want any civilians involved in the two-job."

"I'm on it."

Robin's body had been removed from the car and put on a gurney beside the coroner's van. Judy zipped up the black bag halfway. "We know the MO is different, but I'm pretty sure it's the same perp."

Kellogg checked his notes. "I'm inclined to agree with you, but why are there no ligature marks and the wrists weren't tied?"

"I know, it's a complete departure from the other two vics." She held up Robin's purse. "And this. Everything's intact."

"Perhaps he's sending a message. He let us have the woman's full ID, address, phone number, where she worked, and the whole enchilada."

"I can't be positive yet, but I did manage to perform a preliminary exam." She zipped the bag closed. "There's no obvious sign of sexual contact."

Matt jotted a note. "It can't be a copycat at work here, that's impossible."

"Correct, but I have a working theory."

"And that is?"

Judy nodded to the coroner's assistants. "Get the body to my lab without delay and say nothing about it to anybody. Are we clear?"

"Yes ma'am, not a word."

"That had better be the case. I can't prove it, but somebody leaked information about the other two vics and I'm sure you enjoyed reading the details in this morning's *Trib.*"

The two young men looked at each other. One of them said, "It wasn't us."

"I sure hope not." She glared at both of them. "Get her out of here."

Judy and Matt stepped out of the way so the two men could slide Robin's remains into the back of the van.

Kellogg said, "Your theory?"

"Sorry, I just needed to make a point with those guys. I don't trust them."

"They seem to enjoy their work."

"Too much so. They're like ghouls. I had a pair of them fired last year for taking and posting pictures of dead bodies on a sick Web site."

"Good for you. May I hear your theory?"

"Okay. No strangulation, no tying the wrists, no apparent sexual assault and leaving her purse to be found. Not only those things, but putting the vic in her own car?"

"Which tells you what?"

"He knew her, Matt—or at least had some earlier contact with the victim."

He leaned against one of the patrol cars. "Remorse ... you may have something, Judith." He stood up. "We might have found a chink in the perp's armor."

"It's just an observation."

"And a damn good one."

Ken came around the back of the Chevy. "Incoming at two o'clock."

"What?" Kellogg turned to his left to catch site of an attractive, tall, young blonde approaching from the storefront. "Shit." He walked out around to the opposite side of the black and white.

The woman came toward him with her press pass swinging from her neck.

"Hey, Kellogg, what the hell's going on?"

"Hello, Amanda. What brings you out on this fine morning?"

"Cut the shit, Detective. Is this connected to Marks' story in the Union?"

Judy patted Matt's arm. "I'm heading to Kearney Mesa. I want to be there when the ghouls deliver the body."

"Yeah, okay. Take the vic's purse to Tony. I'll check in later."

"Have fun with Amanda."

"Oh, I shall."

The reporter stopped in front of Matt and looked up at him with a big smile. "Spill it. You have another *Legs* murder and I want it."

"I have no idea what you're talking about."

"Matt, you have to give me the story."

"You want more on the *Legs Collector* story. Attend the press conference at noon, downtown."

"I intend to, but the Sentential has a right

to know what's going on here."

"Okay, you got me there. Get out your notepad, or recorder. I'll give it to you once."

"If you lie to me, I'll make you look bad."

"You want the story?"

"Go."

"We've found the body of a young woman in her car. We don't know the cause of death at this time. Our investigation continues. That's all we have right now."

"Kellogg, you're a rat."

"That just might be true. Sorry, Amanda, see you at the press conference." He and Ken walked away and headed for the bookstore. "We're going inside, Ms. Price, No reporters allowed."

"Matt!"

"Have a nice day."

* * * *

When they entered the store Matt said to Ken, "Call the crime lab and find out if we have the composite from Alexandra. If we do, I want copies at the press conference."

"Got it. That could be a major break."

"Have you had a chance to feel out the two witnesses?"

"Marge and Chuck?"

"There are no others who saw the body."

"The woman is totally blown away, but I think she knows something."

"And you think that because?"

"She told the manager the vic was pretty chummy with a male customer yesterday afternoon."

"Great, what about Baker?"

"He's rattled, but he doesn't remember the victim chatting with a customer. The man's completely shook."

"I would think he would be. I'll interview them." He looked at his watch. "Terrific, we have a press conference in less than two hours and every male employee in this place is a potential suspect, including the manager."

"This is mushrooming, Matt. It's gonna be hell on wheels to get downtown by eleven thirty."

"Tell me about it." He opened the front door and they walked into the store. To Ken he said, "Call the lab about the composite. If there is one, ask Tony to send it to your cell."

Chuck Baker and three female employees sat on a brown leather sofa doing what they could to console Marge and themselves. Chuck stood and came up to Kellogg. "I've contacted corporate in LA. They've agreed to let me keep the store closed today."

"That's a good move. Are all your people here?"

"My three counter clerks just came in."

Matt turned around to see two young women and an older man looking puzzled. "Is that it?"

"For the day shift, yes. In all there are eight … Robin would've made it nine."

"I'm sorry. How many on the later shift?"

"Counting me, it would be six."

"How many are men?"

"Four."

"Including you, that's five." He looked at Baker. "You're here at night too?"

"It's part of being a manager."

The older man came forward. "Chuck, what's happened?"

Kellogg answered the question. "We're going to bring you all up to speed right away."

"Who are you?" His query did not have a friendly tone.

"Detective Kellogg, Special Victims, San Diego PD."

"Special Victims?"

"Exactly. Chuck, I need you to gather all your people into the coffee shop area. Have Mrs. Harrison stay where she is."

"It's Ms."

"Okay, fine. I need to talk to her alone now that I know she saw a man with Robin."

"She's pretty upset."

"That's understandable. My partner will fill your people in and ask a few questions. Where are the folks who work the coffee shop?"

"It's self-serve right now. My girls handle the confection counter and make change, but there are no other people involved. We're putting in a Starbucks in October."

"That's good news. I'll have to stop by."

"Please do. Detective, I'm getting the impression my people are suspects."

"Good observation. The men are, until we rule them out."

"That include me?"

"You're a man and you knew the victim."

"I resent the hell out of that. Robin was half my age and I have a wife and two kids."

"Wouldn't be the first time an older, married, man took up with a lovely young woman."

"You're disgusting."

"So's the crime. Where were you between say, midnight and four AM?"

"At home with my wife and children."

"Prove it and you're off the hook."

"I don't have to prove anything."

"I'm afraid you do. Now get yourself together and act like a manager."

"You're a sonofabitch."

"Perhaps. Lock the front door and get on the phone to all of your male night employees. Include those who work weekends."

"What am I supposed to tell them?"

"Explain what we're dealing with and get their asses in here ASAP. If any one of them fails to show up, we may have a prime suspect." Matt grinned. "Does that make sense to you, Mr. Baker?"

"I don't like the way you conduct yourself."

"Sometimes, I don't either." He patted Chuck's shoulder. "Go take care of your people and let me have some time with Marge."

* * * *

Ken had gone back out to the parking lot to make his call to the lab. He flagged the tow driver. "Hey, this is a hot one." He gave the officer/driver Matt's card. "Make damn sure you have the receiving guy tag this car as priority evidence assigned to Detective Kellogg."

"Not a problem. Is it connected to the *Legs Collector?*" He grinned and pulled the lever that started hauling Robin's car up onto the flatbed.

"It might be. Just get it to the garage."

He addressed one of the uniformed

officers still at the scene. "You guys were a great help with the mess this morning, thanks for that."

"Anytime, Detective. I'll tell you what, when I saw that woman in the car, I puked."

"Try working homicide for a while."

"No thanks, I'm happy on patrol."

"I hear that. Take care."

Ken's cell rang. "Black here." He watched the tow truck drive off with Robin's Chevy. "Tony?" He shaded the screen from the sun. "Send it." The composite came up clear as a bell. "That's perfect. Thanks, now we're cooking."

* * * *

A minute later Ken was at the *B&N* front door just as Chuck was locking it. He held up his badge.

Baker opened the door and stepped back. "I know who you are."

"Thanks, Chuck."

"Your partner is getting on my nerves."

"Yeah, He gets on mine a lot."

Ken walked up behind Matt just as he was about to interview Marge. "Excuse me. You need to take a look at this." He showed him his cell screen."

"Fantastic. Go interview Baker's people.

Take it easy on the women and grill the men." He hesitated. "We're in for a long session here. You and I won't make the captain's conference."

"I didn't want to be there anyway." Ken tapped the cell screen. "This dude doesn't look like any of the men here."

"I'm sure he isn't, but we need to be positive."

"Okay, I'll see what I can shake out."

"Give me your phone, I'll show the picture to Marge."

"You got it." Ken handed over the cell and went to talk to store employees.

Kellogg looked down at Marge.

She was holding a handful of crumpled tissues and crying. "I'm sorry."

"I understand how you must feel. Hang on a minute. I have to make a call." He dialed Ann's cell.

"Hey, Kellogg."

"Ken and I will not be able to make the press conference."

"Sawyer will be livid."

"It won't be his first. We have evidence that makes the perp an official serial killer."

"I believe we saw it coming."

"I'm sending a composite of a likely suspect. Have copies printed and take them to the conference. That'll ease things a tad."

"Is this a break?"

"You bet your lovely ass—and I have a witness who may have seen the perp with our current victim."

"I love it. The Captain will be pissed that you and Ken won't be here, but we'll cover you—good job."

"I'll call you later."

"Looking forward to it."

* * * *

Matt pulled out a chair and sat in front of Marge. "Ms. Harrison, I know this is difficult for you, but I understand you saw Robin talking to a stranger yesterday."

The woman wiped her eyes with a tissue and took a drink of water. "Yes, sir, I did. Robin was always over friendly with customers."

"You said one stands out, could you tell me about him?"

"For sure. He wanted to buy the *Angela Tipton series,* which I don't approve of. So I just told him where to find the books. Well, he ran into Robin. Of course, she loved those books. She must've caught his attention. They chatted for a while, and he bought the books."

"You know he bought the books?"

"Yes. Robin checked him out herself."

"Do you know how he paid?"

"I'm not sure, but, I think it was cash."

"That doesn't help us right now. Did that man leave with Robin?"

"Of course not, she hadn't finished her shift. It was about two or three. Robin wouldn't be off work until four."

"I'm going to show you a composite photo of the man who may have chatted with Robin. Tell me if you think it's him."

Matt opened Ken's cell phone and displayed the Picture. "Is this the customer?"

Marge took a short breath. "It's him! That's the man Robin was talking to."

"You're absolutely sure?"

"It's him—that man bought those books and Robin checked him out."

"Okay, Ms. Harrison, you've been very helpful."

"What now?"

"We'll find him and get some answers." Matt closed the phone. "I'm sorry you had to go through all of this."

"Thank you … I feel so bad for her parents."

"Are they local?" He pulled out his notebook.

"No. They live in Wisconsin, Madison, I think." She wiped her eyes again.

"I'll ask Mr. Baker about Robin's next of kin. Would you like one of the girls to sit with you?"

"Yes, please. Ask Sarah, they were best of friends."

"That's good to know. I'll send her right over."

* * * *

Matt went to where his partner sat in front of the other employees. He tapped Ken on the shoulder and spoke to the group. "Please be patient. We want to clear this up as soon as we can." He smiled. "Give us a minute."

He gave Ken his phone back and gestured toward the front of the store. The two of them walked to the checkout counter. Matt said, "We caught a break, maybe. Marge identified the composite as the guy who bought the books after having a conversation with the victim." He hesitated. "I don't believe in fairy tales. Something tells me the face in the picture is phony."

Ken opened his phone and brought up the picture. "Okay, I tend to agree. This dude could be anyone anywhere. The woman's in a state of emotional chaos. She'd put the finger on me if she saw a computer generated composite of my handsome face."

"I'll give you that. Would another ID change your mind?"

"Possibly, let's give it a shot."

Matt stepped back toward the mumbling group. "Is Sarah here?"

A young brunette, about twenty-three, raised her hand. "That's me."

"Would you come over here please?"

When she approached the two men it was obvious she had been crying.

"Hi Sarah, I'm Detective Kellogg, you've met Ken."

"I want to help in any way I can."

"Marge would like you to sit with her for a while."

"Of course, I will."

"She tells me you and Robin were close."

Tears welled up. "She was so lonely … my heart went out to her. She missed her family back east. She didn't have a boyfriend here or any other girlfriends." Sarah's voice cracked. "I warned her to be careful. Robin was so vulnerable."

"Warned her about what?"

"Going out with that stranger so soon."

"Sarah, this is important. What stranger?"

Ken opened his phone and displayed the composite.

"Him—he's the man who talked with Robin."

"You're sure?"

"Positive, his eyes were smaller and closer together, but that's the guy."

"You said she went out with him."

"Robin told me he'd asked her to have dinner with him."

"Did she go?"

"She had to meet him later because her shift didn't end until four. She was so excited. I had to feel happy for her."

"Did Robin say where they would meet?"

"It's nearby." Sarah pointed out the windows. "TGI Fridays. It's over there at the southeast end of the parking lot. She walked from here."

"Sarah, you have no idea how helpful you've been, thank you."

"Do you think that man murdered my friend?"

"If he did, we'll find out." He touched her shoulder. "Marge needs you right now."

The young woman nodded and went to comfort Ms. Harrison.

Matt put his notebook away and grinned at Ken. "Now is that a lead?"

"Actually, Matthew, it could be a damn good break." He hesitated. "If your doubts are true—we got squat."

Chapter Twelve

The Press Conference

SDPD COMPLEX
REAR PATIO – WEDNESDAY
11:30 AM:

𝕸𝖔𝖘𝖙 𝖔𝖋 𝖙𝖍𝖊 𝖗𝖆𝖉𝖎𝖔 𝖆𝖓𝖉 𝕿𝖁 technicians had finished checking their equipment and the reporters paced around waiting for the chief's grand entrance.

Amanda Price buttonholed Hal Marks and was giving him the what-for about his exclusive with the *Union Trib.* "Why the hell didn't you give me a heads up on this?"

"The nutcase called me. What was I supposed to do, share the piece with the rest of the media? Get real, Amanda."

"We're friends for Christ's sake. We're chipping away at the same rock to make something out of what we do."

"You may be, but I'm not chipping at any rock. I have the big pie on this one, you don't."

"Take a deep breath, big shot. There's been another killing in the North County and I got it from Kellogg this morning. Guess what, *Clark Kent.* It's connected to the *Legs* story and I have it."

"Sorry, I knew about the new victim before you crawled out of bed. The perp told me a body would be found, but not exactly where. And I'm sure Kellogg didn't give you anything other than the fact that it was a woman. You don't know it's another *Legs* murder and neither do I, but I'd bet on it."

"You're a shit. You know that—a total shit."

* * * *

The chief's assistant stepped up to the podium. "Good morning ladies and gentlemen. Chief Arnold, Chief of Detectives, Fuller, Captain Roy Sawyer and members of the SVU squad will be addressing you momentarily. Please take your seats and have your questions ready after the chief issues his statement. Thank you all for coming on such short notice."

Hal looked down at Amanda's crossed legs. "Just a suggestion, but it would be a good idea if you wore slacks for the duration of this mess."

"My legs?"

"The very same." He smiled.

"You're not such a bad shit after all."

He patted her knee. "I never said I didn't like you."

"I'm flattered, but I'm still pissed."

* * * *

THE OLD VICTORIAN
IN THE DEN
AT THAT SAME TIME:

Samantha had curled up on the leather recliner near Michael's desk. She licked at her front paws after finishing an early lunch.

Michael kept an eye on a small TV that sat on a bookshelf not far from his computer monitor. "They should be starting the press conference any time, Sam." He displayed one of the digital images of Robin's face on the twenty-four inch LCD screen and a second picture of her legs. "What do you think? Did I do a good job or what?"

The cat stopped cleaning her paws, blinked, and went back to business.

A Vons Grocery commercial ended and a handsome anchor, with a two hundred dollar haircut, appeared on the small screen. "Good morning, this is KGTV-Ten with a special LIVE report from the San Diego Police Complex downtown. Roberta Sanchez has the story."

"Alan, the atmosphere here is tense to say the least." The camera pulled back to show other members of the media seated near the podium. The attractive Hispanic reporter continued. "This morning's newspaper account of the so called *Legs Collector* has all but created a panic among San Diego County's female population."

"Roberta, we understand another body has been found in the North County?"

The screen split with Alan on the left and Ms. Sanchez on the right.

Michael nodded at the TV. "I see you're not wearing slacks. Maybe we'll run into each other sometime."

Roberta's camera person moved in to a tighter shot. She went on, "A deceased female has been found in a vehicle at Carmel Mountain Plaza. That's all we know at this time."

Michael spoke to the TV again, "Hang in there, lady, you'll find out soon enough."

The reporter hesitated, and then looked off camera. "They're about to start the conference."

The lens closed in on the chief's Press

Secretary as she stepped up to the bank of microphones.

"This is gonna be good, Sam."

Chapter Thirteen

Michael's Paper Trail

TGI FRIDAYS
CARMEL MTN. PLAZA
ONE HOUR EARLIER:

𝕿𝖍𝖊 𝕳𝖔𝖘𝖙𝖊𝖘𝖘 𝖑𝖔𝖔𝖐𝖊𝖉 𝖆𝖙 𝖙𝖍𝖊 composite again and shook her head. "I can't be sure. We were pretty busy yesterday all the way through the dinner crowd."

Kellogg said, "How about around four or a little after? Were these booths full?"

"Closer to five, I had to bring in an extra waitress from the lounge."

"I'll need to talk to her. Is she on duty?"

"She's working the lounge. Ask for Penny. Excuse me. I have guests coming in."

"Thanks, Janice, I appreciate your time."

"Detective, is this connected to the story

in this morning's paper?"

"I really can't say it is,"

She pointed toward the bookstore. "How about what was going on in the parking lot?"

A young couple stood inside the entrance and appeared impatient.

"We don't know that either." He smiled. "I need to get to my partner in the lounge."

* * * *

A few minutes later Matt and Ken sat in a booth with a bubbly redhead named Penny. She studied the image on Ken's cell. "Sure, he was in here with a good looking girl a little older than me. I remember him because he tipped well." She tilted the phone left then right. "His eyes were different and I think he had a higher forehead."

Ken tapped his receding hairline. "Kinda like mine?" He grinned.

"Yeah, but he was younger than you."

"Thank you very much." He took back his phone and closed it.

Matt chuckled. "Anything else outstanding?"

"Not so much about him, but the lady was all caught up in the books they brought with them."

"How so?"

"Well, she explained that they should be read in order. When I came back with the check she had put the books back in the *Barnes* and *Noble* shopping bag."

Ken said, "How did he pay?"

"Credit card. Yeah, American Express."

Matt looked at Ken and said, "We'll need a copy of the receipt."

"See that good looking guy behind the bar? That's Jerry, he's the manager. Ask him."

Ken climbed out of the booth. "I'll deal with Jerry."

Matt said, "Penny you're a delight, you've been very helpful."

"Hey, you guys are fun. I love cops. My brother's on the Highway Patrol."

"Good for him, that's a responsible job."

"Is this guy you're looking for in a lot of trouble?"

"I think he just might be."

* * * *

THE OLD VICTORIAN
12:00 NOON:

Michel sat back and gave his full attention to the small TV. "Here it comes, Sam."

The chief's press secretary addressed the

throng of reporters. "This has been a tough morning. Thank you all for your patience. I present the San Diego Chief of Police, Cal Arnold." She stepped back.

The chief stood before his audience in full dress uniform. "Ladies and gentlemen, I have a difficult message to deliver. I confirm the story you've all read in the San Diego Union Tribune early this morning." He paused to take a breath. "We have, in our midst, a wanton serial killer who is preying upon the young women of our fine city and county." He sipped some water. "I have a young daughter and wife and I fear for their safety." The chief gritted his teeth, raised his chin and looked into the rolling cameras.

"Whoever you are, wherever you may be, I assure you, we will find you and bring you to justice." He gestured to his left. "Captain Roy Sawyer of the Special Victims Unit will answer your questions."

* * * *

Michael applauded the chief. "Wow, what a speech. I'm so pleased to know you'll track me down. I can't wait to find out just how you're going to do that."

* * * *

"Thank you Chief." The captain looked out at the pack of reporters that were about to bombard him with questions. "Before we get started, I need you to know that our four dedicated officers of the SVU are on this case as we speak. Detective Matt Kellogg is the lead investigator. He and his partner, Ken Black, are on a murder in the North County that could be connected to the serial killings. The incident turned up early this morning and the team is working it."

Amanda shouted, "Did the North County victim have her legs cut off?"

"I can't answer that at this time."

Pedro Gonzales from the *Chula Vista Times* spoke next, "Are these butcher-murders involved with the *Oaks North* mayhem eighteen months ago?"

"We have no proof of that so far."

A reporter from the *East County Californian* waved her hand. Sawyer pointed to her, "Lisa?"

"I have it on good authority, that the two victims reported in the Union this morning were from La Mesa. Can you confirm that?"

"Yes, that has been confirmed." He held up his arms. "Thank you all for coming. That's as much as we know right now." He pointed to the lower left of the screen. "You all have that picture and I'd like to see it published in every paper and shown on every TV news report. It's being circulated in LA as well. Thank you." Sawyer left the podium as more questions were being asked.

The press secretary moved up to the mikes. "The other officers, team members, and Chief Arnold, will be available for individual interviews in twenty minutes. Thank you all again."

Michael reached over and turned off the TV. "Samantha, they don't have shit." He laughed hard enough to bring tears to his eyes. "You stupid cops. That picture isn't me. I'm glad you bought it though." He laughed hard again and turned back to his computer. "Now let's see. I need to arrange these pictures and print them out for my favorite detective, Matt Kellogg. He will really appreciate my work."

The cat gave out a soft cry.

"Are you hungry again, Little one?" He pushed his chair closer to the recliner and scratched Sam's neck. "I'll fix you a nice snack in a few minutes."

Chapter Fourteen

American Express Leads

SDPD COMPLEX
SVU SQUADROOM 1:45 PM:

𝕶𝖊𝖓 𝖍𝖆𝖉 𝖉𝖎𝖛𝖎𝖉𝖊𝖉 𝖙𝖍𝖊 𝖈𝖔𝖑𝖑𝖊𝖈𝖙𝖎𝖔𝖓 of fifty three credit card receipts and put the odd one on Matt's stack. "This one's just for you."

Kellogg waited on hold for the ME to come back on the line. He held his hand over the mouthpiece. "How many of those slips were signed by women?"

"It's hard to tell, some are illegible, others used an initial and scribbled their last name. We got a mess here, Partner."

Judy came on Matt's phone. "Sorry, I had to double check a test result."

"No prob. What have you found out for sure?"

"There were no fluids and no sign of any

sexual contact."

"COD?"

"He used potassium chloride. That's another twist in MO."

"Where in hell is he getting this shit?"

Kellogg took a deep breath. "Your theory plays out. The perp shows remorse on this one. Anything useable from the vic's purse?"

"Tony dusted every item in Robin's shoulder bag. The only prints are the victims. He found one thing helpful. Her parents' phone number."

"Let me have it." Matt opened his notebook and wrote down the number.

"Are you going to do the notification?"

"What's the vic's age?" He stood, walked over to the window and looked out onto the back patio. Some of the techs were packing up equipment. A few reporters had stayed after the conference to get more from Ann and Jack as well as from the Chief of Detectives, Ray Fuller.

Judy said, "Her Cal license puts her at thirty-four."

"That would make her parents in their fifties or even sixties."

"I suppose. Is that something to be concerned about?"

He noticed Amanda and two female TV reporters having a chat. All three women wore skirts. Skirts exposing their well-shaped legs. He whispered, "They're taking a chance."

"What?"

"Sorry … just thinking out loud." He cleared his throat. "Yes, the parents' ages are a concern." Matt went back to his desk and sat down. "I *will* be handling notification through the Madison PD."

"I understand. I've wanted to do something like that on many occasions."

"I'll have them send a couple of officers to the house with a social worker. I'll make it clear that her father needs to call me. I'll work out the details and bill San Diego for their round trip flight."

"Can you get away with that?"

"It's been done before and America's Finest City can sure afford it."

"You're getting involved in this one, Kellogg."

"Yes, I am. It started when I heard the girlfriend tell her tale about the vic." He pushed his chair out from the desk and stood again. "Robin Anderson had a Life. She had a *future* until she crossed paths with a sick sonofabitch who ripped it all away from her."

"Are you okay?"

He slammed his fist down on his notebook. "No, I'm not okay—I want this bastard!"

Ken sat back in surprise. "Matt?"

Judy said, "You'll get him."

Kellogg glanced out the window again. The patio was clear. "Sorry." He sat back down and nodded at Ken. To Judy he said, "How many times have I said, *I'm sorry for your loss?* I guess it might be a hundred. You know what? When I say it to Robin's parents, I'll really mean it and it will cut a hole in my heart."

"I believe you. Can I get you back on track here?"

"Yes, go ahead."

"Ready to take another note?"

"I said, go ahead."

"The vic—I mean, Robin, lived in an apartment on Rancho Bernardo Road about five or six miles from the bookstore. It's the RB Estates on the south side of the street. They're all ground floor units, she had number 136. There are no other addresses."

"Okay, got it thanks. I'll have Ann and Jack check it out and seal it off." He wrote down the information and took a breath. "Listen, Judy, I'm sorry I blew my cork."

"No apology necessary. You're human, Matt … I love you for it. I don't have anything else."

"Thanks. We're done today, I'll let you know when Robin's parents are arriving."

"Thanks. Say hi to Ann for me."

"I will. Bye." He hung up and rubbed his hands across his face. "Ken—"

"Not a word. I know exactly where you're coming from."

"What'd we get on the surveillance tapes?"

"While you were on the horn with Judy, I heard back from Aaron at the A/V lab. You won't believe this, but the bookstore and Fridays have the same system."

"I don't think I'm ready for it."

"I wasn't either. Unless something happens during the day's business, the tapes are automatically erased."

"Erased?"

"Exactly. At closing the manager hits *clear.* The tapes are then rewound and bulk-erased and reset for the next business day."

"We're blank on any security tape images of our perp?"

"Clean as the driven snow."

"Anything from the Carmel Mountain Plaza security cameras?"

"Apparently, the parking lot camera, for the northeast sector malfunctioned. It showed nothing but static, and it's been like than for over a month."

"Jesus Christ."

"Devine intervention would be helpful."

"Cute. I need a smoke."

"Go have one. I'll get started on the credit cards."

"Forget the names." Matt stood and slipped into his suit coat. "Use the power of the PD. Contact American Express, run the last four digits of the numbers we have and get names and addresses."

"I take it we're going to be doing some leg work."

"You should be more careful of your choice of words." He started for the patio. "I want this perp."

"I couldn't agree more."

* * * *

THE OLD VICTORIAN
MICHAEL'S DEN:

"See those, Samantha." Michael looked at the images on his screen. "Detective Kellogg will be so pleased."

The cat lazed on the recliner and twitched her ears.

Robin's face, in death, had been carefully edited into *Photo Shop* and showed a lovely picture of her with equally crafted images of her legs, high heels and all, positioned around her head.

Michael added a frame to the picture. "I think burnt oak is a flattering touch." He hit the button for print and the photos started to process.

He scratched Samantha's ears and smiled. "After I enjoy these pictures for myself, off they go in an envelope to Detective Matt Kellogg at SDPD. I'll deliver them personally. He'll be so pleased." He dropped his smile and glared at the screen. "You'd better keep a close eye on Ann Beck, Detective—I am."

The cat sat up and licked her chops.

Michael scratched the animal under her chin. "You never get enough. Okay, more special bacon treats?" He picked up the finished pictures from his color laser printer. "Robin, you're so beautiful. Why were you there? Why did I have to run into you? It could've been anyone else. I'm so sorry." He covered his face with his hands and shook his head.

His mother's voice came out of the computer speakers and filled his mind.

Sorrow won't absolve what you've done, Mickey! You're an abomination!

Michael covered his ears and squeezed his eyes shut. "Go away, Mother."

You're sick, Mickey, you always have been.

"I didn't mean to hurt Robin. It just happened."

The echo of his dead mother's voice came from every corner of the room and pounded in his mind.

Nothing just happens with you, Mickey. You made the same excuse when I caught you with your Cousin, Jennifer. Twice, I found you with her. She was a child, Mickey!

"She was older than me and should've known better."

A wavering image of his mother replaced Samantha in the recliner. *Jenny was sixteen and retarded.*

"I did *not* hurt her." He lunged at the specter.

It vanished.

The cat flew off the chair and ran out of the den.

"Stay dead, Mother—why won't you leave me alone?"

The gold drapes billowed out from the closed window. A cold wind rustled through the room and slammed the door shut. The drapes settled back against the glass.

Another apparition from the deceased, Elizabeth Moran, formed on the closed oak door *Jenny had the mentality of an eleven-year-old, Mickey, and you took advantage of her. You shamed me in the eyes of my sister.*

Michael flopped down in the recliner and stared at the ceiling. "I never, not once, did I ever harm Jennifer and you know it."

"You were always a sneaky, dark-minded, bad boy, Mickey. Now, you're a cunning, evil, grown man. A killer, Mickey—that's what you've become—a killer!

Michael closed his eyes and pressed his fingers against his throbbing temples.

Shards of ice seemed to crawl up his arms as if they were living things. Like the pricking of needles they stung the back of his neck.

Chapter Fifteen

The Legs of Jennifer Warren

THE OLD VICTORIAN CELLAR
TWENTY-THREE YEARS EARLIER:

𝔐𝔦𝔠𝔥𝔞𝔢𝔩 𝔢𝔫𝔧𝔬𝔶𝔢𝔡 𝔟𝔢𝔦𝔫𝔤 𝔦𝔫 𝔱𝔥𝔢 huge basement of the big house. He played there often and thought of it as a magic place where he could be a solider and torture imaginary prisoners.

One of his favorite fantasies involved becoming the Frankenstein monster. The best part required Halloween makeup, old ragged clothes and putting on his special pair of *Ked* sneakers. He had cut and shaped two pieces of thick wood to fit the bottom of the sneaks. Michael nailed the *Keds* to the wood from the inside and then painted the creations black.

What a sight he was. He would clomp around the shadowed cellar imitating Boris Karloff in the original 1931 film. On occasion, he lured his sixteen-year-old cousin, Jennifer to his *imagined* castle and scared the hell out of her. Actually, she loved the play and always became excited.

Jennifer was retarded.

* * * *

One Saturday afternoon, the game changed.

* * * *

The sound of his racing slot cars covered the opening of the cellar door and Jennifer's footfalls on the stairs. She stopped on the second landing and watched.

A bright yellow and red racer lost it in a sharp curve and flipped off the track.

"Damn!" Michael shut down the second car and reached over the table to retrieve the first. He caught sight of his cousin.

"What cha doin', Mickey?"

He hadn't seen Jennifer in nearly two years. "Don't call me that, I don't like it."

"Are you gonna be all mad at me now?"

She came down the rest of the stairs and set a large shopping bag on the floor. "I brought all my new dollies from New York to show you."

"I'm not mad." He stared at her and sat on a stool holding his yellow and red racer.

"What's wrong then? Yer lookin' at me funny."

"You're different." He put the car down. "I mean, older an' all."

She put her hands on her hips and turned from side to side and then all the way around. "Do I look prettier?" She stepped closer. "Smell. I put on some perfume that mom says costs a lot."

"It's nice." He took a swallow of iced tea. "I like it."

"Can I have some?"

"Sure." Michael let her sip from his glass.

"That's good. Yer mom an' mine are havin' cold drinks on the porch out back."

It had been a hot August afternoon. Jennifer was dressed for the weather. Her yellow chiffon blouse fit loosely and she had tied it around her bare middle. Her dark blue, cut-off, denim shorts rode high on her thighs with frayed, loose ends against her tanned skin. What had been awkward skinny legs had filled out and were now gorgeous.

The little girl who went away twenty-two

months earlier had physically matured
beyond her years. Unfortunately, Jennifer still
had the mentality of an eleven-year-old.

She moved closer to him and pushed
herself between his legs as he sat on the
stool. "A nice boy in New York played a game
with me."

Michael started to become aroused. "Like
our monster game?"

"No, not like that, but it made me feel all
nice down there."

"Down where?" He pulled her against
himself.

"You know." She leaned back and put her
hand down the front of her shorts. "Down
here. I feel all tingly now."

He swallowed a gulp of iced tea. "What's
the game?"

"It's not got a name, silly, but I made one
up." She pushed herself against him harder
and giggled. "Legs … you feel my legs an' I
touch myself down there. It's fun, Michael,
let's do it. I want you to rub my legs." She
stood away. "C'mon, let's do it." Jennifer
rubbed her thighs. "Do you like my legs?"

"I think they're beautiful and so are you.
How do we play the game?"

Jennifer looked around and pointed to an
old Morris chair. "There—I'll sit in that an' you
can feel my legs. Please, Michael, it makes

me tingle all over. Will you kiss them?"

"What?"

"Kiss my legs. It makes me feel nice down there."

* * * *

Thirty minutes later, Mrs. Moran came down the cellar stairs. The kids didn't hear her, they were too involved. She stopped on the second landing. "Mickey, Jennifer, are you down here?" She saw the two of them in the Morris chair and screamed. "What are you doing to her, Mickey?"

Michael got up off his knees. "Nothing, Mother."

"You dirty boy!" Elizabeth came off the stairs, ran to her son, smacked him across the face and knocked him to the floor. She pulled Jennifer out of the chair. "Are you hurt, child?"

"No, Aunt Liz, I'm not hurt."

"What did that nasty boy do to you?" She hugged Jennifer.

"We were just playing a game."

"I can imagine what kind of game he came up with."

Michael pulled himself up. "We didn't do anything bad."

"Bad is all you are, Mickey—you've violated this innocent child!"

"Please, Mother—I didn't hurt her."

"Shut your filthy mouth." She started walking Jennifer toward the stairs. "I'm locking you down here until your father gets home. You'll be lucky to survive the beating you'll get."

Michael sat in the Morris chair. "It was Jenny's idea."

"Take advantage of a retarded child, what kind of animal are you?"

Jennifer said, "My dolls, Aunt Liz."

"We'll get them later, sweetheart. Right now we need to get you into a hot bath."

Michael heard the cellar door slam shut and the metal scrape of the bolt-lock being shoved into place. He looked up at the dark stairwell and drew a long breath. "I didn't do anything to hurt Jennifer."

He walked to where his cousin had set down her shopping bag. He opened it and dumped the contents onto his slot-car table. There were a dozen dolls of varying shapes and sizes.

"I'll give you a *legs-game*, Jennifer!"

One by one, Michael tore off the legs of each doll and scattered them across the cellar floor.

* * * *

Six months later Michael and Jennifer were caught playing the same game. Michael was confined to the basement for ten days.

Jennifer was admitted to a facility for the mentally retarded. She will never be alone with a man again.

Perhaps it wasn't Michael's fault at all.

Chapter Sixteen

Sorry for Your Loss

SDPD COMPLEX
SVU SQUADROOM 2:00 PM:

𝕸att came back from his smoke break, walked to the captain's office and tapped on the open door. "Got a minute, Cap?"

"Oh, sure, Detective, I have all the time in the world. It's nice to see you're back from the North County." He shuffled some papers on his desk to make space for a manila folder. "I hope you and your partner had a productive investigation and gathered a trunk full of leads and clues regarding this morning's murder."

Kellogg stepped into the small office and closed the door. "We have a lot of good information, and a couple of solid leads."

"That's great. It's just what I want to hear. I'll need to pass all that along to Arnold and Fuller. They both had a grand time chewing my ass before and after the conference."

Matt sat in a chair facing his boss. "I'll bet you looked great on camera and handled the media well."

"Detective, my patience is a bit thin at the moment."

"Okay. I'm doing the notification for Robin Anderson."

"Robin who?"

"This morning's murder victim."

"You got ID so soon?"

"The perp left Robin's purse with everything intact."

Captain Sawyer sat back. "Are we talking about the same killer here?"

"It's the same nutcase with a few alterations to his MO."

"Why wasn't I brought up to speed on this right away?" He scooted his chair to the credenza and filled his cup from his private coffee maker.

"I believe you were pretty well up to your ass with two chiefs and a press conference. By the time we got the details you were out of reach."

"Yeah, this morning was shit-city. So what's the hold up on contacting next of kin?"

He stirred cream and sugar into his mug of coffee.

"I need a travel voucher."

"Are you going on a trip? The crimes are local, I'm not following you."

"Robin's parents are in Madison, Wisconsin."

"Pick up a phone, Matt, you know the drill." He added more cream to his coffee and took a sip. "What's with a voucher?"

"I think the city owes the family on this one. All I'm asking is round trip air fare and a couple of nights in a hotel plus the extra cost of shipping Robin's remains back to Madison."

Captain Sawyer shook his head and grinned. "Right. You want the department to pick up the tab for this vic. Hell, why not throw in *Sea World* tickets and put the folks up at the Hotel Del? Let's order a fruit basket and a nice bottle of champagne."

Heat rose behind Matt's ears and on the back of his neck. He stood and leaned on Sawyer's desk. "Her name is Robin Anderson. She came here to find a new life. She lived alone and had one good friend. Robin was lonely and missed her parents. She was passionate about her minimum wage job and she was vulnerable—that's what cost the woman her life."

He stepped away from the desk. "Robin's elderly parents are going to see the mutilated body of their daughter and make positive ID. Our city owes them an apology."

"You let this vic get to you."

"Her name is Robin. She was brutally murdered at the hands of one of our town's scumbags."

"I'm in hot water already because of these three homicides. Asking for an expensive travel voucher is pushing it."

"Captain, this isn't about you or me, it's about doing the right thing. If I know you, the gesture will put a shine on our unit and you'll come out smelling like a rose."

"I'm not so sure about that." He took another sip of coffee. "I'll see what I can do."

Matt started for the door and turned back. "Here's the deal, Cap. I'm having the Madison PD send officers and a social worker to the Anderson home this evening with the news of their daughter's death. I will instruct them to have Robin's father call me. I will tell him that the expenses *are* covered." He opened the door. "If *Americas Finest City* can't cough up the money—I'll pay for it myself."

"Matt … wait." Sawyer stood. "I'll process the voucher."

"Thank you."

"If the city won't give, I'll pitch in with you."

He smiled. "Get out of here an' make the call."

* * * *

SVU SQUADROOM 2:45 PM:

Ken passed a printed list of names and addresses over to Matt. "I got full cooperation from a nice lady at American Express. It didn't take as long as I thought, so I ran all the credit card receipts from *Fridays.*" He sat back and rubbed his eyes. "The hard part was trying to read all the small and blurred names and numbers. Now we got 'em."

"Yeah, great, the tough part will be running them down. That means chasing all over the city." He studied the list of names and addresses.

"That's what I thought too, but as you can see, they're all in the North County area except one, he's in La Mesa."

Matt leaned forward and grabbed a yellow highlighter from a cup of several on his desk. "That one interests me." He highlighted the information. "Michael Moran, I believe we need to check out Mr. Moran right away." He paged through his notebook. "First, the call to Madison."

* * * *

Ken stood and paced around behind his desk. "Just stretching my legs. Your call to MPD sounded positive from this end."

Matt checked his watch. "They said it would be about a half hour to round up a social worker and get to the Anderson home. I really feel for those folks. I can't imagine what it would be like to hear such horrible news."

"I can't believe you asked for a travel voucher?"

Kellogg smiled. "It's in the bag. The captain sees the good media reaction." He studied the list of names again. "Out of all the others there's just one from La Mesa. Quite interesting."

Ken came back to his desk and sat down. "Considering the first two vics lived in La Mesa, we may have something here."

"Did we hear from Ann?"

"Yeah, she and Jack have released the second vic's apartment back to the complex manager. They're going to interview people who worked with her at *PETCO.* There may be a lead there."

"It's Sally Patterson, Ken. She was a person."

"I hear you, I understand. I think you need to take some time off."

"Perhaps, but at the moment we're up to

our eyeballs in this and I believe there's more to come."

Matt's cell rang.

"This is the call from Wisconsin."

"Good luck with that." Ken got up to get a cup of coffee and let Matt have privacy.

"Detective Kellogg."

"This is Jason Anderson." The man's voice shook. "The officers told me to call you."

"Is the social worker there with you?"

"Yes, she's sitting with my wife now." He drew several shaking breaths. "I can't believe this has happened to our Robin."

"Neither can I, sir, and I assure you, we'll use everything in our power to catch the person who did this and put him where he belongs."

"I appreciate that, detective, but our Robin is gone. Nothing—nothing will bring her back."

"Mr. Anderson, I want you to know that the City of San Diego will cover all your expenses to travel here and take your daughter back home."

"Robin went out there to start a new life, now she's a corpse in your city's morgue." His voice wavered. "Does my wife have to be present for positive identification?"

"Not unless she wants to."

Jason lost it and broke into sobs. "I'll be

Coming alone."

"Please call me and let me know when you'll arrive and on what airline and flight. I'll pick you up at the airport personally."

"Thank you, detective, I'll call you tomorrow."

"Mr. Anderson, I need you to know, I am sincerely sorry for your loss." His voice broke on the words and a sharp pain sliced through his heart. "Call my cell when you have it all together."

"I will … thank you."

Matt closed his phone and took a deep breath. "Let's pay a visit to Michael Moran."

Chapter Seventeen

The Camera the Gate & the Box

THE OLD VICTORIAN
SEVERIN DRIVE
MT. HELIX, LA MESA - 3:30 PM:

Kellogg and Black managed to stay ahead of the daily exodus out of downtown San Diego. Matt drove east on the eight to Severin Drive. He said, "I put in for a portable GPS unit a month ago."

"Don't hold your breath. Take it easy on this road, it curves like a bitch."

"I came up here about a year ago. Finding an address is a nightmare."

Ken spotted a cluster of mailboxes. "Pull up here. Nope, we got a ways to go. These numbers are in the forty-eight hundreds.

Moran's house will be over the top where the road levels out."

* * * *

Ten minutes later they found the place. Matt stopped the car in front of an elaborate wrought iron gate. "Jesus, that main gate has got to be fifteen feet tall."

"Don't look now, but we're on camera."

* * * *

Michael sat at his computer working with more pictures in *Photoshop* when he heard the buzzer. He grinned at the wall-mounted security monitor.

"I didn't think this would come so soon." He looked over at Samantha. She had curled up on the leather recliner. "We have company." He slid his chair over to a small console and pushed a button. "Who are you and what do you want?"

Matt flashed his badge. "I'm Detective Matt Kellogg and my partner is Detective Ken Black. We're from the San Diego Police Department."

Michael thought. *I know who you are.* He said, "Okay, now what do you want?"

"We're interviewing people who bought

books at a Barnes and Noble store yesterday at Carmel Mountain Plaza."

"Well I guess you've wasted a trip, Detective. I don't go to the North County and I haven't purchased any books lately." He opened a supply closet. *Keep Talking, I've been well prepared for your visit.*

Kellogg looked into the camera. "It would be a lot easier if we could talk face to face. Just a few questions and we'll be out of your hair."

Michael took what he needed from the closet and closed the door. "I'm afraid I won't be much help."

"Mr. Moran, this is a serious police matter and we have to talk to you. Would you please open the gate?"

"All right, Detective. I'm going to let you in. Give me a few minutes and I'll greet you at the front door. I have to come all the way up from the basement." He reached over and pressed a red button.

They heard the metal clank of the locks disengage. The huge iron gates swung slowly inward. The red light on the camera went out as did the green on the call-box.

Matt drove through.

When the car rounded a curve and passed a stand of eucalyptus Ken said, "Will you get a load of that?" The three story old

Victorian stood solid on a knoll of perfectly landscaped ground.

"The damn driveway is about a hundred yards long and the house looks like it was built yesterday."

Ken took out his cell and clicked a picture. "Who the hell lives like this anymore?"

"The Michael Morans of the world, I guess."

They parked and walked up the sloping steps onto an ornate front porch. "What do you think this pad is worth?" Ken checked out the nineteenth century *gingerbread* work along the overhang of the porch.

"Up here on Mount Helix... I'd put her at two point two mill easy." Matt rang the bell. A pleasant chime sounded from inside.

A whirring sound followed.

The detectives looked at each other.

"Another second please." Michael's muffled voice came through the solid oak front door.

The cops stepped back.

Moran pulled the door open. "Come in gentlemen." He moved his electric wheelchair back. "Don't be shy."

Matt said, "Sorry for the intrusion, we won't be long." He looked down on a man in his late sixties, bald and showing age spots on his hands. He stroked a gray and white cat curled up on his lap. "I didn't mean to be so cranky with you, Detective, I just don't like unexpected visitors."

Kellogg took out his notebook and the receipt from the credit card purchase. "Your American Express was used at TGI Fridays yesterday at Carmel Mountain Plaza and your signature is on the slip. Can you explain that?"

"It wasn't me. The information was lifted off the Internet three weeks ago and hit my account several times. I've notified American Express and they've straightened it out." He laughed and pulled up the pant legs of his trousers. "Does this look like I'd be bopping around a Fridays in the North County or anywhere else?"

Kellogg looked at the metal braces on Michael's legs. "Physically challenged people don't have to be home bound if they choose not to." He showed him the slip. "Is that your signature?"

"Not hardly. Give me your pen?"

Michael took the slip, turned it over and wrote his signature with his left hand. "They're, not even close."

Matt studied the signature. "I have to agree, Mr. Moran, they're not the same. For the sake of argument, do it again with your right hand."

"I'm not right handed." He held the receipt and pen out to Kellogg.

"Humor me. Just give it a shot … go ahead. Then we'll know for sure and you're in the clear."

"Clear of what, Detective?"

"Murder, Mr. Moran. Whoever signed that slip bought dinner and drinks for a young woman who turned up dead this morning." He handed the slip and pen back to Michael.

"Sign it with your *right* hand."

"I'll play your game, Kellogg." He clicked the ballpoint and wrote his name in wobbly scrawl and handed the paper and pen to Matt. "Doesn't look anything like the other two does it?"

Ken took the receipt and studied the signatures. The one from the receipt read: *Michael Moran*. He glanced at Matt and read the signature from the man's left hand: *Michael Moran*. Below that, the right hand penmanship looked entirely different, even foreign: Michael Moran. The detective grinned. "I have to say, the handwriting doesn't match up." He folded the paper and handed it back to Matt.

Kellogg said, "We'll have it analyzed just be sure. It's standard procedure."

"Good luck with that, detectives. Will there

Be anything else?"

Ken said, "How is it that there isn't a wheelchair ramp out front?"

Michael grinned. "I have one in the garage entrance and there are three elevators in the house, I get around just fine."

"I'll bet you can do pretty much anything you want." He shook Michael's hand. "Love the cat."

"Thank you, Samantha's my best friend."

"You live alone in this big house?"

"It's Sam, and me, we manage on our own."

"I'm curious." Ken looked around the huge foyer and living room. "No offense, but how does a physically impaired person, of your age, keep a place like this so shiny clean?"

"That's none of your business. I resent the question."

Matt said, "You drive, Mr. Moran?"

"Yes, my vehicle is equipped with the latest electronic hardware for a cripple like me."

"Then you could've gone to the North County to buy books, correct?"

"If I wanted to, but why go through all that effort when I can order anything I want on the Internet?"

"That's a good answer."

"Why would I lie, detective?"

"Maybe because you're not what you appear to be."

Michael glared at Kellogg. "Are you accusing me of anything, Detective?"

"Just an observation as a cop."

"Well, you can take your observation and your partner and get the hell out of my house."

"The next time we visit your humble abode, we'll be armed with a warrant."

"Good luck with that too, Kellogg—get out!"

The detectives moved toward the front door. Ken added, "Thanks for your cooperation."

When Michael closed the door he held both hands over his mouth to stifle his laughter. He took a few breaths and hugged Samantha. "Are they idiots or what?"

* * * *

Matt started the car. "I don't like it."

"What?"

"There's something wrong with this picture."

"Yeah, whatever. We were on the edge of harassment in there."

"C'mon, Ken. That dude is as phony as a three-dollar bill."

"You have to prove that."

"I will. Did you notice the color of his legs when he showed us his braces?"

"They looked fine to me."

"That's my point. A person's legs don't have a healthy color when they're wearing braces. His did."

"I think you're grabbing at straws?"

Matt pulled away from the front of the house and drove toward the open gate. "Did you get a look at the muscle tone on his crippled leg?"

"I didn't pay that much attention."

"The man's legs are strong, the braces are a sham." He pulled through the gate and turned right onto Severin drive. "Michael Moran is not handicapped and I'm betting he's our perp."

"What about his signature on the receipt?"

"That's sham number two. Moran isn't left-handed."

"And you believe that why?"

"He petted and scratched his cat with his right hand."

They reached the intersection and pulled out onto I-8 West toward downtown.

Ken said, "I noticed that."

"His wheelchair controls we're on the right side of the chair?"

"It could be the way it's made."

"I don't think so." Kellogg brought the *Crown Vic* up to sixty-five and swung into the fast lane.

Chapter Eighteen

Chasing Shadows

GROSSMONT CENTER–LA MESA,
PETCO AT THAT SAME TIME:

Sergeants, Ann Beck and Jack
Towne sat with store manager, Bob Russell
in his office. He said, "I just can't believe
someone would do such a thing. Sally was a
happy person." He sipped from a bottle of
water. "She was all excited about her
promotion … I just don't get it."

Jack made a note. "This isn't your
everyday homicide, Mr. Russell. You've read
the papers, seen the TV reports. Ms.
Patterson had to have been targeted and
stalked." He showed the suspect's picture
again. "Nothing rings a bell with this face?"

Bob studied the image once more. "I can't be sure. I'm not on the floor most of the time, and we get a lot of traffic in here seven days a week."

Ann looked at her notes. "Sally's car never left the lot Monday night. What time did she get off work?"

"She was administrative, her day ended at five-thirty."

"Who would've seen her leave?"

"One or both of our checkout clerks. Sally was a friendly person, she would've said something on her way out."

"Are those people on duty now?"

"They should be." He looked up at his office security monitor. "They're both on checkout."

Jack said, "We need to talk to them, in here, one at a time. Can you arrange that?"

"Sure thing, give me a few minutes." Russell got up from his desk and left the office.

Beck stood and watched the manager come into view on the screen. She rubbed the back of her neck. "I'll talk to the girls."

Jack closed his notebook and paced around the cluttered room. "I think we're chasing shadows here."

"You never know. I believe we'll be reopening the *Oaks North* cases and nail this sonofabitch for all of those as well as our current three."

"I'd like to see that happen. We do it and you and I will get gold shields."

Russell came back with a slight young woman who had short-cut strawberry hair and pale blue eyes. "Susan, these folks are from the San Diego Police Department. They need to talk to you about Sally." He went behind his desk and sat down.

"Hi, I'm Sergeant Ann Beck and this is my partner, Sergeant Jack Towne. We just need to ask you a few questions."

"Okay. It's awful about Sally. My stomach goes in knots when I see the reports on the news. How can I help?"

Ann gestured toward the sofa. Susan sat down. Beck opened her notebook. "What's your full name and address?"

"Susan Martin, I live at 136 Kenner Road in Lemon Grove."

"Are you married?"

"No, I live with my parents." She shifted her eyes from Ann to Jack and shuddered. "This whole thing has me afraid to be outside alone."

"That's understandable." Ann sat beside the girl. "Did you see Sally when she left the store on Monday?"

"Yes, she stopped by my register on her

way out. Sally was so excited about her promotion she just had to share the news with Roberta an' me."

"Who's Roberta?"

"The other cashier." She pointed toward the monitor. "That's her." Susan caught a quick breath. "Sally was friendly with all the employees."

"Did she talk with a male customer?"

"Not that I saw. She was alone."

"Did you notice anyone who might have met her outside?"

Susan thought a moment and shook her head. "I can't say. I had customers checking out right then."

Ann showed her the composite picture. "Did you see this man in the store at any time before Sally left?"

Susan stiffened. "Oh my God. It's him! He was in the store earlier."

"When did you see him?"

"I saw his picture on TV, but I didn't make the connection. He looks like the man I saw by the cat cages when I came back from break." She hesitated and nodded.

"Yes. He was talking to a tabby and scratching the cat's chin through the cage with his finger." Susan stood and pointed at the image. "That man was in the store. Is he the killer?"

Ann got off the sofa. "We don't know yet, but he's a person of interest."

"Okay, okay—I remember something else. It may not be important."

"Anything can be helpful."

"Monday afternoon, Sally stopped by my register and said she'd seen a good looking guy staring at her and Lauren during lunch. It could be him."

"Who's Lauren?"

"She's the counter girl at Starbucks right next door. They were casual friends."

"You've been a big help. Thank you."

"I just want to see that *slime* caught."

"You can go back to work now."

The manager said, "You want me to get Roberta?"

Ann smiled and closed her notebook. "No, Mr. Russell, I think we're done here."

Jack said, "Next stop, Starbucks."

* * * *

THE VICTORIAN
AT THAT SAME TIME:

Michael's ribs ached from the hard laughing. "I got a real kick out of fooling the cops, Sam." He removed the leg braces and put them back in the supply closet. "I haven't had a good laugh like that in a long time." He stored the wheelchair against the back wall of the large closet. "I do feel sorry for anyone who has to be so confined and really have to really wear braces."

Samantha jumped up on the leather recliner and made a soft cry.

"You're hungry again. Damn, you could eat me out of house and home, I swear." He put his face close to the cat. "How do I look?"

Sam cried again and curled up on the chair.

"This part is always the worst." He pushed his thumbs up under the latex skull cap and lifted it off his head. "There, back to normal." He shook out the powder and put the appliance in its plastic bag. "I hope I don't have to use that again anytime soon."

Samantha gave out another cry.

"I have a nice roast in the slow cooker and it should be ready in less than an hour. Will that suit my princess?" He reached out and rubbed her belly. "In the meantime, I need to get my package ready to deliver to Detective Matt Kellogg."

He turned back to his computer screen and brought up a still frame he caught of reporter Amanda Price at the press conference. "Lovely girl. Your legs are hot."

Chapter Nineteen

Hostile Witness

GROSSMONT CENTER–LA MESA
STARBUCKS – TEN MINUTES LATER:

𝕬𝖓𝖓 𝖘𝖍𝖔𝖜𝖊𝖉 𝖍𝖊𝖗 𝖇𝖆𝖉𝖌𝖊 to the counter girl and noticed the name tag. "Hi Lauren, I'm Sergeant Beck and this is my partner, Sergeant Towne. We're with the San Diego PD. We'd like a word with you."

"Is this about Sally?"

"Yes, I'm afraid it is."

"Good, I was going to call the police when I saw the story in the paper."

Jack said, "Why didn't you?"

"I've been so upset I couldn't think straight." She turned to a man behind the counter. "Jeff, take over for me, I have to talk to these cops." She addressed Ann. "My shift is over in ten minutes, but we can talk now."

"Is there someplace private?" Beck glanced around the shop. "It's pretty busy in here."

Lauren took off her apron. "Go around to the rear patio, I'll meet you there. You want coffee?"

Jack smiled. "I'll have a small regular with cream and sugar."

Ann said, "No, I'm fine, thanks."

Lauren waved toward the entrance.

"Outside, turn right. Give me a minute."

When they stepped out Jack chuckled. "I have a feeling this woman is on a mission."

"What gave you the first clue?"

* * * *

The back door opened and Lauren came out with Jack's coffee. She handed it to him and joined them at an umbrella table. Cream and sugar sat in a service basket in the center of the table.

"This is where employees take breaks, private enough?"

Ann already had her notebook out. "Before we get started, I need your full name and address."

"Williams, Lauren Williams. I live in an apartment on Fletcher Parkway in El Cajon. It's *The Timbers* I'm on the second floor, number 273."

"Are you married?"

"No, I live alone, except when my *sometimes* boyfriend drops by."

Jack unfolded the composite picture. "Is this the guy who may have stared at you and Sally?"

"How the hell do you know about that?"

Beck smiled. "Sally told an employee at *PETCO* and said you were friends with her. That's why we're here."

Lauren tapped the picture. "That's the creep. I knew it when I saw his mug on TV." Her voice fluttered. "I warned Sally that she was being stared at. He even winked at her." Her dark eyes flashed. "If I see that bastard in my shop again, I'll throw scalding coffee in his face."

Jack said, "I don't really think that would be in your best interest."

"Yeah, well somebody has to do something." She shook back her long black ponytail and tapped the picture again. "That sonofabitch killed my friend—I'd bet on it."

Ann reached over and patted Lauren's hand. "You have every right to be upset."

"I'm pissed, angry to the core, I want to

find him and rip his face off."

Jack stirred his coffee. "Okay, take it easy. You said the flirting came later, how so?"

"Right. That scum must've heard Sally and me set up our lunch date." Her voice shook. "We made plans to have lunch at *Hooleys,* and he was close enough to hear." She clenched her fists and her eyes misted. "That shit waited and followed us to the restaurant."

Ann made notes and said, "Where's *Hooleys?"*

"Here in the center, it's just a short walk from my shop."

Jack looked at her and sipped some coffee. "You've said *my shop* twice. Are you the manager?"

"No, Jeff is. What the hell has that got to do with anything?"

"We're just getting information."

Beck scribbled another note. "What happened at lunch?"

"Nothing really, I mean the creep didn't actually do anything. He was just *there.* I saw him a couple of tables away while Sally and I were eating and chatting. He was staring at us." She shivered. "Christ, his eyes sent chills up my arms. I told Sally we were being watched. I said, *don't look.* She did anyway.

The jerk smiled and winked at her." Lauren's voice wavered. Sally thought it was a compliment. She was so excited about her promotion and the weekend she had behind the scenes at the zoo, I could feel her excitement." She drew a deep breath. "She'll never have that again ...."

A gust of Santa Ana wind rushed through the patio and forced the umbrella to turn all the way around. The metal pole squeaked when it turned in the hole of the table.

Sergeant Beck wrote a final squiggle in her notebook. "Thank you for your time. If there's anything else, we'll be in touch."

Jack said, "You're an attractive young woman. The guy knows who you are and where you work. You need to be extra careful." He handed her his card. "If anything suspicious comes up, give us a call."

"The day that bastard tries to pick up on me will be his last. I'll cut off his manhood and shove it down his throat."

Ann said, "Be careful and stay aware of your surroundings at all times."

"Actually, I hope the pig tries to confront me."

Towne added, "Be careful Lauren."

Ann's cell buzzed. "Beck here. Hi, nice to know you're alive and well. Hang on." She glanced at Jack. "It's Matt." Into the phone she said, "What's the latest?"

Kellogg replied, "We're back from Mount Helix, are you clear there?"

"Yeah, we're wrapping an unexpected interview with one of Sally's friends. I think it's been a productive afternoon."

"Great, the captain wants a meet before we close shop."

"We're done here, give us a half hour and we'll be there."

"I'll tell him … Love you."

"Me too. See you in thirty."

* * * *

THE OLD VICTORIAN
AT THAT SAME TIME:

Michael laid out the color print of Robin's headshot and her severed legs positioned around it. He showed it to Samantha. The cat sat in the leather recliner beside him. "What do you think, Sam? Is that good work or not?"

She sniffed the photo held in front of her nose, but didn't offer any response.

"Okay, I understand. You have no opinion, but I think the picture will do just fine." He studied the image for a moment and turned it around several times. "I know what will shake up Kellogg … a lot."

He picked up a black felt-tipped pen and wrote a message on the photograph:

Keep an eye on Ann Beck, I sure am.

"That should churn Kellogg's cream." He looked at Samantha. "How about I mention my lust for Amanda Price?" He thought a moment, scratched the cat's chin. "No, I think Ms. Price should be a complete surprise." He laughed and slipped the picture into an envelope and sealed it. "Tomorrow's good enough to make the delivery."

* * * *

Ten minutes later, at the kitchen table, Michael sliced off two rare pieces of the roast. "Those are mine." He cut up small chunks of meat and put them in the cat's dish. "C'mon, Samantha, dinner's on."

The cat jumped up to her place at the table and licked her chops.

"Good girl, I've spooned on extra gravy for you, I know you love it."

Sam began lapping at the gravy.

Michael spread a linen napkin across his lap. "I think it's great that we can share family dinners together." He cut a small piece meat, dipped it in hot gravy and put the morsel in his mouth. "Samantha, this is just heavenly."

The cat chewed away on her meat and purred as she did.

Chapter Twenty

At the End of the Day

CONFERENCE ROOM – SDPD
WEDNESDAY - 5:15 PM:

𝕿𝖍𝖊 𝕾𝖁𝖀 𝖙𝖊𝖆𝖒 sat around the huge table with notebooks ready.

Captain Roy Sawyer stood in front of a large marking board. "It's *Showtime* ladies and gentlemen."

He picked up a red dry-marker and wrote:
Three days –3 bodies – no suspects – bum leads!

He looked at his weary team. "Why is that, folks?"

Kellogg stood and went to the service bar.

"We're being played by a very clever

perp." He poured a cup of coffee. "There's no crime scene, he's contacted the media directly, promised and delivered a third victim." Matt returned to his seat. "The composite picture we're showing around is as phony as a three-dollar bill."

Ann said, "Jack and I had two productive interviews with two women who saw the possible perp face-to-face."

Matt sat down next to her. "The people we've talked to saw what the perp wanted them to see." He sipped some brew. "The composite photo isn't real. That man is history. His face will never show up again—count on it."

The captain added to his notes on the board: *witnesses who saw the face of a man who doesn't exist.* "Okay, Matt, you know this because?"

Kellogg leaned forward and picked up the composite photo. "This dude is *make believe.* The real perp is hiding behind a mask. If there's another killing, and I'm sure there will be, any face that might be seen will be just as fake."

Sawyer wrote: *A mystery man in a mask.*

To Matt he said, "And you're sure?"

The detective looked around at the team. "Sorry, the Captain knows this, the rest of you don't."

He stood and paced before the group.

"I worked undercover narcotics with NYPD for six years, on and off, out of the two-seven precinct, which is a tough place to be."

Ann said, "You never told me."

"I didn't share it with anybody."

He stopped at the window and glanced out at the hustle and bustle of San Diego closing another work day.

"There are people who can change how they look, who they are, what they do, and their entire persona at the drop of a hat."

He looked at his fellow squad members.

"They're not serial killers, far from it, but they will kill without hesitation. I've been there and seen it happen."

He walked back to the table and sat down.

"Our perp will never appear the same way again."

The captain said, "How the hell do we nail a killer with a hundred faces?"

"That's going to take some doing. Unfortunately, there may be another killing or two and we can't stop that. He's a loose cannon."

Sawyer picked up the marker and wrote:
Dead end!

He drew a short breath.

"Everything you people accomplished

yesterday and today is apparently all for naught. We're chasing the *Joker* for Christ's sake."

He capped the marker, and set in down.

"The brass won't see anything funny about it."

Jack rubbed his eyes, and closed his notebook.

"We're stuck in limbo here. No crime scene, no prints. There's no evidence, and nothing to go on."

Ann said, "Matt, you and Ken followed the credit card lead on the Anderson case, anything there?"

"Nothing we can take to the bank. He signed the back of the receipt with his left hand, and of course, it didn't match. I believe he's right handed. I had him sign again with his right hand. Not even close. Moran appears to be a cripple, in his sixties, and confined to a wheelchair."

"Appears?" She added. "You sound doubtful."

"Sometimes things aren't quite as they seem to be."

Ken stood and stretched his arms.

"I think, Mr. Moran is more than a person of interest. I could be wrong … there's something off center with the guy. Can't say what, I just sense it."

Kellogg pushed away from the table.

"I'd like to keep an eye on him for a while."

The captain added: **MICHAEL**

MORAN to the board. "We have a different ballgame now, folks. Go home, get some rest, tomorrow starts early."

He shook his head.

"Jesus, I don't believe this."

Ken slipped into his suit coat.

"How about, we all go to the *Top Gun* for a cold one? First round's on me."

Jack said, "You're on, Detective."

Matt helped Ann into her jacket.

"Would you rather pick up some Chinese and go to my place?"

"That's the best offer I've had all day."

The captain rolled down his sleeves.

"Matt, the Anderson travel voucher is approved. I pushed it through."

"Thank you very much. Robin's father called me when we were on the way back from Mount Helix. I'll pick him up tomorrow at four-thirty."

He hesitated.

"It'll be the saddest day of the man's life."

"I hear that. You two have a good night."

Ann nodded.

"We shall."

* * * *

BERNARDO CENTER– NORTH COUNTY
TWO HOURS LATER:

Michael dialed a number from his cell.

"North County Sentinel. How may I direct your call?"

"May I have reporter, Amanda Price."

Amanda picked up on the second ring.

"Yes?"

"There's a guy on three who wants to *have* you."

"That's funny, Kathy." She punched the blinking line. "This is Price."

"Ms. Price, I have the story of your career."

"That's nice, who are you, and what have you got?" She turned over a doodle-covered page on her legal pad and wrote: *Prank call 7:30 P.M.*

"My name is Frank Waverly and I have solid information about the *Legs* killer." He coughed. "Excuse me. I have a touch of the flu. I know things the police don't."

Amanda jotted: *Older man - ill.*

"What things are those, Mr. Waverly?"

He coughed again, and wheezed.

"The crime scene, I know where the murders have been committed."

"Okay, where would that be?" She wrote:

Crime scene location.

"In the basement of an old Victorian house in La Mesa."

He coughed again.

"How do you know this?" She wrote: *Old Vic, La Mesa.*

"I have to tell you in person." Another wheeze. "I'm at Bernardo Center in front of the *Subway* sandwich store." He coughed again. "It's well lit, and I'm sitting at an outside table. I'll wait one half hour."

Amanda chuckled. "You expect me to just bop over there to get your trumped up story?"

He wheezed into the phone once more.

"I'm sorry I offended you, Ms. Price"

Another cough. "I'll just click off here, and call Hal Marks. He'd love to have the piece for the *Tribune.*"

Amanda stiffened. "Wait—wait! I'll be there in twenty minutes. How will I recognize you?"

He wheezed again for effect. "I'm an elderly gent with a white beard. I'm wearing a gray leather coat, and a San Diego Padres ball cap." He coughed. "I walk with a cane."

"You'd better be on the level, Mr. Waverly." She wrote: *Old man with cane.*

"I assure you, Ms. Price, you'll get the best story you will ever write."

"I'm on the way." Amanda grabbed her keys and tape recorder and headed for the back door.

The night editor looked up as she went by his desk. "Where are you going?"

"To get a story, Richard. I'll call it in."

* * * *

Michael closed his phone, and grinned. "Damn, my acting is getting better."

He cleared his throat, and delivered the famous line by Marlon Brando from the movie, *On the Waterfront.* *"I coulda been a contender."* He laughed.

Chapter Twenty One

Kellogg and Beck

BREE MANOR – EL CAJON
MATT'S APT
ONE HOUR EARLIER:

𝔄nn set the table and put out utensils for 𝔐att. She opened the containers of cashew chicken and white rice. "You want the won ton or egg flower soup?"

"I'll go with the won ton." He came into the dining room from his home office. "I just confirmed Mr. Anderson's flight and arrival time for tomorrow."

Ann spooned soup into a bowl and set it on Matt's placemat. I have no idea how I'd handle what those people are facing."

"Yeah. I'm a little nervous about it

Myself. Best thing is; he's coming alone. I don't think his wife could take it."

Ann put more Won-Ton in Matt's bowl.

"I got the shivers when you told the crew to expect more killings and we can't do anything to prevent that." She sat opposite Matt, and opened her chopsticks. "You should learn to use these."

"I'd starve to death in the process." He took some soup. "Excellent." He enjoyed another spoonful. "That's the frustration of law enforcement."

"Which is?" Ann had started into her cashew chicken with experienced use of the chopsticks.

"Not being able to *prevent* a crime. It's even worse with what we're dealing with. More women are going to die, and we can't do *jack."* He opened the carton of pork Chow Mein, and used a fork to put some on his plate.

"What would you do if you could?" She took a sip of a rich California Merlot.

"For starters, I'd run Moran through the wringer. DMV would be the first step, but no, I can't do that *legally."*

"But you could. That is, if you wanted to." She skillfully used her chopsticks to load some Chow Mein onto her plate.

"That gate's closed, Ann, I have no legal

reason to run him." He swirled the red wine in his glass. "Now that's really funny."

"What's funny?"

"We're dealing with the *legs collector murders,* and I'm checking the *legs* of my wine." He poured more for both of them.

"Suppose you had a way to open the DMV *gate?*" She sipped some wine. "I'm sure you *fudged* a few things while you were living your secret *undercover* life with NYPD, which you haven't told me anything about."

"There's latitude when you're undercover, especially with narcotics." He cut a clump of noodles, and used a fork to eat them. "I didn't say anything about my work with the two-seven because I didn't want to flaunt my experience in the *Big Apple."*

"I can appreciate that, but it would've been nice to know I was in the company of one of the cream of the crop." She raised her glass. "To Detective Matt Kellogg, undercover Nark."

"Cream of the crop, shit. When I worked that assignment, I was in the sewer with the rest of the rats." He finished his wine, and poured another glass. "Where were you going with the DMV issue?"

"Okay, I just happen to have a close girlfriend who just happens to be a supervisor of the downtown office of the Department of

Motor Vehicles." She grinned. "My friend and I could have lunch. I give her Moran's name—"

"Stop right there, Ms. Beck. You'll do no such thing. Are you nuts?" He took a sip of Merlot. "You'd be putting yourself, and your friend, on the line. It's not worth it. You want a gold shield, that's not the way to get it."

"I want to stop the bastard from killing another woman."

"So do I, but we can't do much about it." He took her hand. "Ann, listen to me. We'll nail this prick, but we do it by the book. We're not going to sacrifice our careers for the sake of this piece of human waste. Are we clear here?"

"Yes, I'm sorry. I'm a woman … I ache for the three victims, and their families, and for whomever the next one will be."

"I hear what you're saying, and I agree." He smiled, and brushed a lock of auburn hair off her forehead. "I love you. Let's finish our dinner, and watch a stupid sitcom."

"I'm all for that." She drank the rest of her wine, and held out the glass. "I'll have some more please."

* * * *

BERNARDO CENTER
THE SUBWAY SANDWICH SHOP
AT THAT SAME TIME:

Amanda managed to get a parking spot fairly close to the *Subway* store. She climbed out of her *Ford Explorer* with her shoulder bag and tape recorder, and walked toward the outside tables. She mumbled, "I don't see anybody. He bailed out on me—shit!"

Michael came out of the shadows with the silent swiftness of a cheetah. "Miss Price?"

She turned to see a tall, good looking man coming toward her. "Yes?"

"Well, don't you look lovely tonight?"

"Who are you?"

He reached her in a split second. "I'm Michael." He smiled and stuck the needle in her upper right arm. "There isn't any old man with a beard and cane. I'm surprised you bought all that."

Amanda's strength began to slip away, her vision blurred. Her cry came out as a whisper. "What do you want?"

"Your legs, I must have your beautiful legs." He caught the tape recorder she was about to drop. "Easy girl. I'll walk you to my car. You'll be just fine."

The drug claimed its toll on Amanda. She Fought it and tried to speak. "You … son …

of … a … bitch …."

Colors flooded into her vision; all kinds of rolling colors.

Michael held her up. To a casual witness they would appear as a loving couple waltzing through the parking lot. He shifted her weight.

"My, my, you smell nice. Just one more row and we'll be at my car."

He cut between two vehicles and came up to the passenger side of his Mercedes.

"Here we are, Amanda."

When he had the door all the way open he lifted her into the passenger compartment, and hefted her legs into the vehicle.

"Love your legs. You should've worn slacks, my dear. I'm going to have to spend extra time with you."

He closed the door, and went around to the driver's side, and got in.

"Very soon you'll get to see the crime scene Kellogg would love to know about."

Michael started the engine.

"Let's go to my house."

Chapter Twenty Two

An uneasy meeting

LINDBERGH FIELD – SAN DIEGO
TERMINAL TWO – 4:45 PM:

𝕿𝖗𝖆𝖋𝖋𝖎𝖈 𝖜𝖆𝖘 𝖆 𝖍𝖆𝖘𝖘𝖑𝖊 all the way from downtown to the airport. Matt managed to arrive a half hour early.

He stood with a crowd of people waiting for friends and relatives. He was one of a few who held signs displaying names.

A flood of travelers started riding down the escalator into the main entrance area. Matt's nervousness kicked in. *Maybe this wasn't such a great idea.*

He spotted an elderly couple that looked lost. *Shit, the wife came anyway.* He held up his sign. Sure enough, the man waved. *This is going to be a bitch.*

Mr. Anderson helped his wife step off the moving stairs and they approached Matt.

"Detective, I'm Jason and this is my wife, Paula. She insisted on coming." He shook Matt's hand. "I wish we didn't have to meet under these circumstances."

"I agree." He smiled at the woman. "It's difficult for all of us."

Paula studied him for a moment through bloodshot gray eyes. "Young man, you don't know the half of it." She didn't offer her hand.

Telltale signs of embarrassment crept up Matt's neck and around his ears. "I'm sorry … your luggage will be coming in over there." He led them away from the escalator to the baggage area for American Airlines. "How was your flight?"

Jason said, "It was bumpy all the way from Wisconsin to Denver. Otherwise it was okay."

These people don't know what to say and neither do I. "We'll pick up your bags and get you checked in at the Holiday Inn. It's not far from here and they have a nice restaurant."

Mrs. Anderson stopped and glared at Matt. "You're acting like we're here on vacation. I want to see my dead daughter and take her home—that's *all* I want to do."

"I understand that, ma'am, but we have to wait until tomorrow. There's paperwork and arrangements to process." He led them on toward the baggage area.

"Detective Kellogg has gone out of his way to help us and I think we should be thankful." He hugged his wife and kissed her on the cheek. To Matt he said, "I'll go grab our bags, we just have two suitcases."

To Paula, Matt said, "I can imagine how you must feel—"

"You have no idea what I feel and don't pretend you do." She stared at him with cold eyes and continued with ice in her voice, "This paradise you call, *America's Finest City,* took the life of my baby and you have the nerve to say you can *imagine* how I must feel?" She stepped away and sat on a nearby bench.

"There's a psychotic beast running around your town and I feel sorry for his other victims and their families. My only child is dead and so is part of me—you have no idea."

"We're going to catch him and put the man away for good."

"Sure you will—maybe."

Jason returned with their luggage. "We're all set."

"Let me take those and I'll drive you to the hotel."

* * * *

THE OLD VICTORIAN
FIVE HOURS LATER:

Michael sat in the leather recliner with Samantha curled up on his lap. He watched Amanda start to wake up. She was strapped into a wheelchair and positioned in front of his computer. "C'mon, Girl, it's time to write your story."

She came out of a drugged stupor to see a blurred image of a man sitting in a chair. She blinked and strained her eyes. "You … what did you do to me?"

"I let you rest through the night and all day so you could be up to writing your award winning final piece for the North County Sentinel. Of course, I couldn't resist enjoying your beautiful legs."

"You did what?" Her vision cleared and the realization of what was happening shot through her like an electric shock.

"Not to fear, Amanda, dear. I haven't hurt you. I merely made love to your legs."

"You sick sonofabitch—you're the killer!" She fought against the straps.

"Hey, what the hell, you've got the exclusive." He stroked Samantha's neck. "Oh, forgive me. Amanda, I'd like you to meet Samantha, she's my soul mate."

I'm going to die! She tried to move the

wheelchair, but it was locked. She screamed, "You're a sick bastard!" She struggled again against the binds.

Michael lifted the cat off his lap and set her on the floor. "Go get something to eat, sweetheart, I have to deal with our guest."

"What kind of animal are you? I'll never do anything you want. I won't write any story, but my own about you."

"Of course you will. You'll do whatever I desire, or you'll know more pain than you can imagine." He got off the recliner and released Amanda's hands and arms. "I have two choices with you. I can keep you here and enjoy your legs as often as I wish." He reached down and rubbed her naked thighs. "That might be nice, but it would soon become boring. In the meantime you'd be looking for a way to escape. I can't risk that." He grinned. "That leaves the alternative."

"The cops are onto you and they're coming after you."

"Now you sound like my dear departed mother and that can really piss me off. You don't want to do that." He stood behind her, reached over and moved the mouse to clear the screen saver and clicked on MS-Word.

"My second choice is to go as planned. You will write your final article for the *Sentinel,* and it will be published nationwide. Who knows, maybe worldwide."

"Why are you doing this?"

"To answer your question on the *why,* you'd have to speak with my dead mother, she's always around here somewhere." He petted her hair as he would Samantha's.

"You're a lovely young woman, Amanda. You shouldn't have flaunted your beautiful legs at the press conference."

"You're a demented piece of shit—I won't write anything you want." She made a fist and drove her right hand up and hit Michael in the mouth.

"You Bitch!' He grabbed a scalpel from a shelf above the computer, cupped Amanda's right, exposed, breast and cut a two-inch incision.

She screamed.

Hot blood ran down her breast and dripped onto her thigh.

"Fight me again and I'll cut off that nice firm tit—you hear me?"

"You can go to hell!"

"Now we're communicating." He sat in the recliner. "Take a minute to get yourself together and then write this line: *I, Amanda Price, submit my final story. I have met and fallen victim to the legs collector.*

Michael blotted his cut lip with a tissue. "You're lucky I need you, or I'd slice you up right now."

"Write your own damn story."

"I could, but it wouldn't have your snappy style." He tapped the side of the blade against her breast. "Get to work, you're on a deadline."

Amanda began typing.

Chapter Twenty Three

Positive Identification

SAN DIEGO CITY/COUNTY MORGUE
KEARNEY MESA - THURSDAY - 10:00 AM:

𝕸𝖊𝖉𝖎𝖈𝖆𝖑 𝕰𝖝𝖆𝖒𝖎𝖓𝖊𝖗, 𝕵𝖚𝖉𝖞 𝖂𝖆𝖐𝖊
pushed the gurney up to the viewing window.
She carefully uncovered Robin's face and
folded the sheet down just below the woman's
shoulders. The incisions from her autopsy
weren't something Judy wanted the waiting
parents to see.

She pressed the talk button on the wall-
mounted intercom. "Let me know when you're
ready, Matt."

* * * *

In the hall outside of the covered window,

Kellogg stood with Mr. and Mrs. Anderson. He whispered, "Are you both okay?"

Jason held his wife close. He nodded. "Yes … go ahead."

Matt stepped away and clicked the intercom on the wall near the window.

"We're ready, Judy."

The curtain slid open to reveal Robin's head and shoulders. Wake didn't want to expose the empty sheet below the abdomen.

Kellogg steeled himself for the reactions he knew would come.

Mrs. Anderson let out a pain filled cry. "My baby—my little baby girl." She started shaking and reached out to touch the glass. "Robin … oh, Robin, honey." She ran her fingers across the window as though she were feeling her daughter's face. "We're going to take you home … home, Robin where you'll be safe."

Jason spoke through sobs, "That's enough … it's our daughter." He held on to his wife to keep her from falling.

Matt keyed the intercom. His voice cracked. "Thank you, Judy."

The curtain closed. Mrs. Anderson drew a deep breath. "Home, we have to take our baby home now."

* * * *

NORTH COUNTY SENTINEL
RANCHO BERNARDO DRIVE
AT THAT SAME HOUR:

City Editor James Roberts left another message on Amanda's voice mail. "This is the fourth time I've called this morning, Price. Where the hell are you? There better be a damn good reason for two day's absence. Get back to me, I mean like pronto."

Reporter Avery Davis looked over into the editor's cubicle. "I ran late the other night and I heard Amanda tell the night editor she was going to get a story."

Roberts stood and picked up his *San Diego Chargers* coffee mug. "Did she say what it was about?"

"Nope. She did say she'd call it in." He came out from his workspace with his coffee mug. "I think she might be working on the *Legs* story."

"Walk with me." They headed for the kitchen. "I'm pissed at her, but it's not like Price to just take off. What time was it when she left?"

"If I remember right it was around seven fifteen. It was starting to get dark."

"That's what I mean. Price works all day and she's going out on a story after seven in the evening? Something's out of whack here.

I'll call Richard and see if he knows anything."

* * * *

SDPD COMPLEX – SVU
SQUADROOM – 4:30 PM:

Kellogg came in, walked to his desk, took off his sports coat, and hung it over the back of his chair. He looked at Ken. "Partner, that was a rough one."

"The Andersons?" Ken sat back. "You've done a lot of them."

"Yeah, but, I let myself get too involved with this one." He opened a desk drawer and pulled out a form. "Now, the extra paperwork. How'd you guys do with the Sally Patterson case?"

Ken stood. "We caught a break on next of kin."

"Great, I'm not handling that one."

"You want some coffee?"

"Yeah." He handed Ken his cup. "What came up?"

"Turns out the vic has an uncle in Pasadena. He's driving down tomorrow to claim the body." Ken went to the service bar. "You want your usual sugar and cream rush?"

"Please. Anything on Mary Jane Ott's

case?" He started filling out the form to cover his extra time to transport the Andersons to and from the airport.

Ken came back and handed Matt his coffee. "You'll love this. Ms. Ott was a seventies *Flower Child.* Ann and Jack dug up the kicker." He sat at his desk and sipped some coffee. "They pulled a few VHS tapes and DVDs from Mary Jane's closet. She became a porno queen in the late nineties and worked under the name, *Candy Topps.* We both know she has a couple of good ones."

"Ken, your humor, as usual, sucks." Matt continued writing on the form.

"Okay, Beck and Towne tracked down a producer for *Candy's* adult work. A dude named, Harry Wallace. He was broken up when he got the news of Mary Jane's demise. Very touching. He's coming down from LA to claim the body." He laughed. "Now, all three vics are accounted for."

"Terrific, and still nothing on the perp." Matt scratched in another answer on the form.

Captain Sawyer came out of his office and stopped at Matt and Ken's desks. "Detectives … I just took a call from the North County Sentinel's Managing Editor." He hesitated. "Amanda Price went missing forty-eight hours ago."

Kellogg stood. "Sonofabitch—he got to her!"

The captain said, "The editor told me she went out on a story and hasn't been heard from since."

Chapter Twenty Four

Amanda's Last Story

THE OLD VICTORIAN
THURSDAY – 10:00 PM:

𝔐𝔦𝔠𝔥𝔞𝔢𝔩 𝔠𝔞𝔪𝔢 𝔦𝔫𝔱𝔬 𝔱𝔥𝔢 𝔡𝔢𝔫 wearing a fresh pair of latex gloves and carrying Amanda's shoulder bag and tape recorder. "I took the liberty of removing your cell from the purse, I hope you don't mind." He opened the phone, and showed her the screen. "There are a load of messages for you. I can let you hear them, if you want, but, I'm afraid you won't be able to answer them. Would you like to hear your boss frantically trying to reach you?"

"No, I would not!" She regarded him through puffy red eyes. "You're insane—you know they're going to get you, you creep."

He sat in the recliner and Samantha jumped up on his lap. "Now who would *they* be?" He leaned back and grinned. "I guess you mean Detective Kellogg and his idiot partner." He closed the cell and slipped it back into Amanda's bag. "You know police procedure, Price. Those nitwits have nothing to go on. Good old Matt and Ken have already stopped by." He laughed. "They think I'm a crippled old man in a wheelchair—that's a riot. After they left, I laughed until I ached."

"When they do catch you, Michael, I hope Kellogg does make a cripple of you." Bile rose up and burned the back of her throat. "You're a worthless piece of trash!"

Michael flushed and stood. "You sounded just like my dead mother, and that's not wise on your part."

The cat scurried from the room.

"I forgot, I *did* give you my name. Doesn't matter much, does it?"

Mickey, you are worthless.

An image of the departed Elisabeth Moran appeared in the doorway to the den.

"Not now, Mother—I don't need your ranting. Go away."

Startled, Amanda watched and heard the man in a psychotic break. Fear clutched at her heart. "Oh my God." *He's losing it!*

"Shut up, Mother—just shut up." He

bumped the wheelchair in his rush to the apparition. "Stay dead, you old bitch."

Amanda's catheter pulled out, and she winced in pain. "God help me."

"She's gone." Michael stepped back and flopped into the recliner. "Did you see her or hear what she said?"

"I saw and heard a raving lunatic who thought he was talking to his dead mother. I need to add that to my story."

"No … no you don't, I don't want that in the piece." He picked up the two page copy of the story. "Your writing is fine as it is. I love the part about me being handsome. Did you really mean that?"

"I think you're the ugliest piece of shit on the planet." She swallowed the lump in her throat and it felt like a hot coal.

"Okay, I've had enough of your sarcasm and insolence." He folded the two pages, and slipped them into an envelope. He waved it in front of her face. "This, my dear, will be found with your remains wherever I decide to drop them." He glared at her through cold eyes.

Despite her crawling fear and hopelessness, Amanda said, "Fuck you, Michael *Moron!*"

"That's it—that's just it." He unlocked the wheelchair and pushed her out of the den toward the kitchen. "I've had enough of your arrogance." He wheeled her to the elevator. "Now you'll see the crime scene first hand." Michael pushed the button, and the doors opened. "Too bad you won't get to describe all the details in your final story."

Amanda closed her eyes and began to pray. *Please, God ... let it be quick.*

The doors opened into the basement and Michael pushed her into his spotless operating room. "Here we are and everything's ready."

Amanda looked at the equipment, lights, and the waiting table. "There's a place in hell for you, and I hope Kellogg is the one to send you there."

"Sooner or later, we'll all dance with the devil." He pushed her up to the steel table. "You shouldn't have insulted me as you did."

"I'm sorry ... I didn't mean to insult a demented idiot."

"It's time to shut you up once and for all." He took a length of rubber tubing from the table of instruments. "Your troubles are over."

The tubing went around her throat quickly, and he pulled it tight.

Her struggling ended and Michael removed the ligature. "Okay, Amanda, let's get to work. I'm going to make you a special package for Kellogg."

Chapter Twenty Five

Nothing to Go On

SDPD SVU SQUADROOM
THURSDAY – 2:00 PM:

Captain Sawyer paced in front of his team, and scratched his bald head. "We have an APB out, and law enforcement, countywide, has Price's picture. That's been working since eleven this morning. What else do we have?"

Matt picked up his notebook. "I just got off the phone with the Sentinel's City Editor. Security at Bernardo Center found Amanda's Explorer parked and locked in front of the *Subway* shop. I ordered a tow to downtown."

Ken chuckled. "We're collecting cars like some folks collect stamps." He checked his notes. "The boys at the lab have dusted the other three vehicles, and came up empty."

Sawyer sat on the edge of Matt's desk. "Ann, Jack, go to Price's workstation at the paper, and then check out her apartment. Reporters take lots of notes, you might turn something up."

He began pacing again. "I've been trying to put it together since we got the word. Why did the perp grab Price?"

Matt stood, and walked to the coffee bar. "He's working us, Captain. Hal Marks was the first play in the game, and I'm sure the perp spotted Amanda on TV, and read her story in the Sentinel."

The detective filled his cup, and came back to the group. "Price is attractive, and she caught his eye." He sat at his desk, and put cream and sugar in this coffee. "The bastard wants to play in our backyard."

Sawyer thought a moment. "Kellogg, get in touch with Marks. I saw him and Price chatting it up at the press conference. Find out what he might know." He took a long breath. "We're all on gold time. Nobody goes home until we find Price. Crash here if you have to. Get on it, people—I don't want a fourth body."

* * * *

THE OLD VICTORIAN
FRIDAY 1:30 AM:

Michael lifted Samantha off his desk.
"You know you're not supposed to be up
here." He put the cat on the leather recliner. "I
have a few details to take care of." He slipped
on a new pair of latex gloves, and opened the
envelope containing Amanda's last story.
"One more proof read before I release this
gem to the cops."

He unfolded the two pages and read
Amanda's prose. "Excellent opening. I love
the line." *I've fallen victim to the Legs
Collector.* He grinned. "Good work, Amanda.
This article could make me famous. In fact, I
believe it will."

He read further down page one. *This man
is a terror set loose by an abusive mother who
has haunted him from the grave.* "Oh, I like it,
I love it!" He reached over and scratched
Samantha's neck. "I wish you could read, my
pet."

Amanda's closing line struck a sensitive
chord in Michael's black heart. *The Legs
Collector is himself a victim, and must be
forgiven his trespasses for he is innocent of
any wrong doing.*

He sat back, drew a breath and wiped his
eyes. "Such brilliance in those words,

Amanda, so well written." Michael refolded the story, and put it back in the envelope. He sealed it, picked up a black marker, and printed, *Amanda's Last Story* on the front.

"That's bound to get the attention I'm looking for."

Michael rewound the tape in Amanda's recorder, and ejected the cassette. He put it in his machine, set up his voice alteration device, and pressed record.

Hi Kellogg, how's your day going? I'm sorry you had to see Amanda in such a condition, but she brought it on herself. You need to know, the girl fought me right to the very end. She was a spunky bitch, I'll give her that.

Who's next? Could be someone you're more closely involved with. He laughed. *Stay alert and have a great day.*

Michael stopped the tape, rewound it, and listened. "Good work." He ejected the tape, and put the cassette back into Amanda's recorder. "Done."

He gave Samantha a belly rub. "I've done well. I have to run an errand, my pet. When I get back, we'll have a nice breakfast together."

Chapter Twenty Six

Too Close to Home

SDPD MEN'S LOCKER ROOM
FRIDAY – 7:00 AM:

𝕶𝖊𝖑𝖑𝖔𝖌𝖌 𝖉𝖗𝖎𝖊𝖉 𝖔𝖋𝖋 𝖋𝖗𝖔𝖒 𝖍𝖎𝖘 𝖘𝖍𝖔𝖜𝖊𝖗 and tied a towel around his waist. He started a quick shave with the spare *Norelco* he kept in his locker. "I could handle bunking out at the station when I was in uniform, but it ain't no fun no more."

Ken slipped into his trousers and a clean shirt. "I hear you on that. I must be getting old." He sat on a bed across the room and put on his shoes. "You know, I think the bunks are more comfortable at the county lockup."

Matt's cell rang.

He went to the bed and answered it.

"Morning, Judy. I don't think I want to hear

this." Matt sat down and drew a deep breath. "She was found where?" He stared at the floor. "This isn't happening. Okay, we'll be right there. Yeah ... about thirty minutes." He closed the phone.

Ken had his tie half knotted. "They found Price?"

"What's left of her." He grabbed his shoulder holster, and three fifty-seven magnum from his locker, and tossed them on the bed. "The perp dumped her in a vacant lot behind my apartment building."

"Holy shit!" Ken finished knotting his tie, and pulled on his suit coat. "He knows where you live. This is not good." He slipped his *Glock-19* onto his belt.

Kellogg took clean shorts and socks out of a drawer in his locker. "I know where he lives too."

"You can't be sure."

"I'm damn sure now." He pulled on his socks. "Go tell Sawyer what's up, I'll be dressed in a minute."

* * * *

VACANT LOT-BEHIND BLDG 235
BREE MANOR - El CAJON – 8:15 AM:

Kellogg had driven code-three all the way from downtown which is risky during morning traffic. The ME and the coroner's assistants were waiting when Matt drove up to the scene. "There's Gary Rodriquez. He's the complex Maintenance honcho. Wake told me he called it in."

Ken looked at the man in green work clothes. "Well, I'll bet he wishes otherwise. He's as white as a sheet."

Matt climbed out of the car and approached him. "Hi Gary, sorry you had to be the one."

"Yeah, I wish I'd called in sick because I am sick now." He wiped a sheen of sweat off his forehead. "This is that *legs* killer's doing, right?"

"We believe it might be."

"Jesus, Matt, the woman's been chopped up."

"Hang out for a few more minutes, my partner and I have to release the body to the Medical Examiner, okay?"

"Sure, I'll be right here." He leaned against the van and looked away.

Ken and Matt went to where the corpse had been dumped.

Judy said, "It's a tough one, we sort of knew her, you more than me, but I did a couple of interviews with her." Wake hesitated. "Are you ready?"

Matt hunkered down next to the covered body. "Is there something new?"

"Yes ... he took Amanda's arms *and* legs." She pulled the plastic cover down to the victim's waist.

"I can't believe this—it's an outrage!" He stood, and pointed toward the apartment complex. "I live there. This sonofabitch is making it personal."

Ken made a note. "How in hell could he know where you live?"

"That wouldn't be all that hard to find out. My question is, why?"

Judy handed Matt the small tape recorder and the envelope. "You might get some answers from these." She covered Amanda's remains, and motioned to the two coroner's assistants. To Kellogg she said, "You need to know, there's evidence of sexual activity. I'll have to do a full examination to be positive."

"Have you nailed time of death?" He took out his notebook.

"Judging by rigor, I'd say between midnight and three, but that's a guess." She hesitated. "You were up there, in bed, and unaware he was working right in your back yard. Yeah, I'd call that personal." She thought a moment. "It's too close, Matt."

"We spent the night at the station. The captain wanted us on alert until we found Amanda. That's no longer necessary. What about COD?"

"You saw the ligature marks on her throat. Ten to one it's strangulation. I'll know more later this afternoon." Judy patted his shoulder. "I'm sorry, Matt. This whole mess has us all on edge."

"Yeah, four killings in one week, I'd say we're a bit on edge." He held the envelope up to the sunlight. "Ken, let me have your pen knife."

"You got it." He dug it out of his pocket, and handed it to Matt.

Kellogg put on a pair of latex gloves, sliced the envelope open, and removed the two pages. He unfolded them. "That bastard must've forced Amanda to write this story about him." He put the pages back in the envelope. "I have a news flash for that SOB. This story will never be published. That should piss off our perp." He put the envelope in his inside pocket. "What will be released is a statement to the press that we won't make the story public." He removed the gloves. "I'll make that statement myself, and it will be a direct message to this maniac!"

One of the CSI Team approached carrying a clipboard. "I need you to sign off on the envelope and tape machine if you intend to hang on to them."

"Not a problem." He scribbled his name on the form. "Thanks, Ray. Aside from the obvious, did you guys find anything else?"

"Nothing of any value. The perp's covering his bases and damn well knows what he's doing." He looked down at Amanda's remains. "We're being played like a piano, Matt."

"What else is new?" Kellogg gestured toward the apartment building. "He made this one personal. I hate to imagine what's next."

Ray said, "We're done here. A crime scene it isn't. Let us know what you get from the recorder and the contents of the envelope."

"I'll make sure Tony's brought up to speed as soon as we evaluate what we've got."

"That works for me." Ray stepped toward the CSI van, hesitated, and turned back. "This sonofabitch is our worst nightmare."

"Hopefully, we'll become the same for him real soon."

"We're looking forward to it."

"Count on it."

The ME zipped up the body bag.

Ken looked around the lot, and up toward the back fence of the apartment building. Onlookers were chatting, and pointing toward the activity near the body. He shouted, "Show's over, folks. Go on about your business." He glanced at the entrance to the lot, and at the two patrol cars and officers keeping the crowd on the sidewalk. "They got it under control."

The coroner's van and the CSI vehicle pulled out just as Judy headed for her car.

"Hey guys." She held up Amanda's shoulder bag. "He left it." She tossed it on the front seat. "I'll turn it over to Tony, he might find something."

Matt said, "Excellent. We'll come by the lab about four or five, will that work for you?"

"I'll be there." Judy climbed into her blue Crown Vic, and followed after the two vans.

Kellogg jotted a note. "This lot was the home of a family-owned auto parts store. It burned to the ground last December, and that was it." He thought a moment. "We need to find out from El Cajon PD who owns the lot and tell them what happened."

Ken said, "Our killer wanted to get close to you, and he did."

"The perp didn't find this spot by chance, and it served his purpose completely. He shouted to the two officers by the gate.

"Is there a cut padlock around the entrance anywhere?"

"The younger of the two answered, "Yes, sir. It's hanging right where it was cut."

"Bring it here, please." He looked at Ken. "I suspected it. The perp knew the fence was locked ahead of time."

The officer came up to Matt, and handed him the lock. "There's no way anybody could cut that tempered steel without a good pair of bolt cutters."

"Good observation, Roberts. Write it up in your report, and have someone from your department put a police lock on the gate." He hefted the damaged lock. "Actually, you can save us some time."

"Whatever's necessary, Detective." The young cop smiled.

"Excellent. When you get back to headquarters, have a clerk run a trace on the owners of this property, and tell them what's happened."

"I'll be on it immediately, sir." The officer beamed. "Are we clear here?"

"Absolutely, you're free to go back on patrol."

"Thank you."

"You're most welcome." He shook the young cop's hand. "You guys did a great job."

The officer went back to his partner, and

gave a high-five to the other cop. They climbed into their black and white units and drove away.

Ken said, "You made his day."

"We were there once upon a time, and he will save us a trip to El Cajon PD." He started pacing around near where the body was found and noticed Gary leaning on their car. "We'll be right there." To Ken he said, "A perfect drop spot in the middle of the night. It's all concrete and blacktop. There's no way he'd leave footprints or tire tread impressions."

"Of course, he had all that figured out." Ken looked out across a four way intersection and into the lot of the huge *El Cajon Ford Dealership.* "At three in the morning this end of town would be deserted. However, that car lot would be lit up bright."

Matt made another entry in his notebook. "Those lights wouldn't reach into this lot, hardly at all."

"Nevertheless, the perp took major risks. He had to stop his vehicle, get out, cut the lock, open the gate, and drive in." He pointed up at the apartment complex. "Your building has security lights spaced along the walkway on the other side of the fence."

"Ken, you're a cop, you don't think like Joe Citizen. Most people don't pay any attention to half of what's going on around them." He waved at Rodriguez. "Let's talk to Gary before he passes out."

* * * *

The Hispanic man stepped away from the car. "I can't tell you much, Matt." He appeared no less shaken than he was twenty minutes earlier.

"Anything is helpful." He opened the back door of the car. "Climb in, we'll give you a ride around to the front entrance so you don't have to crawl up the bank of ice plant, and scale the fence."

A bright yellow *Hummer* pulled up in front of the lot, backed up, and drove in.

Ken said, "What the hell is this?"

The vehicle stopped, and Hal Marks got out carrying a mini-cassette recorder. "What the hell is going on, Kellogg?"

"How did you get wind of this?" He had been halfway into the car. He got out, and met the reporter. "You know damn well we don't put SVU information over the air, so you had to get a tip."

"From the mouth of your perp." He set the recorder on the hood of the *Hummer,* and pressed play.

The familiar, augmented voice began.

Nice to talk to you again, Hal. I hope you ate a good breakfast and have the energy for a productive day as star reporter for the San Diego Union Tribune. I have a great story for you, oh boy, is it ever.

You'll find Kellogg, and his idiot partner, at a vacant lot in the East County. I left this message on your voice mail because I wasn't up for answering dumb questions. You need to go to …

Marks fast forwarded through the address. He said, "Here it comes, and don't you shit me, Matt." He pressed play.

I hope you get there in time. Unfortunately, there's a new vic, as the cops like to call them. Yes, I put her there while you were in La-La land. Beautiful, she was, beautiful she is no more.

Hal stopped the tape. "Pay close attention to this next part. Your nutcase is escalating. Listen." He pressed play.

The pretty, young victim fought me, Hal, I mean she was a sassy, tough bitch. I collected more than her legs. She gave me no choice. Oh, by the way, she's been missing for a while, but now she's been found. Go to work, young man. Write up a great story.

Until the next time, The Legs Collector signs off. Nothing personal, Marks.

Hal stopped the tape. "It's Amanda,

isn't it?" He stared at the two detectives.

Ken said, "This isn't good." He went back and got into the passenger side of the car. He turned to Gary. "Hang in there, just a few minutes more.

Gary sat back in the seat. "How do you guys do this?"

"To tell you the truth, I don't really know."

Rarely a smoker, Ken opened the glove box, and took a cigarette from a pack he had stashed, and lit it. "Do you mind?"

"Doesn't bother me."

Matt reached into the front seat, and grabbed Amanda's recorder. He set it on the hood of the *Hummer.* "I think I have a message from the perp for me."

Hal said, "That's Amanda's machine. Jesus Christ." He made a fist, and pounded the hood of his vehicle. "He killed her."

"Yes, it's Amanda's recorder. She is his latest victim. We can't do anything about that." He squeezed the younger man's shoulder. "Were you and Amanda involved?"

"No, we were just close friends. We competed with each other, but I wanted it to become more. Goddammit! That sleaze took Amanda's life."

"Listen, I haven't checked this tape, it may be nothing." He pressed play.

Hi, Kellogg, how's your day going?

Matt stopped the tape. "I'll deal with it later. Okay, Hal, we both have this asshole's attention. I need you to work with me on this."

He put the recorder back in the car.

Hal said, "I have to run the story." He picked up *his* tape machine, and stood by the *Hummer.* "You have your job, and I have mine."

Matt took a long breath and leaned on the vehicle. "I understand that, but this is not everyday news, and you know it."

He looked Marks in the eye. "I have an article that the perp forced Amanda to write. He thought we'd just be happy to publish it. Guess what? We won't release it to the press."

"Why the hell not?" He put his tape machine in the vehicle. "The public needs to see it."

Matt clutched Hal's shoulder again. "No, they don't—that's just what this *swill* wants."

He stepped back.

"Work with me on this. I'm preparing a press release that will piss the perp off, and hopefully force him to make a serious mistake."

"You'd better be right—I want first notice."

"You got it."

"Can I see Amanda? I know she has relatives here locally."

"I can arrange that, but I don't think you really want to. Just remember her as she was to you, the way you liked to see her."

"Yeah … I think you might be right."

"You'll hold the story?" He looked at the young reporter.

"I'll sit on it, but not for long."

"Good man, I'll get back to you."

Hal got into his vehicle, and drove off.

Matt slid into the Ford, and craned his neck to see Gary in the back seat. "Sorry for the delay. Tell us what you saw."

He fired up the car, and headed out of the lot.

"I came around the south wing of the complex and saw what looked like a body down below in the vacant lot. It shook me up."

"Go ahead, Ken's taking notes." Matt pulled out onto the street, stopped, got out, shoved the gate shut and climbed back in the car. "What'd you do then?"

Gary cleared his throat. "I hopped the fence, and worked my way down through the ice plant."

Matt turned onto the end of Main Street, and around to the front entrance of the apartment complex. "You didn't see anything other than the body?"

Gary gagged, shook his head and said, "I don't want to see anything like that again."

Matt pulled the car up to the main entrance of Bree Manor. "I hope you never have to. You've been very helpful. We appreciate your efforts. Maybe you should take the rest of the day off."

"You know what, Detective? I believe I'll do just that."

"Excellent. Do something, go to the mall, have a few beers. Anything. Try to get that image out of your head."

Chapter Twenty Seven

Photography by Michael

THE OLD VICTORIAN
FRIDAY MORNING
TWO HOURS LATER:

𝕸𝖎𝖈𝖍𝖆𝖊𝖑 𝖘𝖆𝖙 𝖆𝖙 𝖍𝖎𝖘 𝖈𝖔𝖒𝖕𝖚𝖙𝖊𝖗 working in *Photoshop.* He had three new images on the screen. He petted Samantha. "What'd you think, should I keep the shots separate or put all of them into a collage?"

The cat dozed on a bookshelf near a small TV. She opened her eyes briefly at the sound of her master's voice, and then continued her nap.

"Nope, these shots, along with those of Robin, need to be separate prints." Michael manipulated the pictures of Amanda's legs and arms into one image and added a frame.

"Classic Gold works well with these photos." He saved the file. "Now, the picture of Ms. Price showing head and shoulders should be darker." He increased the contrast.

"Excellent. I think a black frame looks right for the portrait." He added the frame.

"Perfect, Matt will really enjoy my work." He reached over, and scratched Samantha's ears. "Did I do a good job?"

The cat blinked, and yawned.

Michael processed the color prints, and snapped on a new pair of latex gloves. "Okay, Kellogg, special delivery will be on the way soon." He took the prints from the tray, and put them in the envelope with those of Robin Anderson. "You'll remember this day, Matt."

Samantha let out a soft cry, and sat up.

"You're hungry again?" He rubbed her chin. "Let's have an early lunch, and watch TV. The noon news will be on in a while, and I bet my handiwork will be the lead story."

* * * *

SDPD COMPLEX – SVU SQUADROOM
AT THAT SAME TIME:

Captain Sawyer took another call from the media.

"I understand Dennis. Don't go live with

this yet. I'm calling an emergency press conference for two o'clock. We'll release what we have then."

"I'm sorry Roy, I can't hold off on it. Conference or not, I have a reporter at the site where the body was found, and she's ready to do a live teaser for our noon broadcast."

"We aren't sure next of kin have been notified."

"Trust me, no identification will be mentioned."

"Dammit, you know everybody thinks its Price." He jotted a note, and underlined Dennis' name. "Put me in a jam on this, and you'll be hard pressed to get *any* information from my unit."

"I can't help that, Captain, I have a story, and I have to go with it."

"You have part of a story."

"What I have is an exclusive—if I wait for your press conference the piece will be on the noon news from here to LA."

"Put it out before the conference, Dennis, and you're on my shit-list!"

"I'll take that risk Roy."

Captain Sawyer hung up and went out into the squad room.

"Kellogg, has Price's kin been notified?"

"So far as I know. They run a gift shop in The Vista Mall and the local PD has been sent to do the deed. What's come up?" He pushed away from his desk, and went to the coffee bar.

"The press is on it, somebody leaked what you found this morning."

Kellogg looked at Ken. "I had a feeling it would get out."

Sawyer continued. "I just got off the phone with the news director at KUSI. He has a reporter at the vacant lot, and he's authorized a live feed before the noon news."

Ken said, "Who the hell leaked the information, Marks?"

Matt walked back to his desk with a fresh cup of coffee. "I don't think so. It had to be somebody from the scene."

The Captain sat in Ann's chair across from Matt. "Have you finished writing up your statement?"

Kellogg brought the document up on his desktop computer. "I need to listen to the rest of the perp's taped message to me before I wrap my statement."

"I want to see it before the conference. I'd rather not have any surprises in front of the press."

He stood, and started back to his office.

"Trust me, Cap, I believe you'll agree with every word."

Matt took Amanda's recorder out of the

top drawer of his desk.

Ken rolled his chair around to Kellogg's area. "I can't wait to hear this."

"Neither can I." He rewound the tape. "In a way, I'm glad this arrogant sonofabitch has the balls to taunt me directly. His ego is going to be his undoing sooner or later."

"Hey, he called me an idiot on Hal's tape."

Matt pressed play.

Hi Kellogg, how's your day going? Sorry you had to see Amanda in such condition. But, she brought it on herself. You need to know the girl fought me right to the very end. She was a spunky bitch, I'll give her that.

He stopped the tape. "There it is."

Ken said, "There's what?"

"The reason he cut off her arms. Amanda must've given him a rough time. Why else would he change his MO?"

Matt pushed play.

Who's next? Could be someone you're more closely involved with.

Kellogg stiffened when he heard Michael's maniacal laugh.

The tape continued.

Stay alert and have a great day.

Ken looked at his partner. "Jesus H. Christ."

Matt stopped the tape and went to the captain's door. "Where's Beck?"

"She and Towne are at the Sentinel sifting through Price's work area again."

"Call them back here—the bastard just made an open threat aimed at Ann."

"Jack and Beck are both armed, Matt."

"I don't give a shit if she's packing a bazooka! I want her with me twenty-four-seven until we burn this lunatic."

"What about Ken?"

Kellogg looked at his partner.

"No problem, Cap, I'll team with Jack."

Matt nodded. "Thanks."

Kellogg remained standing in the doorway.

Sawyer looked up.

"Something else?"

"Actually, there is … got a minute?"

"Be my guest."

The detective stepped into the office and closed the door. "It's about Moran."

"I'm all ears."

"I want to run him through the mill."

"And that would be what?"

Matt took a seat across from the captain.

"Beck suggested we do a DMV check—I told her there's no legal cause."

"Good call, you're right, there isn't, and you can't." Sawyer took a sip of cold coffee. "So what do you have in mind?"

"I'm thinking financials, medical records,

The whole package."

"Have you slipped a cog in your brain?"

Sawyer pushed back to his private service bar and dumped the rest of the cold coffee into the small sink.

"What about probable cause?"

The captain rinsed his mug.

"You've already interviewed Moran and came up empty."

"Look, Boss, the guy's a phony. The cripple act is a ruse. Medical records would prove that."

"Matt, we can't just pull medical records—you have to show *cause.* Getting financials requires the same thing."

The detective stood.

"Moran's little game with the handwriting samples was just more bullshit."

He clutched the back of the chair.

"We have everything at our fingertips to come down on this asshole like a ton of bricks—and we can't do shit."

"Listen, Matt, I hear what you're saying. Don't go off on your own with this."

Sawyer rubbed his eyes.

"We're being played, big-time by the perp, and he knows it. Bring me solid evidence and *SVU* will go after him with both barrels."

* * * *

THE VICTORIAN – 11:30 AM:

"Here we are."

Michael set a saucer of broth in front of Samantha on the dining room table. The cat started lapping it up immediately.

"That's from my favorite home made chowder."

He sat at his place, and put a handful of oyster crackers into his steaming bowl.

"I don't fix this very often so it's like a treat."

He sipped a tablespoon full.

"It's scrumptious with just the right amount of seasoning."

He smacked his lips. "Am I a good cook?"

Samantha licked her saucer clean without response.

The television on the large dark oak hutch was on, and tuned to KUSI-TV. Michael saw the news logo come on and he reached over and turned up the volume.

"Look, Sam, they're doing a special report. I wonder what's so important?"

He laughed and enjoyed another taste of chowder.

A handsome anchorman appeared on the tube.

"Good morning, I'm Steve Thomas. We have a live feed from the East County. Lonnie

Chong is on the scene. Lonnie, what have we got?"

"Steve, an unidentified female body was found in the vacant lot behind me early this morning, and the authorities are being tight-lipped with any details."

Michael waved at the screen.

"It's Amanda Price you, morons."

The TV screen split and Steve appeared on the left, the reporter on the right.

"Could this be connected to *The Legs Collector* Killings?"

"It's possible, but as I said, the police will only confirm that the remains of a woman were found in this lot."

Steve added, "That makes four female murders in less than a week."

"Yes, it's hard to believe. We hope to have more information within the hour. In El Cajon, I'm Lonnie Chong for KUSI news."

The screen went back to a full shot of the anchor.

"Thank you, Lonnie. I've just been informed that Captain Sawyer, of the San Diego Police Department, SVU team, has called a two o'clock press conference. KUSI News will be there, live."

"Did you hear that, Sam? Another press conference all about my work. I can't wait. I'll set the *DVR* so I can capture it all for posterity." He grinned, and sipped a spoon of chowder.

"Kellogg, you better articulate Amanda's last story just the way I wrote it, no fudging on details."

He switched off the TV. His mother's face appeared on the screen. The room went cold.

Michael pushed his chair from the table. "Go away, you witch."

Mickey, Mickey, Mickey. You are so stupid. They're going to come for you.

"Shut up, Mother. I don't want to hear you ever again."

They will find you, Mickey, you will not get away with the horror you've done.

The screen went blank.

Michael stared at it and shivered. "It's all your fault, Mother …."

Chapter Twenty Eight

Emergency Press Conference

SDPD COMPLEX
FRIDAY – 2:00 PM:

𝕴𝖓 𝖙𝖍𝖊 𝖜𝖆𝖐𝖊 𝖔𝖋 𝖙𝖍𝖊 𝖋𝖔𝖚𝖗𝖙𝖍 brutal murder, in less than a week, San Diego County's press core came out in full force.

Three TV stations from LA sent crews to the event and Fox News had joined the media circus.

The cacophony of reporters and technicians settled down when the captain approached the podium and stood in front of the battery of microphones.

"Good afternoon ladies and gentlemen. I'm Captain Roy Sawyer with the San Diego Police Department's Special Victims Unit. My people and every law enforcement agency in the county are on the grim mission of tracking down a vicious serial killer."

He hesitated, looked down and caught a breath.

"It saddens me deeply to officially release the identity of the perpetrator's fourth victim."

Visibly moved by the intensity of the moment, he gripped the edges of the podium.

"Early this morning, the body of Amanda Price was found in a vacant lot in El Cajon."

Sawyer fetched a short breath.

"Ms. Price was a working reporter for the North County Sentinel. Our sorrow and prayers go out to her grieving family."

The Captain's voice cracked.

"Amanda was a colleague, and one of your own."

He paused, and the questions started.

The Fox News reporter jumped in first.

"Captain, was Ms. Price on a story at the time?"

"We believe she may have been."

Lonnie Chong from KUSI asserted herself.

"Captain, do you have any—"

Roy recognized her.

"You'll all have a chance to ask questions after our statements."

He held up his arm.

"I want to introduce the lead investigator on the case."

Sawyer looked back at the *SVU* team.

"Some of you have worked with him. Here's Detective Matt Kellogg."

Roy stepped away from the podium.

Matt faced the cameras.

* * * *

THE OLD VICTORIAN:

Michael sat on his huge black leather sofa in front of a wide screen TV with Samantha curled up beside him.

"Sawyer sure gave a lame presentation. All that fake emotion for Amanda, and not much about me."

When Matt came on, Michael turned up the volume.

"Here comes the best part, Sam."

The cat licked her front paws.

"Hey, Kellogg looks pretty dapper for a flatfoot."

He lifted a glass of white wine to the big screen.

"Nice suit—do me right, Matt."

The camera moved in on the detective.

Kellogg said, "I've been a cop for sixteen years. Ten of those have been served with the San Diego Police Department. In all that time, I have never encountered a more narcissistic criminal than the perpetrator of the four heinous murders we are now investigating."

Michael applauded.

"Matt, you're outdoing yourself. This is award winning."

He patted the cat.

"You hear that? I'm one of a kind in Kellogg's career. Outstanding."

Matt took an envelope from the inside pocket of his suit coat and held it steady on the front edge of the podium.

"Can you get a close up of this?"

"I gotta love you for this performance, detective, you're all right."

Michael applauded again.

The camera went in tight on the envelope.

The words, **Amanda's Last Story** filled the screen.

"See that, Sam? That's my work."

Michael beamed with pride.

"My work, yes, it'll be all over the news tonight at six and eleven and probably go nationwide. This is exciting."

The TV now showed Matt in a medium shot. He continued, "Inside the envelope is a two-page story Amanda's killer forced her to write before he took her life. The murderer had taped the envelope to the body knowing I would find it and release it to the press."

"That was the idea, Kellogg." Michael grinned. "Go for it. Let 'em have it."

Matt held up the envelope. "Ladies and gentlemen." He slipped the story back into his inside pocket.

"What are you doing, Kellogg?" Michael sat forward on the couch. "Read the story!"

Matt continued. "To the killer, I say, no one will ever see the words you forced Ms. Price to write. The story will not be released to the press."

Michael stood and screamed at the television.

"You bastard, Kellogg! You're a shit. You're going to be sorry for this, I promise you."

He shook his fist at the screen.

"Four in a week? Think again, Detective. You blew it. Get your body bags ready, you're gonna need them. Be sure to mark one for Ann Beck." He clicked the remote and the TV went black.

Chapter Twenty Nine

Cold Hard Facts

SAN DIEGO CITY/COUNTY MORGUE
FRIDAY AFTERNOON – 4:30 PM:

𝕾𝖊𝖗𝖌𝖊𝖆𝖓𝖙 𝕭𝖊𝖈𝖐 𝖍𝖆𝖉𝖓'𝖙 𝖘𝖊𝖊𝖓 𝖆𝖓𝖞 of the other victims. Amanda's remains shook her to the core.

"This is an abomination."

She re-covered the body.

"What else did he do to her?"

Medical Examiner Judy Wake sat at her desk signing off on the official cause of death.

"My preliminary examination, this morning, proved to be correct."

She looked up at Ann.

"You're a little pale."

"I've seen a lot in my eight years on the job, but nothing like this."

Beck climbed onto a stool near Judy.

"What more was done to the victim?"

"The perp strangled her, performed his surgery and then violated the body."

"That monster had sex with Amanda after he killed her?"

Ann shivered.

"He did with two of the other three vics."

Judy hesitated.

"He used a blunt object to penetrate Ms. Price."

The *ME* put the completed forms into a manila envelope with the death certificate.

"Do her parents know that?"

"It's all in here."

She sealed the envelope.

"But no, they weren't given all the details."

Matt entered the lab from the viewing room.

"I walked the parents out to their car. They'll be sending someone from the funeral home to pick up the body and paperwork."

He sat in a chair across from the two woman.

"Amanda's mother is in a state of denial and her dad's seething with anger."

The detective looked at Ann.

"Are you okay?"

"Not really—actually, I feel sick for those people. My heart aches for that poor woman. It tore me up to see her crumble when Judy opened the curtain."

She took a deep breath.

"My job has always been doing follow up investigation and interviews. This—this."

She waved toward the gurney.

"It's a whole new ballgame."

Kellogg stood. To Judy he said, "Are you all clear with this case?"

He pulled out his notebook.

"I've finished my reports and they've been filed. I'll release the body when the mortuary guys get here, that's it."

Judy looked up at Matt.

"Nothing personal, but I hope we don't see each other for a long while."

"I hear you on that. However, I do enjoy visiting with you."

The *ME's* desk phone rang.

"Wake … what've you got Tony?"

She held up a hand toward Matt.

"Hang on he's right here."

Kellogg took the receiver.

"Hi, you've found something?" He nodded. "Great. We'll be right down. Thanks." He handed the phone back to Judy. "Tony got something on Amanda's cell."

"I hope to hell it's a break."

"Me too." To Ann he said, "Have you been to the new crime lab?"

"Not yet."

She got off the stool.

"That's where we're going."

"Lead the way."

Ann smiled at Judy.

"Nice to meet you, but I can't say I enjoyed the visit."

"Nobody ever does."

She grinned.

"Take care of my favorite detective."

"I'll give it an honest try."

* * * *

CRIME LAB - SAME BUILDING
TEN MINUTES LATER:

Ann and Matt met Tony in his office. Kellogg made the introduction.

"This is Ann Beck."

Tony shook her hand.

"I'm pleased to meet you."

He held up Amanda's cell phone.

"One of my techs dumped the vic's cell while you guys were at the conference."

Matt corrected him.

"Amanda's phone."

"Yeah, right, Amanda's cell. Anyway, it was clean. There was nothing on it. I put it back in her purse."

He picked up the phone and opened it.

"The tech left the cell on. About ten minutes after the press conference, the phone buzzed. I pulled it from the purse and the screen showed that there was a message."

He held it out to Kellogg.

"Here's what the perp left on voice mail directed right to you, Matt."

The three of them listened. The augmented male voice came across clear as a bell.

You've done it, Kellogg, you really did it. I knew you'd get this message, I know all about your technology. You screwed up, detective. You didn't release Amanda's last story—you bastard.

Get ready to count more bodies, Matt, and include Ann Beck's among them.

Ann shuddered.

"That nutcase is over the top."

Matt looked her in the eye. "He's the reason you'll be with me day and night until we bring him down."

"Gee, I thought it was because you liked me."
She grinned.

"You're making jokes?"

He didn't smile.

"Have you forgotten what you recently viewed in Judy's lab?"

"I'm a trained cop. That slime ball comes after me and he'll get a face full of slugs from my nine mil, Smith and Wesson." She rested her right hand on the grip of her holstered gun.

"You may not have a chance to pull your weapon. Besides, he'll have to go through me to get to you and for the moment, I don't think he's aware of that."

To Tony he said, "I'll need a copy of that message."

"I've already made one."

He handed the detective a mini cassette.

"Good man. Let me have the phone, it's the Price family's property now. Are your people done with the purse?"

"Danny finished dusting the contents earlier. He ran all the prints through DMV and they Matched Amanda's"

To Ann he said, "Nice meeting you. I believe you're safe in Matt's company."

"I'm sure I'll be protected."

She winked.

To Kellogg, Tony said, "The CSI team is still mumbling frustrations about the lack of a crime scene with four consecutive homicides."

He hesitated.

"I'm a bit puzzled by that myself."

"There's a crime scene. It's in one location and I have a pretty good idea where that is."

He slipped Amanda's cell into the right side pocket of his suit coat and grinned.

"I need probable cause to get to it. That is, if I want to stay legal."

"Good luck with that."

"Thanks, Tony, I appreciate your help."

"You take good care of Sergeant Beck."

He smiled at her.

Ann replied, "He's got my back."

Matt said, "We're headed for the impound garage."

They left the crime lab.

* * * *

DOWNTOWN SAN DIEGO
FRIDAY AFTERNOON - 5:00 PM:

Michael parked his black Mercedes on a street five blocks from the SDPD complex. He checked his appearance in the rearview mirror.

"You're a handsome devil, you are for sure."

He combed the false goatee and adjusted the brown long-haired wig.

"Nice touch, I look ten-years older. Well, maybe five."

He put on a ball cap with a bogus *L&L DELIVERY SERVICE* logo.

The envelope lay on the seat beside him.

Michael slipped on a pair of latex gloves, picked it up and wiped it clean with a cloth.

"There's no room for error here."

He opened a small box and removed the fake hands that would fit over his own.

"Damn, they did a good job on these. They're gnarly as hell and well worth the expense."

He got out of the car, locked it and put four

quarters in the parking meter.

"Don't need that much time, but hey, why not be safe?"

Michael put the envelope on the roof of the car and slipped into a blue jacket. The name, Bob was sewn into an oval patch above the left pocket.

"Let's get to it."

He started walking toward the police station.

SDPD IMPOUND GARAGE
AT THAT SAME TIME:

Matt pulled up to the gate shack.

"Hi, Nick."

He handed the officer the impound form.

"Where'd they put it?"

"Right alongside the other three, level four, space two twenty-five."

"Thanks."

To Ann, he said, "I have to deal with the Price family again to release the Explorer, and I'm not looking forward to it."

Beck put her head back against the seat.

"I admire you. I've never dealt with any of this part of it … today's been an education."

* * * *

Kellogg stopped in front of Amanda's SUV and took her cell phone out of his coat pocket.

"I don't think the parents need to hear the perp's message to me."

He opened the phone and deleted Michael's rant.

Ann said, "How do you deal with all this horror day after day?"

He cut the engine and thought a moment.

"It's my job, it's what I do, and I deal with it as best as I can."

He drew a long breath.

"I'd like you to be my permanent partner."

She sat forward and rubbed her eyes.

"After today—I'm not sure I can handle it."

Kellogg patted her leg.

"Will you consider it?"

"I'll think about it."

"That's good enough for now."

He got out of the car and went to the Ford.

* * * *

SDPD COMPLEX
At THAT SAME TIME:

Michael marched up the front steps and went inside. He approached the duty officer. The sergeant looked up.

"Can I help you?"

"Yes, I have a special delivery for Detective Matt Kellogg."

He handed the cop the envelope. The officer took it.

"You need a signature?"

"Nope, everything's in order."

Michael exited the building and smiled.

Enjoy the pictures, Kellogg. Similar shots of sexy-ass, Ann Beck will be forthcoming.

Chapter Thirty

Images of Death

𝕮𝖆𝖕𝖙𝖆𝖎𝖓 𝕾𝖆𝖜𝖞𝖊𝖗 𝕻𝖚𝖙 𝖔𝖓 𝖍𝖎𝖘 sports coat, came out of the office and closed the door.

To Jack and Ken he said, "It's been a long Friday gentlemen, I'm packing it in."

Ken responded, "Have a great weekend, Cap."

He pushed back from his desk.

"I'm hanging out until Matt gets here and opens his special delivery."

"What delivery?"

He walked toward Kellogg's area.

Jack said, "That envelope." He pointed at Matt's desk. "A clerk carried it in here a half hour ago."

The captain looked down at the package.

"What the hell's this?"

Ken said, "Ten bucks it's from our perp."

The elevator door opened. Kellogg and Beck entered the room. Matt started shedding his suit coat and saw the three men standing by his desk.

"What's the attraction?"

Sawyer pointed to the package.

"You have a special delivery."

Matt hung his coat over the back of his chair and picked up the envelope.

"Son-of-a-bitch." He showed it to Ann. "It's from him." He read the bold black printing.

FOR DETECTIVE MATHEW KELLOGG
DO NOT BEND: PHOTOS ENCLOSED

He turned the envelope over several Times.

"Who delivered this?"

Ken said, "A clerk brought it up from the front desk."

"Did you recognize him?"

"It was a *she* and wore an ID badge. Are you going to open it, of do we wait for the next episode?"

"Smart ass."

Matt sat at his desk, used a letter opener and let the pictures slide out.

"Jesus Christ."

The top one showed Robin Anderson's head and shoulders shot, her severed legs and the message Michael had written:

Keep a close eye on Beck, I sure am.

Ann saw it.
"Mother of God."
Kellogg spread out the other photos and quickly shoved them back into the envelope. He picked up the gruesome package and stood.
"No use in dusting it, the only prints on this will be the clerk's the desk sergeant's and mine." He looked at Ann. "You okay?"
"Not altogether jolly, Matt."
Kellogg addressed his team.
"I'll be right back."

* * * *

The detective got off the elevator and went to the front desk.
"Excuse me, Sergeant. Were you on duty about an hour ago?"
"I was, what can I do for you?" The officer seemed distracted.
Matt held up the envelope. "Did you see who delivered this?"
He glanced at the package. "I may have." The officer turned back to what he'd been

doing. "Are you Detective Kellogg?"

"Yes, I am, and this is important, Sergeant Jenkins. It involves four homicides. I suggest you drop what you're doing, and give the envelope some serious thought."

The officer perked right up. "I remember the dude who delivered the envelope. He was weird looking and big, about six-three, six-four. He had long brown hair and a goatee. What caught my attention were his hands."

"And why is that?"

"I don't know, they looked unnatural."

He leaned on the desk, and rubbed his right hand.

"The guy had heavy black hairs growing out of them, and his fingernails were kind of brownish."

"They were fake, Sergeant. That's why there are no prints on this envelope."

He slapped it against the counter.

"You were face-to-face with the *Legs* killer, and didn't think to question a strange looking delivery guy. Did you see any company logo?"

"I don't remember. Do you have any idea how many people come in here every day?"

He glared at Matt.

"No, I don't, but I would suggest a little more diligent observation."

The detective stepped away from the

counter. The front doors swung open, and a disheveled, dirty old man about sixty-five stumbled into the lobby.

"I did it, I'm the serial killer …."

Two officers came out from the desk area, grabbed him, and eased the man down onto a bench.

One young cop said, "Okay, Jimmy, we got you. You're drunk again. You didn't kill anybody."

The delusional vagrant raised his arms. "I killed them all."

Sergeant Jenkins said, "See what I have to put up with every day?"

Kellogg pulled a photo out of the envelope and showed it to the Officer. "This is what I've been dealing with all week."

The sergeant took a breath. "Good God almighty."

"Stay more alert." He walked away from the front desk, and went to the bum. He showed his badge to the cops.

Matt sat beside the homeless man, and put his arm around him. He winced at the body odor, mixed with the smell of urine and cheap wine.

"Hi, Jimmy. I'm Detective Matt Kellogg."

"Hello … are you going to arrest me?" He covered his face with his dirty hands. "I done bad."

"No sir, you haven't hurt anyone. We got the killer, and he'll be punished."

Jimmy looked at Matt through glassy bloodshot eyes. "I didn't kill those girls?"

"You did not. You're not a bad person. I need you to let these officers take you to a shelter where you can get some rest, and maybe a little medical help, okay?"

"Okay, thank you, Mr. Matt."

"You're welcome." He pulled out his wallet, and handed one of the cops a ten. "Get him some food, and take him to Saint Vincent's Shelter. The kitchen will be closed. And Tell Father Paul I sent Jimmy over."

* * * *

When Kellogg got back to the squad room, he found Ann working at her desk.

"The duty officer looked a weird delivery guy in the face, and didn't ask a single question."

She turned around in her chair. "He could've paid to have the envelope delivered."

"Nope, it was him." He leaned against the edge of his desk. "The sergeant told me the guy had ugly hands, long brown hair and wore a goatee."

Matt put the package in his top drawer

and locked it.

"And you think it was all phony?" She swung back, and closed the folder she had been working on.

"I'd bet on it. This perp wanted to show me how close he could get, and he did."

Matt put on his suit coat, and turned off the desk lamp. "Let's go to your place so you can pick up some things, and then we'll get a bite."

"I'm not sure I could eat anything right now." She stood, and pushed her chair into the desk, and took her jacket off the back.

"Here, let me." He helped her. "You look tired."

"Not so much tired, but definitely frazzled." She turned around, and hugged him, and then stood back. "To be honest, I'm not sure about several things."

"Am I in there somewhere?" He smiled, and kissed her on the cheek.

"No, we're fantastic, and I love you." Ann hesitated. "I've been studying hard to make detective, and get that coveted *gold* shield."

She took a short breath, and sat on the edge of her desk.

"After today, I'm not all that positive about it. I mean, seeing Amanda's body—then those horrible pictures."

She rubbed the back of her neck.

"Matt, I don't know if I could do this with you every day."

She pushed a lock of her hair over her left ear.

"Maybe I should stay with interviews, and after the fact investigation."

"Everything you've said is understandable, and today was an unusual bitch."

He buttoned his collar and tightened his tie. "This whole case is a nightmare, but that's not typical of SVU. You should know that."

Matt waved toward a bank of filing cabinets.

"Ninety percent of our vics aren't murdered. Yes, they're abused, beaten or raped—sometimes all three, but not cut into pieces." He hesitated. "You got through the four mutilations with the *Oaks North* killings."

She slid down off the edge of her desk.

"I never saw their faces, or snapshots of the perp's handiwork."

"Okay, here's the deal ... tomorrow, if there are no bodies, you and I will do San Diego."

"Like, how?" Ann cracked a smile.

"We'll ride the trolley, just for the hell of it, and spend a leisurely afternoon at *Seaport Village*. I'll take pictures of you on the Carousel. Then we enjoy a long, romantic dinner at the *Harbor House."*

"And then?" Her expression brightened.

"We hop on the trolley again, and go to *Mission Valley,* and catch a movie."

"After that?" she laughed, and her eyes sparkled.

"That, my dear, remains to be seen." He squeezed her.

"Mr. Detective, with the shiny *gold* shield, I love you to death. What about Sunday?"

"Now that's the best part." He held her away and grinned. "We spend the day at the San Diego Zoo."

"Matt … we both live and work in a zoo."

"Copy that, Sergeant.

They walked out of the squad room.

* * * *

THE OLD VICTORIAN
AT THAT SAME TIME
IN THE FORMAL DINNING ROOM:

Michael carried a hot pot held with two oven gloves. "This turned out perfect, Samantha."

He set the container on a metal holder to keep it from damaging the finish of the solid oak table.

"It's my favorite recipe for homemade stew."

The cat jumped up to her place at the far end of the huge table. She sniffed the aroma, and licked her chops.

Michael spooned some broth and a few chunks of meat into a small bowl.

"It'll be hot, Sam, so you wait a minute."

He filled a larger bowl for himself.

"It's not thick, like some store-bought stew. The dish has just the right mix of potatoes, carrots, onions, broth and perfect cuts of special meat."

He stirred the cat's portion.

"Okay, I think its cool enough."

He walked to the other end of the table and set the steaming helping in front of his princess feline.

"If it's still too hot, just wait a minute."

Michael went back to his place, sat, and

tasted a spoonful of the stew.

"I should have my own cooking show on TV, this is the best."

Samantha began lapping the broth, and munched on a hunk of meat. She purred as she enjoyed her meal.

"How was your day, Sam? I'll bet it wasn't as productive as mine."

He laughed.

"I waltzed right into the cop shop, handed the desk officer the envelope, and he just took it. They're all idiots. I was right there, and he didn't have a clue. But then, how could he?"

The cat licked her front paws and rubbed her face as she always did after a tasty meal.

Michael enjoyed hot, chunky spoonful of stew.

"Tomorrow's another day, girl. I'll be having a Latte at *Starbucks,* and getting acquainted with Ms. Lauren, the lovely friend of the departed, Sally Patterson."

He spooned more stew into his bowl.

"This is great, I have to have another helping."

Chapter Thirty One

No Shoptalk Today

SEAPORT VILLIAGE SAN DIEGO
SATURDAY – 2:30 PM:

𝕬nn and 𝕸att had breakfast in La Mesa
at a downtown café, and then took the Trolley
south to Chula Vista. They had lunch at
Anthony's Fish Grotto.

After a nice seafood salad and two
glasses of a crisp California chardonnay they
rode the train back to San Diego.

Kellogg sprang for a horse and carriage
ride to *Seaport Village.*

They strolled along the boardwalk toward
the gift shops and the carousel.

To the casual observer, Matt and Ann
appeared to be a thirties-something couple in
jeans, sneakers and matching *UCSD*

sweatshirts. no one would suspect they were cops and underneath the long tailed shirts, they both carried snub-nosed thirty-eights.

Ann hooked her right arm through Matt's left, and looked up at him. "Are you sure the captain will let us work together permanently?"

"I'm positive." He jerked her arm. "Hey, lady, no shoptalk today, okay?"

"I've just been trying to get my head around the idea since you said that's what you want."

Matt led her to the seawall, and leaned against it. He held her out at arms length. "Everything depends on your agreement. Then, it becomes a done deal." He hugged her. "Let it be for the rest of our weekend."

"What about Jack and Ken?" She smiled. "Are they a perfect match?"

"You know what?" He grinned, and brushed a strand of hair out of her eyes.

"What?" The breeze from the ocean finished what Matt had started.

"You're impossible." He kissed her with the softness of a gull's feather.

"I promise you, Detective, I always will be." A warm rush worked its way through her heart. "I love you, Kellogg." She hugged him and pressed her face into his chest. "I just plain-ass love you."

He kissed the top of her head. "Yeah … me too." He took a breath, held her away and smiled. "Regarding Jack and Ken, they'll be fine together. Ken's detective first grade, he doesn't pull rank, and Jack will learn a lot from him. That is, if Ken doesn't drive him crazy with bad jokes."

Ann smiled. "Has anyone told you you're a nice guy?"

"Not lately. Is there a reward for that?"

"Yeah, me." She pinched his ribs. "Let's get an ice cream cone."

"First the carousel, I want to get pictures of you riding around on it like a kid."

"So, you're into little girls?" She threw her head back and laughed.

Matt watched her and grinned. "I can't tell you how much being with you means to me."

Ann reached up and touched his face. She whispered, "I do love you."

They walked away from the seawall, and headed toward the carousel.

* * * *

GROSSMONT CENTER
LA MESA - STARBUCKS
TWO HOURS LATER:

Michael Moran, disguised as a senior citizen, entered the coffee shop using a cane to navigate, and hobbled his way to the front counter. "Hi, Miss, I'd like a *Latte* with a spurt of extra cream, can you do that?"

Lauren smiled at the older gentlemen.

"Sure, no problem. Find a seat, and I'll bring it to you."

He paid with a five, and waited for change. He watched her, and thought, *Lauren, you're in for the surprise of your life.*

She came back, and handed him his change. "You get a discount. I'll bring the coffee to your table."

Michael slid into a seat near the front door. *I haven't seen her legs, but I'm sure they'll be just fine.*

Lauren came up to Michael's table. "Here we are." She set the cup in front of him, and opened the sip-flap. "It's hot, so be careful."

"I know, thank you for being so kind." He smiled and nodded. "I appreciate the gesture."

Lauren said, "Can I get you anything else, a pastry maybe?"

"No dear, I'm fine." *Later, I'll take*

everything you have. The mere idea tingled through his loins.

Chapter Thirty Two

The End of the Day

SEAPORT VILLIAGE SAN DIEGO
SATURDAY EVENING
THE HARBOR HOUSE – 6:30 PM:

𝔏𝔬𝔫𝔤 𝔟𝔢𝔞𝔪𝔰 𝔬𝔣 𝔣𝔦𝔢𝔯𝔶 𝔩𝔦𝔤𝔥𝔱 pushed their way through the windows and into the dining area. The sun had just begun to slip below the distant horizon and into the Pacific. It bid farewell to another beautiful Southern California Saturday.

Matt took a sip of his Cabernet Sauvignon, and smiled at Ann across the table. "I'm a pretty lucky guy. I have a successful career, I make good money, my apartment is top notch … and." He raised his glass.

"And what?"

"You're in my life … to you for being exactly who you are." He sipped some wine.

"Kellogg, you're an incurable romantic, and I love it." She sat back, let out a sigh, and adjusted the silverware on the linen napkin.

"Something wrong?" He leaned forward.

"Here we sit, like a couple of love birds, while we try to ignore the evil and death that's all around us every day." She swallowed a gulp of wine.

"Yes, that's what we're doing right now." Matt reached across the table and held her hand. "That's exactly what today was meant to be—an escape from a week of hell."

"I'm afraid, Matt. As tough as I may have sounded in Judy's lab yesterday, I'm scared to death. That bastard has my name on his list." She finished her wine and held up the glass. "I want another."

"Me too." He waved at the waiter. "We're together, hip to hip, you're not getting out of my sight." He squeezed her hand. "Who the hell wouldn't be scared?"

The waiter approached. "You folks ready to order?"

"Two more wines and we will be."

"Sounds good, I'll be right back."

"Thank you." To Ann he said, "You're going to be all right, I promise."

"What if being partners doesn't work out?"

She blinked back tears. "Will that pull us apart?"

"Nothing is going to separate us, I won't let it." He looked into her eyes for a moment. "Where is all this coming from?"

"I've been holding it in." She smiled. "Sorry."

"Don't be sorry about anything. You've let it out, and I understand." He whispered, "You're safe with me."

"I know, I trust you."

The waiter returned and served their wine. "Have you decided?"

Matt opened his menu. "Give us a couple of minutes, and we'll order the two best dishes in the house."

* * * *

GROSSMONT CENTER
LA MESA – 4:30 PM:

Michael limped from the coffee shop with his unneeded cane, got into his Mercedes, and drove the short five miles back to the old Victorian. There he re-masked his face, donned a security officer's uniform, and sported a neatly trimmed, thick brown mustache.

* * * *

One half hour before Lauren got off shift from Starbucks, Michael stood in front of the PETCO store acting like a security guard. He checked his watch, a cheap Timex to replace his Rolex. He didn't think a rent-a-cop would be wearing one. He nodded, and smiled at passers by, and offered greetings.

Too bad you have to be an example, Lauren. I'm sure you were interviewed regarding Sally. Nothing personal, but I have to make a point with Kellogg.

At ten minutes after five, Lauren came out the front door of *Starbucks.* She walked toward the parking lot, and took her keys out of her shoulder purse. When she clicked the remote a late model Chevy beeped and blinked its lights.

Michael started to close in on her. *That's all I need to make contact.* "Miss, are you employed by the Center?"

Lauren turned to face him. "What?" She stepped back.

"Do you work in the mall?" Michael moved closer. "You do work at Starbucks, right?" He reached into his pants pocket and gripped the syringe.

"Yeah, so what?" She moved to her car. "What the hell's your problem?"

"We're cracking down on employees who take front spaces. You're supposed to park away from the prime spots. I'll have to write you a ticket."

Lauren put more space between them. "That's bullshit." She studied his face. "I know all the guards on the day watch, and you're not one of them."

Michael moved closer. "I just came on duty. Calm down and we'll be done here in a minute."

She noticed the officer didn't have a two-way radio on his belt. "You're a phony, who the hell are you?" Lauren backed away, and stepped between her car and another.

Moran went for her. "I'm your worst nightmare." He pulled the needle out of his pants pocket and took off the cap.

Lauren saw it and stepped back. She swung her shoulder bag, and hit him on the left side of his head. "You're him—the killer!"

The hard blow knocked Michael off balance. He fell against the other car and dropped the syringe. "You're dead, bitch."

Unsteady, he reached down to grab the needle.

Lauren swung her purse and walloped him again. She took one quick step toward him and kicked the syringe under the other car. She moved back between the two vehicles and started screaming. "Help—somebody help me!"

Enraged, Michael rose to his full six foot four. He caught sight of two men hurrying toward him. He glared at Lauren. "There will be another time."

One of the two men, about five-nine, approached Michael. "What the hell's going on here?"

Lauren shouted. "He's the Legs Killer—not a security guard." She leaned against her car and started shaking.

Confused, the first young man said, "What's she talking about?"

Michael reached out with his gloved right hand and grabbed a fistful of the man's shirt. "Me, you stupid fuck. I'm the Legs Collector." He pushed him back into the other, would-be, hero and grinned.

A small group of people had gathered on the sidewalk nearby.

Lauren shouted. "Will somebody do something?"

Michael looked her in the eye. "I'm not through with you, Bitch." He turned and jogged off through the parking lot.

The young man with the rumpled shirt said, "Are you all right, Ma'am?"

"Yeah sure, I'm just peachy keen. Sorry, thank you for scaring him off." She relocked her car and stepped up onto the sidewalk.

"I don't think he was anywhere near being

scared." He chuckled. "The guy thinks he's the serial killer."

"Actually, he is. The sonofabitch killed my girlfriend, now he's after me." Lauren started rummaging through her purse for Sergeant Towne's card. "Would you do me a favor?"

"You want me to call the cops?"

"I already have one on the hook who's working the case." She found the card. "There's a loaded syringe under that car." Lauren pointed to the one next to hers. "Would you get it for me?"

"Are you diabetic?"

"That needle was a weapon the big bastard meant to stick in me. The police will love to have it."

"I'll get it." He got down on all fours and retrieved the hypo and handed it to her. "What is it?"

"I haven't got a clue." She remembered the cap. She looked down between the two cars and spotted it. "One more thing. "See that little piece of yellow plastic on the ground?"

"Yeah, you need it?"

"It's the cap for this thing."

He picked it up and gave it to her.

"Thank you, I owe you two guys a free coffee at *Starbucks.*"

"Great, we'll take you up on that."

Two *real* security guards came around the corner of the building in golf cart. One of them said, "Is there a problem here?"

"You missed it. The ruckus is over. The *Legs Collector* just jogged out of here free as a bird."

The other guard climbed out of the cart and approached Lauren. "Were you attacked?"

"I'm sure it was all caught on the cameras. You better save it, the cops will want a copy."

He looked at her. "Are you okay?"

"I am now—I work at *Starbucks,* I'll be in the manager's office for the rest of the evening. You'll be hearing from the police within the hour." Lauren slung her bag over her shoulder and walked toward the coffee shop.

Chapter Thirty Three

Lauren and the Syringe

GROSSMONT CENTER
SECURITY OFFICE – 6:30 PM:

𝕾𝖊𝖗𝖌𝖊𝖆𝖓𝖙 𝕿𝖔𝖜𝖓𝖊 𝖌𝖔𝖙 𝕷𝖆𝖚𝖗𝖊𝖓'𝖘 call
while having dinner with his wife and two
daughters. He contacted Ken and they drove
to Grossmont Center in separate cars.

They met Lauren at *Starbucks*, and she
escorted them to the security office. The three
sat in front of a bank of color monitors.

Security officer Jesus Vasquez brought
up the captured moments of Lauren's
encounter with Michael.

They all watched the video. Ken said,
"The guys attempted assault on Ms. Williams
and the confrontation with those other two
men went on for nearly five minutes. Then
three more fly by before real security gets

there. He stood and looked at the officer. "That's pretty sluggish response time, Vasquez."

Jesus pushed his chair away from the console, and waved across the stack of monitors. "There are fifty-seven cameras working the entire mall, Detective. Five cover that parking lot. We were in shift change, and didn't notice the altercation right away."

"Well then, I guess your cameras work just fine, but the guards don't." He tapped the screen. "Stop the tape and run it back to where the fake guard is standing in front of *PETCO*, and freeze it." The image came on screen. He looked at Lauren. "Is that the same man who tried to attack you?"

"That's him. The sonofabitch doesn't have a radio. I caught that right away."

"Good call." To Vasquez he said, "Your officers aren't armed, but they do carry batons, right?"

"That's part of the uniform, yes."

"Jesus, that guy doesn't have one. The phony security guard stood in front of the store for almost twenty-five minutes, on camera, and never got spotted?"

"I told you, it was shift change and we missed it. irritation crept into his voice. "Besides, Detective, there are monitors at security checkpoints throughout the mall."

"Not much good are they? I guess the best time to commit a crime here is during shift change." He tapped the small screen again. "Where did the perp go when he ran away?"

Jesus skipped ahead to the point where Michael left the scene and hit play. "He headed north across three rows, and got into that black sedan."

Jack leaned closer to the monitor. "It looks like a high end late model. Can you blow that up?"

Vasquez chuckled. "I don't have state of the art equipment like you guys do."

Ken said, "Make me a copy of all that from when the fake guard stands in front of the store to after Ms. Williams goes out of camera range."

"You got it. I'll run one now." He hesitated. "Would you like that on DVD or VHS?"

"DVD will be just fine, thank you." He turned to Lauren. "Do you work the same shift five days a week?"

"Yes, I'm off at five every day."

"Jesus, how many guards are on duty at five?"

"Ten on second watch, why?" He handed Ken a DVD copy of the security camera footage.

"Assign one of them to escort Ms.

Williams to her car every day until you hear otherwise." He held the disc. "You have a sleeve for this?"

"Yeah," He opened a drawer and gave Ken a plastic jewel case. "I can't authorize what you're asking."

"Who can?" He put the DVD in the case.

"That would be head of security, Larry Thomas." He pushed back in his chair, and looked up at Ken. "You know, Detective, you don't have any authority here."

"I beg to differ, Vasquez," He pointed to the screen. "That man is a possible suspect in the killing of four women in the last week. He approached Ms. Williams in a parking lot of your mall. I have all the authority I need. Get Thomas on the phone, and I'll talk to him."

"He won't be too happy to get a call on a Saturday night."

"I wasn't all that pleased to be called here on my Saturday either. Get Thomas on the horn, now."

Jack looked at Lauren and sensed the fear in her expression. "You did well, but it was risky."

"If I hadn't done what I did, I wouldn't be here now, would I?" She shook her head. "Why is that bastard after me?"

"You knew Sally, he obviously knows that and somehow, he knows you were interviewed by us. The perp has targeted you to make an example." Jack took a breath and responded in a way he knew better. "You're going to be okay, we'll protect you." He held up the plastic bag containing the syringe. "What you did to get this was extremely dangerous."

"Yeah, but you're damn glad I did it, right?" She grinned. "That was the bastard's give away. When I saw the needle, I knew it was him."

"How did you put that together?" He slipped the syringe into his jacket pocket. "Nothing regarding a needle has been released."

"C'mon, Sergeant. Who walks around with a loaded hypo in their pants?" She shuddered. "Christ, he came at me with that thing."

"You're fortunate, Lauren, had he stuck you we wouldn't be having this discussion." He stood, jotted a notation and put the notebook in his jacket. "We'll be done as soon as Ken gets off the phone. Then I will personally walk you to your car." He smiled. "I'm glad you're okay."

"Thank you." She looked up at him. "What if he comes back?"

"Chances are, he won't risk a second attempt." He hesitated. "Not with you, you're too tough for him, but stay alert."

"I appreciate you guys, thanks for caring."

"You're welcome … and yes, we do care."

* * * *

Ken finished his phone conversation with Thomas, "That works for me, thanks Larry. Here's Jesus." He handed the receiver to the lead guard. "Your boss."

He glared at the detective. "What's the plan, sir?" He listened to the head of security.

"The plan, Vasquez, is simple. You will provide an escort for the lady every night until you hear otherwise from me. Are we clear?"

"Yes, sir.'

"You're on thin ice. There will be a meeting Monday morning in my office. We're going to develop a new procedure regarding the change of watch. Are we clear on that?"

"Absolutely, sir."

"Get your people shaped up Vasquez."

"I will, sir." He hung up and looked at Ken. "Thanks a lot."

"My pleasure." He turned to Jack. "Let me have the syringe. I'll swing by the crime lab and drop it off, it's on my way home anyway." To Lauren he said, "I'll escort you to your car."

"I'm flattered. Two handsome cops concerned for my welfare." She smiled and stood. "The attention is overwhelming."

Ken gripped Jack's shoulder. "He's happily married with children, I'm not."

Jack smiled, and handed his partner the evidence. "Thanks, I appreciate it." He shook Lauren's hand. "And thank you for helping us on two occasions."

"You're welcome, I hope you get that scumbag soon."

"I assure you, we will. Good night, Lauren, and be careful." He winked at Ken. "I'll see you Monday morning." Jack left the security office.

Ken gestured toward the door. "Shall we?"

Lauren hooked her purse over her right shoulder. "What you said about Jack being happily married with children, does that mean you're not happily married?"

They left the office and walked out into the open mall. Ken smiled at her. "It means, I'm not married."

"Are you flirting with me Detective?" She grinned.

"I shouldn't be, but I guess I am." He dug a card out of his jacket. "Here, my cell number is on the back. Call me anytime."

"About what?"

"Whatever comes to mind."

"You mean about the *Legs killer?*"

Lauren looked up at him.

"Yeah, that too." He took her arm and they headed toward the main entrance. "Are you hungry?"

"Famished."

"You like seafood?"

"Love it."

"Does *Red Lobster* sound good?

"Perfect."

"Excellent. We're on our way to a great dinner." Ken knew it was against the rules, but right then, it didn't matter.

* * * *

EL CAJON BLVD-10:30 PM:

Michael had gone home, changed his facial disguise, and put on an expensive Armani suit, a two-hundred dollar custom-made shirt, and topped it all off with a one-hundred-dollar silk tie, and slipped into a pair of two-hundred-dollar Italian-leather loafers.

He drove along the south end of the boulevard just over the line from La Mesa to San Diego. It was a known haven for street-walking working girls.

Vice cops had not been able to clean up the area for more than a month at a time, but the risk of getting caught didn't bother Michael at the moment. He wanted a quick, easy victim with as little hassle as possible.

* * * *

He spotted a young African American woman about twenty-six. She wore a short, black leather skirt and fishnet stockings on a pair of great looking legs and red stiletto heels.

Michael pulled to the curb and lowered the passenger window. He said, "Are you working tonight?"

"I sure am, Honey, what's your pleasure?" She leaned into the car. "You're not one of those vice dudes are you?"

"No, Ma'am, I'm not any kind of police." He flashed his Hollywood smile.

"Ma'am? I ain't heard that in a long while. You're pretty fancy with this big, car an' all."

Michael studied the woman and grinned. "I'm just looking for a good time." He gave her another big smile. "What do you charge?"

"Honey, I tell you that an' I'm busted."

"Not so, I told you, I'm not a cop ... promise."

"Okay, fifty bucks for a knob job an' a hundred for all the way."

Michael laughed. "You're a delight." He pulled out a handful of bills. "You'll get a thousand for an all nighter."

"Are you for real?" She stepped back "How do I know you ain't that crazy killer runnin all over the county?"

"Do I look like that kind of a nut?"

She laughed. "I've never seen one an' you sure don't look like that face they had all over the news." She leaned back into the window. "Am I safe with you?"

"Absolutely, climb in, we'll go to my place, have a great time, and I'll bring you back here in the morning."

"I need to see that money, honey." She salivated at the thought.

Michael held out ten one hundred dollar bills. "Here it is."

The woman opened the door and slid in. "I guess this is my lucky night." She pulled a pack of cigarettes out of her small purse. "Mind if I smoke?"

"Not at all, what's your name?" He pressed the button and the passenger door locked.

"I'm Darcy."

"Lovely name." Michael stuck the needle into her neck before she could light her cigarette. "Smoking isn't healthy."

Chapter Thirty Four

Deliver us From Evil

ST ANNE'S CATHOLIC CHURCH
28th & SICARD, SAN DIEGO,
SUNDAY – 6:30 AM:

𝕿𝖜𝖔 𝕬𝖑𝖙𝖆𝖗 𝕭𝖔𝖞𝖘, Timmy Farrell and
Jonathan Logan, had the duty for the 7:30
mass that fateful Sunday morning. They
were both in the Sacristy getting things
ready for the service.

Timmy set out the sacrificial water and
wine and took a nip.

Jonathan slapped him on the arm. "Father
Davis catches you and we'll be sacked, man."

"He won't." The boy grinned and took
another sip.

"Yeah well, he can smell your breath,
stupid." He grabbed the bottle and corked it.

"I don't want my ass in a jam because of you."

"Cool it." Timmy popped a few *Tic-Tacs.*
"I'll go light the altar candles, I'm taller."

"You're a trouble maker, Farrell. You're lucky I won't tell." Jonathan put the wine back in the cupboard.

"You'd better not."

Father Davis entered the Sacristy from the side door. "Better not what?"

Jonathan said, "Morning, Father … nothing, we were just arguing about who was going to light the candles." He glared at Timmy.

The priest smiled. "I take it Timmy won."

"Yes, he did, he's taller." He thought, *Farrell, someday, you're gonna get nailed.*

"Well then, you can carry the water and wine."

* * * *

Timmy lit the wick of the candle lighter, and walked out into the sanctuary. He went behind the altar, reached up, and ignited the four tall candles, stepped in front of the altar, genuflected, and lit the two smaller candles.

When he turned and came down he saw Darcy. "Holy God—oh my God!" He dropped the long, brass candle lighter and ran back into the Sacristy. "Father—there's a naked woman sitting in the front pew and her hands are tied."

* * * *

Father Davis approached Darcy. He saw her bound wrists over the railing, and that she was positioned in a posture of prayer. He retched when he realized the body had no legs.

"Mother of God. What has happened in my church?"

He blessed himself.

* * * *

THE OLD VICTORIAN
ONE HOUR EARLIER:

Michael finished scrambling a batch of eggs, and put them on a plate with strips of sizzling homemade bacon. "Here, Sam." He placed eggs, and pieces of the meat on a saucer for Samantha.

"We're having an early breakfast today." He carried the cat's portion to her end of the kitchen table, and set it on the cat's placemat.

"Enjoy my dear." He scratched her ears. "I had a productive night, and I think detective Kellogg will have a fantastic Sunday when he reads the note I left with the remains of Ms. Darcy. God bless her soul." He made the sign of the cross.

The cat chomped on her food and didn't respond.

Michael took a forkful of bacon and eggs. "Excellent, I'm such a good cook."

Chapter Thirty Five

Last Rights for Darcy

ST ANNE'S CATHOLIC CHURCH
SUNDAY – 7:40 AM:

𝕶𝖊𝖑𝖑𝖔𝖌𝖌 𝖆𝖓𝖉 𝕭𝖊𝖈𝖐 arrived at the scene. Matt parked behind two black and white units.

A young priest directed a group of parishioners to the parish hall. There would be no early mass in the church that morning.

Two uniformed officers stood in front of the main entrance. Matt and Ann held up their badges and one of the uniforms opened the door for them. Kellogg nodded.

The vestibule doors were open. When Kellogg and Beck walked in they went into the narthex and stopped. Matt looked at his partner. "Does this bother you?"

"What rattles me is that this is Saint

Anne's." A chill crept up her spine.

"Yeah … I hear that, and he picked it on purpose."

Both raised Roman Catholic, the images at the front of the church did not set well. Judy Wake stood next to the covered victim on the Gospel side of the altar and two coroner's assistants leaned against a gurney nearby.

Bright beams of morning sun fell through elevated stained glass windows and showered multi-colored light over the white sheet that hid the gruesome remains of Darcy.

Matt blessed himself with holy water. Ann did the same and they entered the nave of the church. When they reached the front pew, the reality of desecration told its own tale of horror.

The ME stepped away from the body. "We meet again so soon." She looked at the two cops. "I'm not Catholic, but, as a born Baptist, I'm offended to the core by this defilement of a sacred place." Judy reached over and pulled back the sheet.

Ann grimaced and covered her mouth.

Kellogg opened his note book. "The killer selected this church because it *is* Saint Anne's."

To Beck, Judy said, "I'm sorry."

"Yeah, isn't that a kick in my face?"

Matt moved around to get a different perspective. "What did you find on prelim?"

The ME tilted the vic's head back.

"Ligature marks inflicted by the same type of tubing he used on three of the others. And similar rope used to tie her wrists."

"Any defensive wounds?" Matt wrote down the information.

"None, but he did change his surgical procedure."

Wake pointed to the leg stumps.

"This time, the perp severed the limbs just above the knees."

Matt bent down.

"Yeah … he did that so there'd be enough left to support the torso when the corpse was put in this sick prayer position."

He hesitated.

"Cover her up."

"Wait for a minute."

Ann put on a pair of latex gloves.

"Was there evidence of sexual assault?"

Judy said, "I really don't want to check for that here."

"Understood."

Beck came around to get a better view.

"No purse?"

"Nothing. There's no way of knowing who she is right now."

Matt watched his partner go to work.

She's turned herself around—damn!

Ann examined a necklace around Darcy's neck.

"Could she have been wearing this gold cross when she was strangled?"

Judy said, "It's possible, it rides well below the ligature marks."

"True, but the perp may have put the jewelry on her to make a statement."

She covered the body herself. "This creep will do anything to get at me."

Ann jotted a note regarding the necklace.

Kellogg made a note of the cross. "Good observation, Ann." *She's going to work out just fine.*

He closed his notebook. To Judy he said, "I think you can get her out of here now."

Matt looked up at the pristine altar.

"This sanctuary has been violated long enough."

Wake summoned one of the coroner's assistants.

"Ray, take the body out through that side door."

She gestured toward the exit on the epistle side of the church.

"We're parked in the lot."

"Well, go move your van around the building. I don't want people seeing you cart a body out of this church."

"Okay, Ma'am, we'll bag it and put the corpse on the gurney first."

"Get to it then."

Ann said, "Who found the vic?"

"A young altar boy, he's in the sacristy with the other kid and Father Davis. They're all going to have nightmares for who knows how long."

"We have to talk to them."

Beck added another entry in her notebook.

Judy looked Matt directly in the eyes. "This vic is a *sister*. When I saw that body … a jagged shard of ice stabbed through my heart—get him, Matt."

"I promise you, that piece of human waste has his days numbered."

The two coroner's assistants lifted Darcy's body out of the pew and a white number ten envelope fell to the floor.

Ann held up her hand.

"Hang on a second."

She reached down and picked it up.

"It's for us, Matt."

She handed him the envelope, and moved out of the way of the two young men.

The detective looked at the bold lettering:
TO KELLOGG & BECK – HAVE A BLESSED SUNDAY!

Chapter Thirty Six

The Priest
&
The Altar Boys

Saint Anne's Catholic Church
Sunday – 8:35 AM:

𝕱𝖆𝖙𝖍𝖊𝖗 𝕯𝖆𝖛𝖎𝖘 𝖕𝖆𝖈𝖊𝖉 around the sacristy with his hands behind his back. He studied the oak floor as he walked.

"I'm so sorry you kids had to see what you did. I've asked your parents to wait in the rectory until the police are through here."

The altar boys, Timmy Farrell and Jonathan Logan sat in silence on a bench near the entrance to the sanctuary. Timmy shuddered at the image of Darcy.

"Why was a dead woman in our church with no clothes on?"

"The authorities will sort that out, son. May God bless her soul."

Matt and Ann appeared in the open doorway. Kellogg said, "We need to ask a few questions, Father."

"Of course, come in."

"I'm Detective Kellogg, and this is my partner, Sergeant Beck."

"I can't say I'm pleased to meet you, not under such circumstances."

He gestured toward a sofa opposite from where the boys were sitting.

"Please have a seat."

Timmy nudged Jonathan and grinned.

Ann opened her note book to a new page.

"I have to tell you, Father, I'm Catholic, we both are. I feel personally violated by what happened here this morning."

Matt added, "We're sorry you and the boys had to experience the horror that you have."

Father Davis glanced at the two kids.

"Jonathan and Timmy will carry the images of this day through the rest of their lives."

He stepped back and leaned against the counter where the tray of unblessed water and wine remained. It would not be served with the Holy Eucharist that Sunday morning.

"As for me, I came fresh out of the Seminary, and spent two years in Vietnam. I was the chaplain for a company of Marines. Horror is not a stranger to me, Detective."

The priest took a breath and folded his

arms across his chest.

"Not once did I ever see a violation of a house of worship."

He sighed and looked down.

"This morning, the personification of evil walked down the aisle through the nave of this holy place."

Matt took a breath and looked up at Father Davis.

"Your church is clear now. The victim has been removed and there's no evidence she was ever here."

"That poor woman. I gave her the last rites. Whether she was Catholic or not, it didn't matter, I did what I had to."

Ann said, "If it's any comfort, she was wearing a gold cross. It's safe to assume she was a Christian."

"Thank you, it does make a difference."

He hesitated.

"Was this the work of the killer the newspapers and TV can't get enough of?"

Kellogg responded.

"We believe it may be him. Father, let me ask you, is the church left unlocked during the night?"

"Up until this mess, we haven't locked our church. That policy may have to change."

Beck jotted a note.

"Actually, Father, I don't believe locked

doors would've made any difference. This perpetrator wanted in and a lock wouldn't have stopped him."

She smiled at the two boys.

"Which one of you guys discovered the victim?"

Careful, you're questioning two kids who've just seen a mutilated body.

"I did." Timmy said, obviously thrilled to be part of a police investigation.

"Tell me what you were doing at the time."

She wrote a note that the boy had been first to see Darcy.

"Well, I went into the sanctuary to light the candles on both sides of the tabernacle. After I did that, I walked around to the front of the altar and lit the candles on each end of it."

"Is that when you saw her?"

"Yeah ... I blew out the wick on the lighter and stepped down—there she was. I almost lost my breath. The lady was naked and her hands were tied."

"Did you approach the woman?"

Ann wrote her own shorthand in her notebook.

"No, Ma'am—no way. I dropped the candle lighter and ran back to the sacristy shouting for Father Davis."

"What did you see, Jonathan?" *This boy is more rattled. Go easy.*

"All I ever want to see, ever."

He sat on the edge of his chair and held his head down.

"When Timmy came screaming for Father Davis, I thought he was pulling one of his pranks, but he wasn't. He was scared to death."

"Did you go into the sanctuary?"

This young boy will have serious nightmares for a long time.

She noted the fright still visible in his eyes.

"I wasn't sure what Timmy was yelling about. I followed Father Davis out into the sanctuary."

The boy shivered.

"I saw the naked woman with her head down like she was praying."

He swallowed hard.

"Her hands were tied. She wasn't in prayer."

Jonathan shook his head.

"I got closer and saw the stumps of her legs."

The lad looked over at Ann.

"I puked on the altar steps."

He started to cry.

"It's okay, there's nothing to be ashamed of, or feel guilty about."

She jotted another note.

"We're through with you boys now, you

can go home when Father Davis says it's okay. Thank you both for helping us."

Timmy said, "Will our stuff be on an official report?"

"Yes it will."

"Cool." He patted Jonathan's arm.

"Hey, Dude, we're gonna be famous!"

"Yeah, right."

The boy looked up at Father Davis.

"Can we go now?"

"Yes, your parents are in the rectory, as I said. If they need to see me, I'll be right along."

The boys got up and left through the side door.

Ann closed her notebook and put it in her jacket pocket.

"Those two are going to need some counseling. Is the parish able to handle that?"

The priest pinched the bridge of his nose. "Yes, we have professionals available to deal with such trauma. I may need to visit one myself."

He sat in one of the chairs the boys had used.

"The Bishop is coming up from San Diego University. I contacted him right after the body was found."

He drew in a long breath.

"We're having a special service at noon to

address this morning's incident. What do we tell our parishioners?"

Matt said, "Father, The media will soon be all over this story, if they're not already. I suggest you tell the truth. Simply say, an unidentified woman was found dead in your church and you have no further information. Actually, that *is* the truth, isn't it?"

"I think I'll smooth the edges a little."

"You might as well, we don't have any more information."

Matt closed his notebook and put it away.

"To be honest, Father, I believe what happened in your church today *is* the work of the *Legs Collector*. He chose St Anne's because it's the namesake of my partner and he has targeted her as a victim."

Father Davis looked at Ann.

"Do you believe this to be true?"

"It is, and we're prepared to take him out when he makes his move."

"Dear God ... you'll be in my prayers, Sergeant."

"Thank you, Father, I appreciate that."

* * * *

When Kellogg and Beck came out the front doors they were met by a gaggle of reporters and TV cameras rolled.

Matt spotted the big KGTV-10 and KUSI vans and knew they were on *live.* He didn't recognize most of the reporters because the majority worked weekends.

That Sunday gave them a shot at the big story.

A young reporter with Channel Ten stuck his microphone up at Matt.

"Was a woman murdered and mutilated in the church?"

"No one has been killed here. Now, if you'll excuse us, we have work to do."

"Detective, two men removed a body from that church about a half hour ago. Was it dropped here by the *Legs* killer?"

Kellogg noticed her press pass. She worked for Channel Thirty-nine.

"An unidentified female body was found in the church this morning. Her corpse had been compromised, and it may be the work of the so called, *Legs Collector.* That's all we know at this time."

He and Ann took a couple of steps down and the group moved with them.

An aggressive, more experienced reporter called out above the din of the others.

"Detective Kellogg, I'm Ben Hanson with

Fox News. This is day seven and you've been presented with a fifth homicide. How do you account for the fact that SVU doesn't have a suspect or a person of interest?"

"Actually, Mr. Hanson, I don't have to account for anything to the media, and you don't know if we have a suspect or person of interest, do you?"

"What about the note that the killer left for you this morning?" He hesitated. "Is it like *Amanda's last story* that you refused to release?"

Matt glanced at Ann and responded to Hanson's question,

"I have no comment."

They took two more steps away from the church and Hanson followed.

"Was it addressed to you, or Beck?"

Matt's irritation showed. "I said, no comment and I mean, no comment. Step aside and let us through."

A female reporter from KSDO Talk Radio shouted, "Ann, has the killer made a statement to you by dumping the body here at Saint Anne's?"

"I have no comment. Get the hell out of the way and let us go back to work."

* * * *

Matt drove away from the church and headed downtown. He glanced over at Ann.

"You got a little testy with the press."

She stared at the envelope from the killer.

"You snapped at the *Fox* guy."

She started opening the note.

"Yeah, I did, he's an arrogant sonofabitch, but then, they're all just doing their jobs and I can't fault them for wanting to know why we have no suspects."

He decided to take Twenty-Eighth Street into the city rather than the freeway.

Ann unfolded Moran's letter. She caught a short breath.

"Good God."

"What's it say?"

"He's promised another victim for tomorrow morning." She looked at Matt. "I don't believe this."

"For Christ's sake—read it."

Ann drew another breath, cleared her throat, and started reading out loud.

* * * *

Hi guys, I hope your morning visit to saint Anne's was spiritual. BTW: I picked the church especially for the lovely, Ms. Beck, I thought it would be a nice touch.

If it helps any, the vic's name is Darcy.

She was a street walker on El Cajon Boulevard, and just happened to be there for me. You can blame, Lauren, the Starbucks lady for that. She got away from me on Saturday and I had to improvise.

I won't hunt the same area again. However, I will have something for you tomorrow morning. There are so many places to find young ladies with great legs.

I'm going to get you, Ann Beck—count on it!

Fuck you, Kellogg, kiss your sweet Ann goodbye.

* * * *

Matt cut across town to Sixteenth Street. "Who is Loren?"

"She's a friend of Sally Patterson. Jack and I interviewed her. It's all in my report."

"Okay, we were out of the loop yesterday. Something happened. We have to get up to speed."

Chapter Thirty Seven

The Wrath of Michael

THE OLD VICTORIAN
TWENTY MINUTES EARLIER:

𝕸𝖎𝖈𝖍𝖆𝖊𝖑 𝖜𝖆𝖙𝖈𝖍𝖊𝖉 the special live broadcast coming from in front of Saint Anne's and became enraged. He got off the huge, sectional sofa and paced before the widescreen television.

"Did you hear that bullshit, Samantha?" He shook his fist at the TV. "Smart ass, Kellogg avoided the sharp Fox reporter's questions with his, *No Comment* crap. He wouldn't admit that I, *The Legs Collector,* left Darcy in the church. However, everybody now knows a note was found with the remains. I have no idea how that leaked, but I'm glad it did."

Sam busied herself with the cleaning of her right rear foot and paid no attention to the ranting of her master.

"Okay, Detective, you've really pissed me off."

Michael wagged his finger at the screen.

"All of a sudden you and Beck are partners."

He clenched his fists and screamed at the TV.

"You son-of-a-bitch!"

He grabbed the Sunday paper off the coffee table and pitched it at the screen.

The cat jumped down from the sofa and ran into the dining room.

"Kellogg, you're an idiot. You think strapping Ann to your ass will stop me?"

Michael's face turned red and the veins in his neck gorged with blood.

"Think again, Flatfoot—the longer it takes me to get to Beck, the more legless bodies will turn up and you can take that to the bank, my friend."

An apparition of the dearly departed, Elizabeth Moran appeared in the doorway to the dining room.

You're on a downward spiral, Mickey.

"Go away, Mother."

The image on the TV went still and the living room became as cold as a frozen winter day. The specter of Mrs. Moran continued her haunting.

I saw the evil in your eyes the day you were born and I was sorry I birthed you.

Michael started picking up the newspaper pages and putting them back together.

"I don't want to hear you, Bitch—go back to your grave and leave me alone."

You do hear me, Mickey. It took thirteen years for the demon in you to come out. The day you violated your retarded cousin you became the beast you are now.

"I never hurt Jennifer."

He screamed at the phantom.

"We were just playing—you knew that. You wanted to punish me and you kept on punishing me for nothing."

I never felt sorry for you, Mickey—you were always bad, and you will burn in hell.

"You witch—go away!"

He threw the newspaper at the ghost image and the pages scattered into the dining room.

* * * *

The freezing cold ended. Michael sat on the sofa and stared at the TV screen to see Kellogg and Beck walk away from the reporters. "Pompous ass, Kellogg—you pompous ass." He grinned. "Mark my word,

Detective, I'll get to Beck. Count on it."

* * * *

He got up and called for his cat.
"Samantha, I didn't mean to frighten you."
Sam trotted in from the other room.
"There you are."
He picked her up.
. "I'll fix you a nice early lunch. Daddy has to get ready for a Sunday evening hunt."

Chapter Thirty Eight

Sunday Night Surprise

WESTFIELD MALL
EL CAJON, CA– 4:00 PM:

𝕸ichael parked his 𝕭enz in the *Wells Fargo* lot near the main entrance to the huge indoor mall. He had just two hours to hunt before most of the stores closed and the crowd would start to thin out.

He checked his appearance in the mirror.

"I have to say, you look just like one of those bronco riders, Hoss."

Michael grinned at his image, put on a hundred dollar *Stetson,* and climbed out of the car.

Any other time he would stand out in his Western garb. Not this weekend.

A nationally sanctioned rodeo event had

been running since Friday at the Lakeside Arena, just four miles away.

Cowboys from all over the country flooded the East County. Michael would be one among many.

His steel-toed *Tony Lama* boots, at two hundred forty bucks a pair, made him an inch taller than his six-foot-four. They looked great with his boot-cut *LEE* jeans. The tailored blue and white-checked shirt, with *Mother of Pearl* snaps instead of buttons, fit perfectly on his muscular frame. He had topped it off with a short, denim jacket. Just for effect.

Michael went the extra step to carry a can of *SKOAL* chewing tobacco in the upper left pocket. He made the perfect image of a good old cowboy from Texas. The four-day growth of whiskers he had applied to his face rounded out the disguise.

Michael looked down and tapped the big brass buckle on his belt. It displayed the raised image of a rider on a bucking bronco.

"I guess we're good to go."

* * * *

Inside, the mall remained busy with Sunday shoppers. As Michael anticipated, many cowboy hats were easily spotted.

Five minutes later, he had purchased a double cheeseburger with fries and a *Coke* and sat at a table in the food court.

B*eer would go better with this shit.*

A blonde woman, about twenty-four, carried a tray of food to a nearby table.

Not bad, young, but what the hell.

Thirty seconds later a man pushed a stroller up to her table in which a toddler was fussing.

Michael took a bite of his burger, *So much for that one.* He checked his watch. *Four thirty … I'm losing time here, dammit.*

When he had eaten all of the sandwich and continued nursing his drink, a tall brunette wearing a medium length skirt slid into a seat two tables away. He grinned, tipped his hat and wiped his mouth on a paper napkin. *This is more like it.*

The woman noticed him and smiled.

She has a great pair of legs. Love the black heels, honey. He sipped some *Coke. Go for it.*

"Excuse me, Ma'am."

"Yes?" Her smile gleamed and dangling gold earrings danced when she turned her head. They sparkled in the multi-colored lights of the food court.

"Is there a W*al-Mart* in this Mall?"

Beautiful amber eyes. Lovely lady.

"There sure is and it's a big one."

She pointed away from where they were seated.

"Go all the way to the end of the court and turn left. You can't miss it."

She took a bite of a French fry.

"You must be from out of town."

"Yes, Ma'am, I flew in from Austin, Texas for the Lakeside rodeo. This place here is close to bein' as big as the one we got down home."

Watch the country accent; you're not that good at it.

She drank some *Dr. Pepper.*

"Did you ride a bronco?"

"Boy—did I ever."

He gave her one of his cute smiles.

"You can be sure that eight seconds on the back of one of them raging animals seems like forever."

You're making headway … don't overdo it.

"Did you win something?"

Her eyes sparkled.

"Did fer sure. Came in second in saddle bronc an' won me back the cost of my plane ticket an' then some."

She's ready—get her outside.

"Well, congratulations are in order." She raised her soda cup. "To the winner from Austin, Texas."

"Thank you, Ma'am."

He lifted his drink and winked.

Two boys about nine and twelve walked down the center of the food court and came toward the woman's table. She turned and greeted them.

"There you are."

She smiled at Michael.

"My two little men, Robert and David."

He stood and tipped his hat.

"Hi guys."

The younger kid looked up at him.

"Are you a cowboy?"

"Sure am, son." *Goddamn brats and a mom.*

The woman dug in her purse and handed a five to the older boy.

"This nice gentleman is visiting from Austin, Texas. He won second place for bronco riding at the rodeo."

The smaller child said, "Wow, that's cool."

Robert looked at the towering cowboy and put the five in his jacket pocket. He wasn't impressed.

"Mom, you shouldn't be talking to strange men."

"Mind your manners, Robert, that's rude. Now go get you and your brother a hotdog and fries."

She looked up at Michael.

"Sorry, he just wants to protect his mother."

"I sure can relate to that."

The boy didn't move away from the table and kept staring at the tall man.

Michael said, "Ma'am, you're a lucky woman." *You have no idea how lucky.*

"Yes, I believe I am."

He tipped his hat.

"Ya-all have a good evening."

"Thank you."

She smiled and nudged Robert.

"Go get the food."

"As soon as Tex leaves, Mom, I will."

"Good boy."

Michael touched the brim of his *Stetson* again and walked away.

Little fucker—I'd love to kick his young ass.

* * * *

Forty minutes later the crowd of shoppers had dwindled considerably.

The place is closing down and my pickings are getting fewer by the minute.

Michael started to get angry.

Dammit, Kellogg, I'm going to have a prize for you tomorrow morning—one way or the other.

A good looking woman came out of *Victoria's Secret* carrying a shopping bag and headed toward the main entrance.

He started following her.

Great, she's oriental, small framed and a pair of excellent legs.

Heat rose in his tight jeans.

The woman walked with the grace of a New York model.

She got within twenty yards of the big doors and Michael made his move.

"Pardon me, Ma'am, maybe you can help me."

The woman stopped and faced him.

"What is it?"

"Well, I feel kinda dumb."

He gave her his radiant smile.

"I was told I could find a *Wells Fargo ATM* in the mall and I haven't found the darn thing yet."

"It's not in the mall."

She grinned and gestured toward the street.

"The bank is across the way. There's an ATM over there, I'm parked in their lot."

How convenient.

"Mind if I walk with you?"

"No, not at all."

They started toward the entrance.

"You're not from here?"

"I came in for the rodeo from Austin, Texas. It was a long, expensive, trip for a whole lotta nothin' … I didn't place in any event."

"Sorry to hear that."

"Yeah, better luck next time." *I like this little lady.*

They crossed the driveway from the mall into the bank's parking lot. The woman waved toward the building.

"There it is. The ATM is around the corner to your right."

"I'll walk you to your car."

"Thank you, but that's not necessary."

"I think it is."

He reached into the right side pocket of his denim jacket and gripped the syringe.

"It's most necessary."

He moved closer.

The woman stepped back and shivered at the grin on the cowboy's face.

"Get away from me!"

The images of recent newspaper headlines and TV reports flashed across her mind. She dropped her shopping bag, opened her purse, pulled out a small container of pepper spray and let him have a full blast.

"You creep." She sprayed him again.

Michael fell back against a car in burning agony.

"You bitch."

His right leg buckled and he went down. Violent coughing started. He tried to protect his face and eyes with his left hand.

The woman sprayed him again.

"You're a pervert." She grabbed her shopping bag and ran back into the mall.

Michael threw his head back, the *Stetson* fell off. He grabbed it, got to his feet and stumbled to his car.

"Fucking bitch."

His face, hand and eyes were on fire. He fumbled for the remote and unlocked the Mercedes. "Christ, I can't see worth a shit."

He found a bottle of water, opened it and flooded his eyes.

"Son-of-a-bitch."

He started the car, drove over the sidewalk, and went through a stop sign.

Two security guards rushed out through the entrance. They caught a glimpse of the Speeding black car take a right onto Broadway.

Chapter Thirty Nine

Sunday Brunch

EL PATIO RESTURANT
OLDTOWN– SAN DIEGO
FIVE HOURS EARLIER:

𝕶𝖊𝖑𝖑𝖔𝖌𝖌 𝖆𝖓𝖉 𝕭𝖊𝖈𝖐 relaxed at a shaded table and enjoyed sips from their margaritas.

Matt said, "This all seems so unreal from the horror that started our day."

Ann drew in a long breath.

"Yeah … and we're no closer to this monster than we were a week ago."

She scooped up some salsa on a warm taco chip.

"He wants me, Matt, so he can spite you."

She crunched the chip and took another swallow of her drink.

Matt leaned toward her.

"That isn't going to happen."

He let out a sigh.

"If the sonofabitch saw the news coverage this morning, at the church, he knows you're now my partner. He has to go through me to get to you."

He sat back.

"The perp's a dead man if he tries."

"Are you sure?"

Ann had another sip.

"Are you really sure?"

"I'll bet my life on it."

His cell buzzed.

"Yeah, Kellogg."

He listened.

"We're at the El Patio. Not a problem, join us. See you in a few." Matt closed the phone.

"That was Ken, he's coming over."

"Does he have something from yesterday?"

She dipped another chip.

"Apparently, the lady you and Jack interviewed had a threatening encounter with our guy."

"That has to be Lauren, the counter girl at Starbucks. I guess she got away from him?"

"Ken says she did. We'll know more when they get here."

He crunched a chip.

"They? You mean Jack and Ken?"

"No, I mean Lauren and Ken." He grinned.

"He hustled Lauren?"

She sat back and chuckled.

"I need a refill, you're driving, I'm not."

Matt waved down a waiter, pointed at Ann's glass, and held up one finger.

* * * *

Thirty minutes later Ken and Lauren arrived. Ken introduced her.

"This young lady met up with our perp yesterday afternoon. I'd like you to meet Lauren Williams."

Ann smiled.

"I've had the pleasure."

Matt stood and shook her hand.

"Apparently you're a lucky lady."

He gestured toward two chairs.

"Please, join us … how did you manage to get away?"

She held up her shoulder bag.

"I hit him twice in the head with this."

Lauren hefted her bag and smiled.

"Here's the best part."

Ken laughed.

"We have the whole scene on DVD. It's a riot to watch. I had the security guy run us a copy. And there's bonus material."

He patted Lauren's arm.

"When she whacked him the first time he fell against a car. The second blow put him down on one knee and he dropped the syringe."

"You got it?"

Ken grinned.

"This brave one did the getting for us."

"I had help."

She enjoyed the attention.

"A young man, who came to my rescue, snatched the thing out from under the car."

"She's being modest."

Ken smiled.

"The help came after the attempted attack. You can't see in on the DVD, but Lauren kicked it under the vehicle while the perp was down. By then two guys made an attempt to come to her aid."

He put his arm over the back of her chair.

"That was a joke. The perp was wearing a security guard's uniform and it confused the onlookers. This guy's big, Matt. I'd say six-three, maybe four, and built solid."

Lauren laughed.

"He grabbed my, would be, hero by the shirt and nearly lifted him off his feet."

Goose bumps crawled up her arms and she shivered.

"He swore at the guy and claimed he's the *Legs collector.*"

Ann fetched a breath.

"You're the only one of five women who came face to face with the killer and got away. Jack and I told you this might happen. Thank God he didn't get you."

"Time out."

Ken held up his hand.

"You said five women?"

"Didn't you see Matt and me on the news this morning?"

He glanced at Lauren and then Kellogg.

"No, we didn't."

Matt pulled out Michael's note and handed it to him.

"The killer left his fifth victim at Saint Anne's this morning. It got leaked to the media before we could clear the scene. They swarmed all over the front of the church and went live with the story. We were caught in the flood."

Ken folded the paper and gave it back to Matt.

"This is bad. The captain will be a roaring volcano tomorrow morning."

Ann looked at Lauren's pale face.

"Are you okay?"

She pulled a lock of hair over here right ear.

"Ken … I need a drink."

She shuddered.

"That victim was supposed to be me."

Ann reached across the table and gripped Lauren's hand.

"It wasn't, you'll be all right now."

"Will I … will I really?"

To Ken, Matt said, "The syringe, do you have it?"

"I dropped it off at the lab last night and tagged it as evidence. Tony will analyze the contents tomorrow."

He hesitated.

"How did the press get wind of the body in the church?"

"The Fox News reporter knew about the letter I just showed you. My guess is, one of the coroner's assistants tipped him off.
Beside Ann and me, they're the only ones who saw the envelope. I'll alert Judy first thing in the morning."

"Good, she'll have heads rolling."

* * * *

THE OLD VICTORIAN
SUNDAY EVENING 7:00 PM:

Michael washed his face and hands for the third time in cool, soapy water. He flooded his eyes again with *Bausch & Lomb* soothing eye solution and looked in the mirror. Most of the bloodshot had dissipated.

Samantha jumped up on the bathroom counter and gave a soft cry. The cat sensed something troubled her master.

"Yes, sweetheart. Daddy's hurting a little right now, but I'll be all right."

He carried her into the living room.

"I'll fix a tasty Sunday dinner for us shortly. You have to eat more than just meat, honey. How about a few asparagus spears with lots of butter to go with a small steak just for you?"

The cat purred as he cradled her in his arm.

He sat on the large sofa and held Sam on his lap.

"Let's watch that news report from this morning one more time."

Michael clicked the remote on his DVR. Kellogg and Beck filled the widescreen.

"See those two Bozos, Sam?"

He laughed.

"That pretty little woman cop is my next target."

Chapter Forty

Syringe Content Results

SQUADROOM SDPD COMPLEX
MONDAY – 7:45 AM:

𝕾𝖊𝖗𝖌𝖊𝖆𝖓𝖙 𝕿𝖔𝖜𝖓𝖊 𝖍𝖊𝖆𝖙𝖊𝖉 his cappuccino in the microwave and listened to Ken finish telling a bad joke.

"So, after this guy picks up the chick in the bar they go to his place."

Jack walked to his desk.

"Let me guess, when he gets her in bed he finds out she's a he."

"No, that's another story."

He chuckled.

"They make love and get up. The woman smiles and says; *'That was great. Can we do it again sometime?'* The dude steps into his boxer shorts and they hear a soft popping sound coming from the rumpled bed."

Ken Chortled.

"The woman says, *'What's that?'* The guy grins. *'It's my memory foam mattress forgetting you were ever here.'*

He roared.

"Get it?"

"It's a little better than most of yours, but I wouldn't try it out at the *Comedy Store.*"

Captain Sawyer stood in his office doorway.

"Very funny, Detective, perhaps you've missed your calling."

He did not laugh.

"Kellogg and Beck are on the way over from the crime lab. They have the report on the syringe and more info about yesterday's fifth killing. We'll all meet in the conference room in thirty."

He went back in the office and closed the door *hard.*

Jack and Ken looked at each other. The sergeant said, "I believe the shit has hit the fan."

* * * *

CONFERENCE ROOM – 8:30 AM:

The captain entered the room carrying a thick black loose-leaf notebook. The buzz of chatter ceased immediately. He dropped the heavy item on the shiny table and all four cops sat up straight in full attention.

Sawyer took his seat at the head of the table and opened the cover.

"You've all contributed eloquently to this murder book with finely detailed reports of your various follow-up investigations regarding the four homicides recorded herein."

Ann held up a file folder.

"The fifth one is in here, Captain."

"I'm sure it is, Sergeant, and in your usual pristine form."

He smiled at her without humor.

"However, it isn't finished is it?"

"No, sir, but we have good Intel on the vic."

"That's nice, Beck, I'll let you enlighten us in a few minutes."

Roy snapped open the metal rings of the book and laid out each of the four separate files.

"Number one, Mary Jane Ott, she was mutilated and dumped in the surf. Vic two, Sally Patterson."

He tapped the folder.

"Same MO, strangled, legs cut off, strapped in a rented wheelchair and left to be found in *Balboa*

Park. by a security guard.

Sawyer studied the faces of his team.

"Here we have victim number three, Robin Andrews."

He opened the folder.

"Slight change on this poor girl, the perp didn't choke her to death. He must've had an attack of conscience, but the sonofabitch cut off her legs anyway and left the body in her car. Now we come to Amanda Price, our fourth victim."

He opened that file.

"A young reporter we all knew and had worked with."

The captain stared at the photos and took a breath.

"It turns my stomach. This woman was practically left on your doorstep, Kellogg and the bastard chopped off her arms as well."

Matt stood to get coffee.

"He's made it personal, Cap. He wants Beck so he can get at me for defying him."

"Sit, Detective, I need your rapt attention."

He put the folders back into the murder book in their respective order and closed it.

"We have all this information and not one shred of hard evidence pointing to a person of interest let alone a suspect."

"With all respect, Captain."

"Yes, Ken?"

"We can't come up with evidence that isn't

there in the first place."

"It's there, Detective, you have to look harder to find it."

Sawyer sat back and folded his hands on the book.

"This is day eight in a series of killings that has now claimed five lives."

He drew a quick breath.

"The assistant chief chewed on my ass for the first half hour of my Monday morning after he heard about the Saint Anne's horror."

His face stiffened.

"Shit rolls down hill and now you're getting it."

Matt said, "We can't manufacture a suspect."

"Don't push it, Kellogg, you know better."

He looked at Beck.

"What've you got on the syringe contents?"

"Tony had no trouble nailing the drug."

She opened the folder and pulled out an official looking report.

Sawyer said, "Would you be kind enough to share it with us?"

Tension in the room had become palpable.

"Okay, it's technical, but I can paraphrase most of it."

"Please do."

Ann cleared her throat and read from the report. "The drug is called: *Rohypnol,* we suspected that. It's a sedative ten times more powerful than Valium."

Ken said, "That's a *date-rape* cocktail in potent form."

"Exactly."

Ann continued.

"It previously came in the form of a white, dime-sized pill that quickly dissolves in liquids and has no taste or odor. The drug-maker, *Hoffman-LA Roche,* has changed the makeup of the drug because it's been used to commit sexual assault. The newer form of Rohypnol now dissolves more slowly and releases a blue dye. It may color light-colored drinks and give a cloudy appearance to darker cocktails."

She skipped over a few lab notes.

"Other names for it include *Roofies, Roaches, Rope, and the Forget Pill.*"

She looked up from the form.

"Of course, our perp pre-dissolves the pills and injects his targets."

Towne asked, "What's the effect on the vic?"

"The drug causes disorientation, dizziness, and/or drowsiness beginning within fifteen minutes to one hour after ingestion; hot or cold flashes, difficulty speaking, partial paralysis or heaviness in the limbs, some or complete inability to remember what happened after ingesting the substance."

Ann paused.

"Tony wrote a side note. The syringe contained way more than the dose of one pill.

Getting hit with a needle full directly into the bloodstream would trigger the effects almost immediately. Using the drug the way he does means eventual death."

The captain said, "Fill us in on the church vic."

She handed the folder to Kellogg.

"Would you?"

He held up the picture from the morgue.

"Her street name was *Darcy*, and she has a *RAP* sheet a yard long. She's been in and out of the system since age fourteen. There's no known driver's license. Tony ran her prints through NCIC and got a series of prostitution busts and a few drug beefs, mostly for possession of crack for sale."

Ken commented, "No matter what life she led, she didn't deserve that kind of death."

"That's not all."

Ann drew a breath.

"Darcy was twenty-six; her real name is Viola Johnson. She lived in a four-room crummy duplex on the seedy end of Severin Drive in La Mesa."

She glanced at Matt.

"Tell them the rest."

"Ms. Johnson lived with her sickly mother and left a five-year-old female child."

The captain took the file.

"It's all a real sad story."

He pointed to the door.

"Across the hall we have three brand new

interrogation rooms. The furniture is gathering dust from lack of use."

He stood and slipped the Darcy file into the black murder book.

"Listen up, people. I want to see a suspect's ass warming a chair in one of those rooms posthaste."

He hefted the book and held it in his right arm.

"Ken, you and Towne go to the crime lab, sit down with Tony's A/V tech guy and go over every frame of that DVD of the failed attempt on the Williams girl."

Ken said, "We've been over it three times."

"Do it six times more. Are we clear?"

"Yes, sir."

"Good. When you're done there, take a long lunch. You're both on night duty."

He pushed his chair up to the table.

"You're going to hit El Cajon Boulevard and talk to the working girls. Somebody had to see something Saturday night. Any questions?"

Jack said, "We're on it."

"That's what I like to hear, thank you."

He gestured toward the door and the two cops left.

Kellogg closed his notebook.

"Captain, I have a request."

"No, the city will not foot the bill for Ms. Johnson's final expenses."

"That's not what I'm asking."

"What is it then?"

He set the book back on the table and leaned on it.

"We'd like to stakeout the Moran house on Mount Helix."

Matt took his suit coat off the back of his chair and put it on.

Sawyer hesitated.

"You know damn well I can't authorize that."

"I'm telling you, Cap—he's a person of interest."

He adjusted his shoulder holster.

"Beck and I will do it on our own time. No one needs to know."

"That's just ducky, Detective. Two members of my elite squad go off on their own without approval, are you nuts? Do you want to answer a harassment charge?"

Sawyer picked up the black book.

"Bring me solid evidence and I'll get a warrant. In the meantime, comb through all your notes and find something you could've missed."

"Captain, I have a better idea."

Both men looked at Ann.

Kellogg spoke first.

"If it's what I think you're getting at—it's not going to happen."

Sawyer asked, "What's your idea?"

Beck stood.

"We bait him."

Shivers *skittered* across the back of her neck.
Matt responded in a loud voice.

"No way. I told you, that's out of the question."

"He wants me now, Cap. The bastard will keep dumping bodies until he gets a clear shot at me."

She leaned on the table.

"Let's give him what he's really after. Draw his attention away from other women."

Kellogg shook his head.

"No way."

The captain looked through a serious expression.

"How do we bait him?"

Matt shouted,

"I don't want to hear this."

Chapter Forty One

An Elaborate Setup

SQUADROOM
SDPD COMPLEX
MONDAY – 11:15 AM:

The Plan had been set in motion within a half hour of the captain's tense meeting. Members of the media were alerted and a few reporters and camera crews already started hooking up equipment on the back patio.

An impromptu SVU announcement had been called to go *live* for the noon news.

"I'm still uptight about this."

Matt sat on the edge of his desk. "It's risky no matter how you slice it."

"Yeah, so's driving on the freeway."

Ann had her back to him and continued. typing notes on her laptop.

"Relax. I'm trying to word my press speech to entice the perp. Nothing dangerous happens until tomorrow."

"That's exactly what I'm worried about."

He stepped up behind her and put his hands on her shoulders.

"I'm concerned about your safety."

She patted his left hand, tilted her head back and looked up at him.

"I appreciate that, I'll be all right."

Captain Sawyer joined them.

"I just got confirmation. We're good to go for tomorrow afternoon at two o'clock."

* * * *

BACK PATIO – 12:00 NOON:

Ann stepped up to the podium and faced the cameras.

"Thank you for coming on such short notice. I'm Sergeant Ann Beck with the Special Victims Unit of the San Diego Police Department."

She looked down at her notes.

* * * *

THE OLD VICTORIAN:

Michael had just sat down to a lunch of angel hair pasta with a nice zesty onion and garlic meat sauce and a glass of robust Merlot.

He had Fox news on the small kitchen TV and glared at Beck's image.

"What the hell is she doing?"

He turned up the volume.

Ann continued,

"The discovery of a body in Saint Anne's Catholic Church, early yesterday morning, brings to five the number of brutal murders committed in our city and county in one week."

Michael pointed at the screen.

"See that, Samantha? My work is getting more coverage. I love it."

The cat looked at him for a second and went back to enjoying her bowl of food.

Beck appeared confident on camera and continued with her address.

"The majority of young women, in our community, are living in fear. The SVU team, and the entire department are doing everything in our power to find the killer."

She paused.

"All other law enforcement agencies throughout the county have joined us to bring this reign of terror to an end."

Michael grinned.

"Hear that, Sam? Now, I'm a terrorist."

He lifted his glass to the screen.

"It all sounds great, Sergeant, but it's not working out too well."

The Fox camera moved in to a medium shot.

"Tomorrow afternoon, at two o'clock, I will conduct a free seminar on the University of San Diego campus. It will be held at Eagan Plaza near the center of the complex. I'm sure employers will allow time for employees to attend."

One of the reporters jumped in.

"Sergeant Beck, how is your meeting going to help catch the killer?"

"The purpose of my seminar is to educate women in ways to be alert and protect themselves. There will be other speakers with professional training."

She smiled.

"The information is aimed at women, but men are welcome."

A well known talk show host from KSDO Radio tossed a question.

"Would you be willing to come on my program in the morning?"

"Yes, John. See me when we're done here."

Another question came from the group.

"Why on the USD campus?"

"It's big, centrally located, and the bishop was kind enough to give us his blessing."

She held up her hand. "No more questions

please. You'll have plenty of opportunity at the event. In closing, I want everyone to know that Hal Marks will run complete details in the editorial section of the morning Tribune. If you haven't already, pick up a press kit, and please, talk it up on the evening news."

Ann started folding her notes.

"One last point, tell your female viewers and listeners not to wear skirts for the duration. That's all I have, thank you."

When the Fox anchor came on Michael switched off the TV.

"The woman has nerve, Sam, I have to give her that much."

He walked to the microwave and heated his pasta.

"Well, Ms. Ann Beck, it doesn't take a rocket scientist to figure out what you're up to."

Samantha let out a soft cry.

"You're still hungry, little girl."

He carried her bowl to the stove and spooned more cooling sauce into it.

"Here we are, sweetheart."

As soon as the food arrived the cat swished her tail and started eating.

Michael removed his lunch from the microwave and returned to his seat.

"You know what, Sam?"

He took a sip of Merlot.

"I think it's high time I taught little Ms. Beck a

lesson and showed her just who is running this dog and pony show."

He raised his glass.

"A toast to the Eagan Plaza seminar."

Chapter Forty Two

The Radio Show

KSDO TALK RADIO
TUESDAY MORNING
SAN DIEGO– 8:15 AM:

𝕶𝖊𝖑𝖑𝖔𝖌𝖌 𝖆𝖓𝖉 𝕭𝖊𝖈𝖐 𝖆𝖗𝖗𝖎𝖛𝖊𝖉 at the station forty-five minutes early. The receptionist recognized them when they entered the lobby.

"Good morning, I'm Nancy, welcome to KSDO."

She stood and pointed to the visitor's log.

"Please sign in. I'll let Carol know you're here."

Matt said, "Thank you."

Two minutes later an attractive, thirty something blonde came in from a door to the right of the front desk.

"Hi, I'm John's producer, Carol Vickers."

She smiled and offered her hand.

"We're happy to have you on the show."

They shook hands all around.

Ann said, "I love the outfit. You took my advice seriously."

"Sergeant, I've been wearing slacks since last Monday morning, and I'll be at your lecture and sit in the front row."

She eyed Matt.

"Detective, will you be on the program?"

"If that's okay with John, yes, I'd like to."

"You're most welcome."

Carol started toward the door she came out of.

"Nancy, would you buzz us in?"

* * * *

In the lounge, Ms. Vickers served coffee for the three of them.

"As you must've heard, our early show was swamped with callers concerned about the monster in our midst. It's been like that all week. Usually, the topics of the day are politics and the economy."

She looked up to spot a young man waving from the doorway.

"John's in studio two. We're ready."

* * * *

THE OLD VICTORIAN:

Samantha jumped up on the bathroom counter and watched Michael finish shaving.

"Hello, Little one. I hope you enjoyed your breakfast."

He reached down and scratched her under the chin.

A portable radio played various comments from concerned callers during the closing minutes of the early show on KSDO. One female voice sounded near tears.

I'm fifty-five and consider myself attractive. I'm afraid to leave the house.

Michael held the blade away from his throat and chuckled.

"You have nothing to worry about, old hen, I like 'em young and tender."

He continued shaving his neck with a straight razor. The feel of surgical steel pleased him.

He glanced at the clock.

"Our cop-friends will be on in a few minutes."

* * * *

KSDO STUDIO TWO
ONE MINUTE TO AIR:

Matt and Ann looked uncomfortable in their headphones with two *Telefuncan* microphones suspended in front of their faces.

John smiled, "You guys okay?"

Ann glanced at Matt.

"All of a sudden, I'm nervous."

The host laughed.

"Relax; it's a piece of cake. Just respond as you would at a press conference."

He put on his headset and adjusted the microphone.

Carol hit the intercom from her booth.

"Go in fifty, all lines are lit."

John said, "We're on seven second delay in case somebody says *shit* it won't go on the air."

Kellogg laughed, "I might be the one who says it."

The show's theme started, the red light came on and they were LIVE.

* * * *

THE OLD VICTORIAN
TWO MINUTES EARLIER:

Michael had carried the radio to his bedroom and finished dressing.

"This outfit will knock 'em dead."

He slipped into a pair of black imported Italian leather loafers, tucked in his custom made white shirt and put on the black vestment.

"Nice ensemble, I must say."

Samantha climbed up on the bed.

"What do you think, Girl, do I look the part?"

The cat blinked at him, laid back and went about her personal house cleaning that felines often do.

"It's early yet. We'll have time for lunch before I leave."

He picked up the radio, his black suit coat, the rest of what he needed for the outfit, and headed downstairs.

Michael stopped sleeping in the ground floor bedroom months ago. He used it to store his collection of purses and trophies from his victims.

His father had died in that room, and it made him ill to stay there.

He went into his den, put the radio on the desk and hung his coat over the back of the chair.

Samantha had followed him down from the second floor.

"It's time, Sweetheart, they're coming on."

He opened a desk drawer, took out his voice-altering device and disposable cell phone.

"I'll be calling in."

* * * *

KSDO STUDIO TWO
ON THE AIR:

"Good morning San Diego, I'm John Foster and this is Perspective.

My guests are Sergeant Ann Beck and Detective Matt Kellogg from the Special Victim's Unit of SDPD.

Our topic today is the so-called *legs Collector.* The number is 858-999-6254."

He turned to his guests.

"Sergeant Beck, your brief press conference yesterday, and Hal Marks' editorial in the Tribune this morning, have stirred up the female population of the entire county.

The issue itself has sent waves across the state and gained national attention.

The spotlight is on your team. How does all this affect the overall investigation?"

"On one level it has helped, on another, we've been hindered."

She glanced at Kellogg.

"I'll let Matt explain."

John said, "Go ahead, Detective."

"In regard to being helpful, the *spotlight,* as you put it, has given us the full cooperation of county-wide law enforcement."

"And the downside is?"

Matt continued. "Chasing false leads and having to deal with bogus confessions are two factors that slow us down considerably."

Beck added, "Another plus, from the attention, is getting immediate involvement from various women's agencies, which made it possible for us to setup my lecture so quickly."

She hesitated.

"May I point out; it was the bishop's blessing that let us hold the seminar at Eagan Plaza."

John saw his producer hold up her hand.

"Okay, we'll take a break and then go to the phones."

Carol cut the mikes and went to commercial.

John said, "You guys are doing great. The fun starts when we come back."

* * * *

THE OLD VICTORIAN:

Samantha started batting her right front paw at the thin cord Michael had plugged into his untraceable cell phone.

"Don't play with the wire, Sam. That's how daddy changes his voice."

He lifted the cat off the desk and set her in the nearby recliner.

"Did you hear all that bullshit?"

He scratched her ears.

"Full county-wide law enforcement—pure fantasy, Kellogg."

Michael laughed.

"If you need all that to do your stupid job, chuck the badge and gun, and take up needlepoint."

He thought a second.

"That reminds me."

He scratched the cat's neck.

"Don't let me forget the special cocktail I mixed just for Ms. Ann Beck. Blessings from the Bishop—what a crock of shit. I'll give her a blessing, won't I, Sam?"

* * * *

KSDO – STUDIO 2:

The spot-break ended and John Foster's voice came from the radio.

"We're back with *Perspective* and my guests, Sergeant Ann Beck and Detective Matt Kellogg of Special Victims. Our topic is the *Legs Collector,* and his week-long killing spree across our county. The number is 858-999-6254."

He pushed line one.

"La Mesa, you're on KSDO Talk Radio, what's on your mind?"

This is Betty and I'm scared to death, John. I work in the same mall as that girl who got away from the killer on Saturday. Now I'm afraid to even go to work.

"I can understand that. Do you have a question for one of my guests?"

Yes, for the lady detective. How can I be safe with that wacko on the loose?

"Hi, Betty. This is Sergeant Beck, I appreciate your concern. My best advice is to be alert and aware of your surroundings at all times. Be especially careful if you're approached by a very tall, well built male."

Is that what he looks like?

"Yes, the man who ran from the Grossmont Center Mall on Saturday fits that description."

What should I do, scream?

"If he tries to get near you in an inappropriate

manner, yelling would be a good idea. That's one of the things I, and other professionals, will be covering at this afternoon's seminar."

"Thank you, Betty. Hello, Lakeside, you're on KSDO Talk Radio."

Hi, I'm randy. I have a message for the legs dude. Over the weekend I taught my wife how to shoot my three-five-seven mag revolver. She'll be packin' it. If that s-o-b gets within ten feet of her, he's history.

"I'll let Detective Kellogg handle that one."

"Hi, Randy, I have advice for you …."

* * * *

THE OLD VICTORIAN:

Michael opened a package of hamburger buns and set one out on the kitchen counter. "This ought to be good. Go for it, Matt."

* * * *

Randy said, *I'm listening.*

"The last thing we need, right now, is to have nervous young women walking around with handguns."

We have a right to bear arms.

"You don't have a right to carry a concealed weapon without a permit. I suggest you put a trigger guard on that weapon and lock it away in a safe place."

Don't hold your breath detective.

"Thanks, Randy. We'll be right back after these messages."

* * * *

THE VICTORIAN:

Michael laughed and took a jar *of Kraft Salad Dressing* from the fridge.

"That's the smartest thing you've said all week, Kellogg. I sure don't need some shaky broad blowing my head off. Christ, what a horrible thought."

He put two frozen meat patties in the microwave. "I'll thaw these slowly, Sam, then fix us an early lunch. Daddy has a busy afternoon ahead.

* * * *

KSDO RADIO:

John Foster's voice came through the speaker.

"Hello Oceanside, you're on KSDO Talk Radio."

I'm a retired homicide detective from NYPD,

I'd like to address detective Kellogg.

"Go ahead, he's listening."

I know you from the two-seven, matt. You should've nailed the perp by now. Five killings in one week? That's unacceptable. Do it the way we did in the big apple. You owe it to San Diego to get the job done.

"Who is this?"

"He hung up, Matt."

* * * *

THE VICTORIAN:

After opening a fresh jar of relish, Michael grinned.

"Hear that, Sam? Kellogg just got his ass chewed in public—I love it!"

He went back to the den.

Samantha trotted behind with her fluffy tail held high.

Michael sat at his desk.

"Now it's my turn."

He picked up the cell and dialed 858-999-6254.

The cat climbed onto the leather recliner and went to work with her feline house cleaning again.

* * * *

KSDO – STUDIO – 2:

Carol Vickers answered Michael's call.

"KSDO, this is *Perspective,* you're twelfth in line, please hold."

"Make me next, Sweetheart, I'm the *Legs Collector.* I know details that haven't been released."

"Yeah sure, and my mom's the Queen of England. Wait your turn."

"Do you see an incoming location on your computer screen?"

Carol looked. The usual prefix locator read 000.

"Where are you calling from?"

"You'll never know."

He clicked on the voice alteration device.

"I'm John's next caller, do you hear me?"

She grabbed a startled breath.

"Okay—I have to tell him, please hold."

"That's much more like it, thank you."

Chapter Forty Three

Michael on the Radio

KSDO TALK RADIO
TUESDAY MORNING
SAN DIEGO– 9:45 AM:

𝕮𝖆𝖗𝖔𝖑 𝖌𝖆𝖛𝖊 𝕵𝖔𝖍𝖓 a frantic *break* signal from the booth.

"I'll take the next call after this time out."

The producer cut the mikes and started a spot cluster, then hit the intercom.

"I have some guy on line five who says he's the killer and his voice is altered. He wants on next."

Foster looked at his guests.

"Could this be for real?"

Matt said, "The perp played the game before. The first time he called Marks, the second time he left me a tape."

Ann shuddered.

"His altered voice gives me chills."

"I'll put him on. It might be interesting."

John hesitated.

"Can you tell if it's the same man?"

"There are details only the perp would know. I'll challenge him." Kellogg added, "If I hold up my hand or nod it will be the killer."

John grinned.

"If it's him, our news department will be all over the tape."

Carol's voice came through the intercom, "You're on in three."

"Here we go."

He punched line five.

"Good morning, you're on KSDO Talk Radio. Who do I have on the air?"

I'm the Legs Collector, Mr. Foster, and I'd like to address your guests.

"First, what do we call you, Mr. Legs? Mr. Collector? Maybe it should be, Mr. Killer?"

Don't get cute, John, comedy isn't your strong suit.

"Where are you calling from?"

Foster looked at the cops. They didn't react.

I'm on top of the Sea World Tower—you think I'm stupid?

"I didn't say that."

He nodded at the detective.

Matt shrugged.

Foster, I'm tired of your dumb chit-chat. Let me talk to Kellogg, now!

"He's right here, go for it."

How's your day going, Detective?

"It was fine until you called in."

Matt shrugged again.

So, you're going to be a wise guy too?

"I don't believe you're who you claim to be. You're just another nutcase looking for attention."

John cut in.

"Do you have a question for my guests? If not, I'll cut you off. You're wasting airtime."

Shut up for once, Foster. You want proof, Kellogg?

"Tell me something only the killer could know."

Matt glanced at Ann and squeezed her hand.

Anger crept into Michael's augmented voice to make it sound more ominous.

Didn't you find Amanda Price's body in a vacant lot close to your apartment building?

Matt held up his hand.

"The body was found in a vacant lot, that's public knowledge and there's no evidence I live near the site."

John looked at the detective and mouthed, *yes?*

Kellogg held up his hand and nodded.

Michael continued.

Did you not find a note and cassette tape with the legless, armless remains? I believe I performed exquisite surgery on the woman.

Ann took a breath and held her hand over her mouth.

Matt said, "All of that could've been leaked to the press. You're just a screwball trying to get his fifteen minutes."

He knew that would infuriate the caller. He also knew he was talking to the real *Legs Collector.*

Well, try this on, Kellogg. I picked up the late Robin Anderson at Barnes and Noble in Carmel Mountain Plaza and bought books from there.

His voice went up in pitch.

Guess what, Detective. I didn't strangle Robin because I liked her. Oh, almost forgot. I left her purse in the car with the body and I did the same with Amanda. Are you satisfied?

Michael's fury rose.

Carol gave John the *break* sign.

He held up his hands and shook his head.

Matt laughed.

"You're nothing but a fake. You're no more the *Legs Collector* than I am."

Michael screamed, *Put Ann on, I want to talk to her!*

Kellogg looked at his partner.

She shook her head.

Matt said, "Sorry, Mr. Phony, she doesn't want to speak with you."

He nodded at John and gave thumbs down.

Foster said, "Thank you, Mr. Fake."

He cut Michael off.

"We'll be right back after this break."

He took off his headset and stared at Matt.

"He's the killer?"

Ann removed her headphones and stood.

"He's real, John. However, I think Matt made him look like a fool."

"Damn, that guy is scary."

Kellogg removed his earphones and got up.

"No one but us cops knows what that caller described about the killings. Thanks for having us on the show."

"My pleasure."

They all shook hands and Ann waved at Carol in the booth.

* * * *

THE OLD VICTORIAN:

Michael yanked the cord out of his cell and flung the phone against the far wall.

The instrument shattered. The battery and broken pieces scattered across the floor and into the dining room.

Samantha jumped off the recliner and followed the debris out of the den.

"Sonofabitch—that bastard."

He opened a desk drawer and dropped the voice device into it.

"Humiliate me on the radio, make me the fool."

He pounded on his desk.

"Keep me from talking to Beck!"

The portable radio continued to broadcast John's show.

Hello, Chula Vista, You're on KSDO Talk Radio.

Who was that moron saying he was the Legs Collector?

Nobody to be concerned about. The two police officers have assured me he was not the killer.

What a creepy dude.

"I'm nobody to be concerned about?"

Michael snatched the radio off his desk and slammed it down on the oak floor. The plastic casing cracked open and the program ceased.

He kicked the remains across the room.

"I'll give you all a lot to be concerned about—mark my words!"

The air in the room became freezing.

Mickey, have you any idea how stupid you are?

His dead mother's specter appeared in the dining room just outside the doorway.

"Shut up, you dead bitch. Don't call me that—I don't want to see or hear you."

His breath blew out as a cloud of vapor.

I can't use your given name because Michael was a saint. You're a demon working your way to hell.

"You're *in hell,* Witch—stay there."

His head began to throb.

"Get out of my house and stay out."

He rushed toward the apparition. It reformed on top of the dining room hutch. That room froze.

Mickey, Mickey, dumb Mickey. You were worthless as a child, and now more so as an adult. You're an abomination; I'm ashamed that I gave birth to a beast.

"Stay dead and give me peace."

Your father had faith in you and you let him down. I never believed in you. What a waste you are, Mickey. You'll never have any peace.

He screamed at the vision.

"Go away from me!"

They will get you. You're a murderer.

He reached for his mother's image and it

drifted away into the space above the hutch.

Michael fell back against the huge oak table and grasped the edge with both hands.

"I'll get Ann Beck before they get me. That's a promise."

The temperature in the room returned to normal.

Chapter Forty Four

The Seminar

UNIVERSITY OF SAN DIEGO
EAGAN PLAZA – 12:00 NOON:

𝕿wo hours before the event and the plaza had already been swamped with sound equipment, campus security, the media and cops. The latter were undercover and wired.

Eagan Plaza looked like it would be staging a *Rolling Stones* rock concert.

USD is a Catholic facility in which, there is a Seminary to educate young men for the priesthood. The campus is spread out over one hundred eighty acres and is the Diocesan center of San Diego. Many members of the clergy were expected to be among the eventual crowd.

Captain Sawyer had managed to get authorization for the SDPD Mobile Command

Center. It stood out against the smaller TV vans that would cover the seminar *live* from gavel to gavel.

Volunteers from four local women's organizations were busy stacking specially prepared blue glassine folders on a long table near the podium. On each, bold red letters read: **STAY ALERT, PROTECTED & SAFE.**

In front of the raised platform, a group of maintenance people set up rows of white folding chairs and two tables of bottled water donated by the *Vons Grocery Company.*

Everything promised to be a major San Diego *happening.*

Inside the police command center, Captain Sawyer, Kellogg, Beck, Jack Towne, Ken Black and five techs prepared for the event.

Sawyer said, "Ken, Jack, I want you two within ten feet of Sergeant Beck at all times, clear?"

"Got it, Cap." Ken grinned, "I feel like I'm back in college." He adjusted his long-tailed USD sweatshirt.

"Good, Jack, any questions?"

"No, sir, we both look like grads hanging out on campus."

He adjusted his *Padres* ball cap and looked at his former partner.

"Ann, I got your back, count on it."

She smiled.

"I feel like some celebrity with all this."

Matt squeezed her shoulder.

"Today, you are. You're also the target of our perp."

She patted his hand and looked up at him.

"I'll be safe with all this muscle nearby."

After a moment she said, "What if he doesn't show and the whole, expensive, ballgame goes down the tubes?"

The Captain chuckled.

"Don't worry about that. Show or not, you will have informed potential victims how to protect themselves against this animal and that alone justifies the cost."

"Thank you, I appreciate all this support."

She hesitated. "I hope I can pull this off."

Kellogg kissed her on top of the head.

"You'll be great."

He smiled.

"And by the way, you're beautiful on camera."

"Thanks, I'm sure that makes a hell of a lot of difference."

Captain Sawyer addressed the leader of the five techs.

"Andy, is your crew up to speed?"

"Yes, sir. We just ran a communications check. All six undercover guys are at their stations and alert."

"Great."

He nodded at Ken and Jack.

"Get on out there, mix in with the activity and

check all rooms near the stage area several times over."

Ken said, "We're on it."

They left the command unit.

Sawyer said, "El Cajon PD followed up on that report from the Westfield mall. Ms. Woo gave her would be attacker a face full of pepper spray. Her description of the guy fit about fifty cowboys from the Lakeside rodeo. Ten to one, he was our dude, but they came up empty."

Matt said, "That makes it two failures in as many days. He'll be after Beck with a vengeance.

He untangled the wire and tiny microphone that would be worn by Ann.

"You haven't been wired before, so I need to make this all clear to you."

She smiled.

"You're going to put that between my boobs, right?"

The detective grinned.

"Yes, my love, that's where it has to go."

He tore off two pieces of white tape.

Ann laughed.

"I'm getting excited."

She kissed him.

"Would you hold still and get serious, please?"

Matt held the tiny mike to Ann's chest and applied the tape.

"Oh, I'm serious, Mr. Detective, quite serious."

She kissed him again.

"What are you doing after work?"

"You're impossible."

Matt smoothed out the tape and closed Ann's blouse.

"Yes, I am."

"Everything you say and everything anybody says close to you will be picked up and monitored here. If something goes wrong, we'll be on you in a heartbeat."

"My heart is beating, Detective."

Sawyer said, "Would you two knock it off, you're on duty for Christ's sake. Excuse my French."

He chuckled.

"I forgot. We're on hallowed ground here."

* * * *

THE OLD VICTORIAN
ONE HOUR LATER:

After finishing his homemade burger with romaine lettuce, tomato and *Vlasic* pickle relish, Michael carried his plate to the sink.

He looked over at Samantha to see that the cat had eaten her chopped meat patty.

"Good girl. I'll leave some treats out for you while I'm gone."

Sam licked her right front paw and cleaned her face with it as she always did after a meal.

Michael picked up her bowl, rinsed it along with his plate, and put them in the dishwasher.

"Daddy's going to have a fun afternoon. I wish you could be there to see me at work."

He grinned.

"I have a real talent for what I do."

The small kitchen TV was tuned to Fox news and since noon the station switched from the studio to the activity at Eagan Plaza several times.

Michael smiled at the screen. "This report, I've got to watch."

* * * *

The split screen showed the studio anchor on the left with the reporter and Ann on the right.

"Fox news *live* coverage of the special

seminar on the USD campus continues. Alice Newland brings us up to date."

"Thank you, Brian. There's a lot going on here at Eagan Plaza."

The TV now had a full shot of the two women.

* * * *

Michael snickered, "You look great, Ann, love the fawn pants suit. It goes great with your auburn locks. I'd bet a hundred bucks there's a pair of fine looking legs hidden in those slacks. I can't wait to see them in the flesh."

* * * *

Alice continued, "In less than an hour the event begins. Sergeant Ann Beck, who's with the Special Victims Unit of SDPD, has made it all happen."

The camera moved in to a medium shot.

"Sergeant, how did you manage all this?"

"I had the help of the entire department, about a hundred volunteers, and the support of the whole San Diego County community."

* * * *

Michael rested his chin on the heel of his right hand.

"Aren't you just the heroine of the day, Ms. Ann Beck?"

He tapped her image on the small screen.

"Enjoy your day of fame, lady ... it's all you're gonna get."

* * * *

Alice said, "What is the main theme of the seminar?"

Ann held up the blue folder.

"These are the words our female population will live by from now on."

She pointed to the cover.

"Stay alert, protected and safe. This folder and our professional speakers will explain just how you can do that."

"Thank you, Sergeant Beck. We'll be back *live* when the seminar starts. I'm Alice Newland, at Eagan Plaza, for Fox News, San Diego."

* * * *

Michael clicked off the television.

"Good luck, Ann, I'm sure you'll dazzle 'em to death with your speech. They'll need a hell of a lot more than a folder and a bullshit lecture to stay safe from me."

He reached over and scratched Samantha's neck. "Ain't that so, Sweetheart?"

The cat stretched and yawned, oblivious to the man her master really was.

He went to the fridge and took the loaded syringe off the top shelf.

"Just for you, my dear, Ann Beck."

He grinned and set it on a dishtowel.

"Time to get ready."

Sam followed him to the first floor bathroom. She jumped up on the counter where Michael had laid out the rest of his outfit and watched.

He put on the salt and pepper wig and secured it in place. He combed it.

"Don't you think that's a nice touch?"

Sam didn't respond. She started playing with the gold chain on the cross Michael was going to wear.

"That's not one of your toys."

He slipped it over his head and adjusted the crucifix against his black vestment.

"Nice, I like it."

He ruffled the fur on the cat's head.

"Now, the final touch."

The white Roman collar slipped into place.

"Perfect."

He stood back and admired himself.

"Do I look the part or what?"

Michael smiled at his image in the glass and held his hands in the posture of prayer.

"Bless me father for I have sinned."

Chapter Forty Five

The Seminar Ends

UNIVERSITY OF SAN DIEGO
EAGAN PLAZA – 3:30 PM:

𝔄𝔫 𝔢𝔰𝔱𝔦𝔪𝔞𝔱𝔢𝔡 𝔫𝔦𝔫𝔢 𝔥𝔲𝔫𝔡𝔯𝔢𝔡 𝔣𝔦𝔣𝔱𝔶 concerned women had turned out for Sergeant Beck's seminar. There were approximately two hundred men in the crowd as well.

Seven qualified speakers had addressed the audience with demonstrations and advice on staying alert and self protected. The eighth professional, Lieutenant Arlene Morrison, a self defense instructor, from the San Diego Police Academy, ended her presentation on a serious note.

"Remember, ladies, everything hinges on being aware of your surroundings at all times."

She held up one of the blue folders.

"Study the information in this document and put it to use. In closing, I must tell you this. Since the first killing, a week ago Monday, countywide sales of hand guns, to females, has increased by fifteen percent."

Arlene hesitated.

"That is not the answer. Forget the firearms or a stun gun and learn how to use pepper spray. Those instructions are in the folder. Thank you for your attention."

She stepped down.

Ann took Morrison's place.

"I want to thank the lieutenant, all of our speakers, and each and every one of you for your attendance. I believe the San Diego Police Department, with the help of our supporters; have made this seminar a success in helping all of you be safer. Thank you all again."

Michael stood twenty feet to the right of the stage.

He smiled.

Very Impressive, Ms. Beck, impressive indeed.

* * * *

THE MOBILE COMMAND POST
AT THAT SAME TIME:

Captain Sawyer pushed back from the console and rubbed his eyes.

"The perp could be right out there in the crowd and we'd never know it."

Matt watched the closed circuit monitor. "If he is, there's no way he'd make a move out in the open anyway. Let's just keep things rolling until Ann's back here with us."

The lead undercover cop checked in.

It's a wrap, are we done here?

Sawyer looked at his head tech.

"Tell him to stay put until we say otherwise."

Andy keyed his mike.

"That's a negative, UC one. Maintain surveillance."

Copy that, command, we're on it.

* * * *

THE STAGE AREA:

The crowd began to disperse. Ann smiled, nodded, shook hands and thanked attendees as they left the plaza. When she stepped away from the stage area she spotted Ken. She reached inside her blouse and removed the wire. She waved at Ken and spoke into the little mike.

"He didn't show, Matt. This thing's driving me nuts. I'm going into the reception room behind the platform and get my things. I'll be right with you."

She handed the wire to Ken.

"Here, take it, I can't stand it another minute."

Ken said, "Where are you going?"

She pointed toward a door between the arches of the main building.

"In there to freshen up and get my stuff."

Ken had two-way contact with the command unit. He spoke into his shirt sleeve.

"Did you get all that, Matt?"

* * * *

THE MOBILE COMMAND UNIT:

Kellogg looked at the monitor.

"I did, you're out of camera range, where are you?"

"About twenty yards right of the stage area."

Captain Sawyer said, "Andy, pan the stage camera and find Black."

"Got it."

Ken came into view.

"There he is."

A group of students and three priests came down the walkway and headed toward the arches of the main building. They were followed by two maintenance workers in a golf cart pulling a flatbed trailer. Ken scooted out of the way.

"It's getting busy around here."

Matt said, "Stay close."

"You got it."

He stepped off the walkway to let three women and two more priests get by.

Kellogg sat back.

"She took off the damn wire—shit!"

Sawyer gripped Matt's shoulder.

"She's a big girl and Ken's right there."

Matt said, "I don't like it."

THE RECEPTION ROOM:

Ann touched up her makeup and fluffed her hair. She grabbed her purse and started toward the front door.

Two soft knocks sounded on the side entrance.

"Sergeant Beck? I'm Father Francis Kelly, may I come in?"

"Of course. I'm on my way out. What is it?"

Michael entered the room and closed the door.

"The bishop would like a word with you before you leave, and he sent me to escort you to his office."

"The bishop? I'm flattered."

He moved closer.

"His Excellency was impressed with your

seminar and the efforts you put forth to make it all happen."

"Well, It wasn't all me, I had a lot of help."

"I'm sure you did."

Michael took two strides and stuck the needle into Ann's neck.

She struggled, reached for her weapon. A scream froze in her throat and her arm went limp.

Chapter Forty Six

Beck is Silent

UNIVERSITY OF SAN DIEGO
SDPD MOBILE COMMAND UNIT
EAGAN PLAZA– 4:00 PM:

𝔇𝔢𝔱𝔢𝔠𝔱𝔦𝔳𝔢 𝔎𝔢𝔩𝔩𝔬𝔤𝔤 𝔰𝔱𝔬𝔬𝔡 𝔟𝔢𝔥𝔦𝔫𝔡 his chair and watched Ken on the small monitor.

"What the hell's she doing in there?"

The captain chuckled.

"She's a woman, let her have some slack."

Matt shrugged into his grey leather coat. He clicked on the mike and spoke to Ken.

"Go knock on the door and tell her to get a move on."

"Roger that."

He walked around groups of people leaving the plaza area, a couple of students, and a few priests. Ken reached the door and knocked.

"Ann, Matt's getting nervous."
Nothing.
He knocked again.
"What's the hold up?"
No response.
He tried the handle.
"It's locked and she's not answering."
Kellogg flew out of the Command Post with Sawyer right behind him.

* * * *

Sergeant Towne and the other six undercover cops heard Ken and converged on the building.

* * * *

THE RECEPTION ROOM
TWENTY MINUTES EARLIER:

Michael had snapped on a pair of latex gloves before entering the side door.

He locked both doors, carried Beck to a long sofa and stretched her out.

"There we are, my dear, nice and comfy."

He removed the spent hypo from her neck and slipped it in the right side pocket of his suit coat.

Ann blinked rapidly. The terror in her eyes was apparent.

He smiled at her and nodded.

"Yes, you can see me, hear me, blink, swallow and breathe, but not anything else. You can't feel anything either, but that's just a side effect of the cocktail I mixed just for my favorite cop, Ann Beck."

She watched her towering assailant remove a black leather case from his coat pocket and take out a small pair of scissors.

Matt, help me!

The cry was only in her head.

"Don't fight the drug, Ann. I own you."

He snipped two starter holes in each leg of Ann's beige slacks.

She squeezed her eyes shut tight.

He's going to kill me!

"Don't be so frightened."

He put the scissors back in their case and then into his pocket.

"I have no intention of hurting you, *today*. That will come another time."

Ann stared at the tall man, who was not a priest at all, and anticipated some kind of horror.

Michael knelt in front of the sofa, poked his fingers in the hole he'd cut in the right leg of her slacks, and ripped it open.

"Oh, my goodness."

He did the same to the left leg.

"What beautiful legs you have, my dear."

He rubbed them with his gloved hands.

"Great taste in patterned high thighs too. Love the little black bows at the top. I'll bet old Matt gets all hard when he sees those."

He kissed the bows on both thighs.

"Lovely, just so feminine you are, and you smell so good. Is that a fragrance Kellogg gave you?"

She screamed in her head.

I should've noticed his gloves. I could've shot him right then—Matt, where are you?

Moran kissed her on the lips with the softness of a gentle, summer breeze.

"You're adorable."

Michael stood and looked down at his prey.

"Be sure to tell Matt we had a great time."

Useless fury rose inside her.

You insane son-of-a-bitch! When the time

comes, and it will; I'll blow your brains out!

As if he could hear her thoughts, Michael's eyes went cold and his expression turned grim.

"Your days are numbered, Bitch and Kellogg can't do anything about it."

He went out the side door, flipped the lock and closed it behind him.

Ann stared at the ceiling and yelled in her mind.

Matt, for God's sake, help me!

* * * *

Michael entered the main building and headed down a long corridor bustling with students and priests.

"Good afternoon, Father," said a young co-ed as she passed him in the hallway.

"And the same to you."

He blended in with the moving crowd and was gone.

Chapter Forty Seven

Saving Ann Beck

UNIVERSITYOF SAN DIEGO
RECEPTION ROOM ENTRANCE:

𝕿𝖜𝖔 𝖔𝖋 𝖙𝖍𝖊 𝖚𝖓𝖉𝖊𝖗𝖈𝖔𝖛𝖊𝖗 𝖈𝖔𝖕𝖘 went to the side door. One of them shouted.

"It's locked, and there's no window on the outside wall."

Kellogg banged on the front door for the third time.

"We're coming in, Ann."

He yelled at two maintenance workers who were loading chairs on a trailer.

"Get security here now—I want this friggin' door opened!"

* * * *

Beck lay on the sofa completely helpless with her vision blurred by tears, and listened to all the commotion. The anguish in her head was a silent cry.

I can't move, matt—help me!

* * * *

Two campus security guards trotted up to Ken, Jack and Kellogg at the entrance. The short, chubby one shouted.

"What the hell are you guys doing?"

Matt snapped around and looked down at a squatty guard.

"I have an officer in there. She may be injured or dead and the door is locked."

"It's not supposed to be during regular hours."

Kellogg glared at him.

"It goddamn well is—open it!"

The taller officer said, "We don't have the key."

Matt raised his voice.

"I have a battering ram in that Command Center over there. If that door isn't opened in the next two minutes it'll be smashed in."

The short one grinned.

"You'll play hell with that. The doors are solid oak and two inches thick."

The other guard keyed his mike.

"This is Jensen. Get the pass keys over to the

the reception room at Eagan Plaza on the double."

His radio squawked, *What for?*

"There's an injured police officer locked in there—get the keys over here pronto."

That's a ten-four.

Matt stared at chubby.

"How come you have the stripes and your partner has all the smarts?"

The little man didn't respond.

* * * *

Ann heard the muffled fracas through the door.

Hurry, Matt … I'm dying.

* * * *

A Fox News reporter and her cameraman stayed after the seminar to get a few reactions from several women who attended the event. They picked up on all the activity and loud voices in front of the Reception room. The reporter recognized Kellogg.

She said, "We have a story brewing over there. Let's get it."

* * * *

At that same moment the heavy door flew open and Matt rushed into the room. He stopped short. His heart thudded and his throat went chalk dry.

"Ann …."

He took two steps closer and saw her blink.

"She's alive. Tell Andy we need EMS now and put a rush on it."

Captain Sawyer came in behind him.

"Holy Christ, the bastard drugged her."

Kellogg squeezed Ann's hand and put his fingers to her throat.

"I got a low pulse."

He pulled an afghan off the back of a leather chair and covered her legs.

"If you can hear me, blink."

Ann responded.

In her mind she pleaded, *Help me … he stuck a needle in my neck, I'm paralyzed.*

"She can hear us. Get that damn bus here now!"

Ken said, "It's coming, they had two units on campus for the event and one is still here. They're two minutes away."

Kellogg took a tissue out of his jacket pocket and gently blotted Ann's eyes.

"Is that better?"

She blinked rapidly and whispered in her head, *I love you.*

* * * *

THE OLD VICTORIAN
5:59 PM:

Samantha climbed up to her place on the dining room table and waited for her dinner to be served.

"Daddy had a fantastic afternoon."

Michael came in from the kitchen with a plate for himself and a bowl of chopped meat for the cat.

"It was like being back in medical school."

He put the bowl in front of Sam and she started into it immediately.

"All those women running around were exciting to see."

He sat at his end of the long oak table.

"No legs to be seen. That damned Ann Beck scared them into wearing slacks, but that'll blow over soon enough."

Michael poured a half glass of a California Merlot and tested the legs.

"Excellent."

He sniffed the wine and took a sip.

The TV on the hutch caught his attention. He picked up the remote and raised the volume. It was tuned to the local Fox News channel. The anchor, with a two hundred dollar haircut, gave a Hollywood smile and said, "We have a report from earlier this evening that was shot following the seminar at Eagan Plaza on the San Diego

University campus. Apparently there was an incident involving police at a reception room near the staging area of the event."

A short clip of men and two security guards gathered at the entrance to the room played without sound.

"I'll have more from the reporter who was at the scene when we come back."

The TV cut to a Burger King commercial.

Michael laughed and took a swallow of wine.

"See that, Samantha, Daddy's work is in the news again—hot damn."

The cat paid no attention and continued enjoying her food.

Michael's demeanor changed to ice.

"I'm not done with the lovely Sergeant Ann Beck yet, Kellogg, count on it. I got to her once and I'll do it again. When you find her the next time she'll be legless."

Chapter Forty Eight

Struggle for Survival

EMERGENCY RUN
SOUTHBOUND I–FIVE - 5:15 PM:

𝕯𝖊𝖙𝖊𝖈𝖙𝖎𝖛𝖊 𝕶𝖊𝖑𝖑𝖔𝖌𝖌 rode in in the ambulance with Ann and held her hand all the way.

"You're going to be okay, I promise, you'll make it through this."

In her mind, she fought the paralyzing chemicals coursing through her veins.

My vision is fading. I'm frightened, Matt!

Her eyes closed. A sound like rushing air filled her head and covered Matt's voice.

I'm dying ....

* * * *

THE OLD VICTORIAN – 6:05 PM:

A string of TV spots ended. The handsome anchor and an attractive female came on in a two-shot. The man said, "We're back with FOX News reporter, Roberta Nester. Following this afternoon's well publicized seminar, on the USD campus, an incident took place at a reception room near Eagan Plaza, where the event had been staged. Roberta, what was going on?"

Michael smiled at the screen. "Sam, watch. They're about to show what I set in motion." He took a sip of wine. "Yes, daddy did good."

The reporter continued, "As you will see, on the video, a group of men and two security guards were arguing at the front entrance to the reception room. I recognized Detectives Matt Kellogg and Ken Black. They're with the Special Victims Unit of SDPD and the team's honcho, Captain Roy Sawyer was with them. Let's go to video."

"Here it comes, Sam, more of my work on the tube—I love it!"

The cat looked up and then went back to the rest of her meal.

After several seconds the video camera zoomed in on the room's front door. It opened and the cops entered.

Roberta came back on the screen.

"About three minutes later, an EMS van arrived. Here's our closing shot."

The last thirty seconds of the video showed paramedics pushing a gurney out the side door of the reception room and into the back of the van.

Michael held up his glass.

"Great job, Roberta, I'll have to take you to lunch."

The TV cut back to a two-shot.

The anchor said, "Was that a cop getting in the van with the gurney?"

"It was clearly Detective Kellogg, and my guess is, the person on the gurney was Sergeant Ann Beck. She organized the seminar and this morning, on KSDO Talk Radio, the so-called, *Legs Collector* threatened to get to her."

"Hey, Roberta, I carried out that threat."

He laughed.

"They've made a big mistake underestimating Dr. Michael Moran."

The anchor said, "I'm wondering what Captain Sawyer and Detective Black had to say?"

"It was the usual, no comment, police business. They promised a press release in the morning."

"Thank you, Roberta for an excellent report."

The camera cut to a full shot of the anchor.

"We have an attempted armed robbery in Logan Heights that put the would-be gunman in the hospital. We'll be back with that after this."

An El Cajon Ford commercial started.

Michael clicked off the TV.

"Wasn't that great, Sam?"

He drank the rest of his wine and poured another glass. His face stiffened and his voice became guttural.

"There *will* be a next time, Beck, and I won't be so nice."

The room temperature dropped rapidly.

Michael saw his breath.

A ghostly image of his dead mother appeared in the kitchen doorway.

You're on your way to hell, Mickey, stupid Mickey.

He stood and screamed at the specter.

"Get out of my house!"

The vision shook its finger at him.

Evil you are, evil you've always been.

Samantha flew off the table and shot into the living room.

You made a mistake, Mickey, dumb Mickey, and it will be your downfall.

"Go away from me—get out of here you hateful bitch."

The transparent image leaned against the doorframe and laughed.

You left your mistake with Amanda, Mickey, and it will bring you down. Stupid, Mickey thinks he's so smart. They'll be coming for you, Mickey, you idiot.

He screamed and threw the glass of wine through the doorway. It shattered against a cupboard and scattered shards all over the counter and onto the floor

The freezing ceased.

"What mistake did I make with Amanda?"

He fell back into his chair at the head of the table.

"What mistake?"

* * * *

THE AMBULANCE RUSHING
ANN TO THE HOSPITAL:

Kellogg watched her eyes close. He squeezed her hand.

"If you can hear me blink."

No response.

The paramedic checked her pulse.

"Her heart rate has dropped and breathing is shallow."

"Can you do something?"

Matt felt Ann's forehead.

"She's chalk-dry and cold."

"I can't give her anything without knowing what's cooking inside."

"Goddammit, man."

Matt rubbed Ann's face.

"Her lips are turning blue."

The medic clicked on his radio.

"This is EMS-five."

Were ready here. Go, Tom.

"My patient's vitals are dropping and she's dehydrating."

Start an IV STAT and get her in here.

"Copy that."

He called to the driver.

"Step on it, Eddie."

The driver responded.

"Got it, we're two minutes out."

Tom looked at Matt's terrified expression.

"I've had my share of overdoses before, Detective. If she's on *Rohypnol,* as you said, she'll come out of it and be a very hung over lady."

"I hope to God you're right."

He squeezed Ann's cold, limp hand.

"Stay with me, baby."

Chapter Forty Nine

Life on a Thread

UNIVERSITY HOSPITAL- ER
SAN DIEGO- 5:30 PM:

𝕬𝖑𝖑 𝖍𝖊 𝖈𝖔𝖚𝖑𝖉 𝖉𝖔 𝖜𝖆𝖘 𝖜𝖆𝖙𝖈𝖍 the doctor and an RN tend to Ann. Matt wanted to hold her hand, be near her, but he had to stay out of the way.

The EKG machine beeped and the screen displayed three different colored rising and falling lines to the rhythm of the beeps. Kellogg had a vague idea of what it all meant. He did know for sure that the undulating lines were a picture of Ann Beck's life.

Dr. Karl Eckles clicked off his penlight and spoke to the nurse, who had just taken fifty CCs of Ann's blood.

"Run her sample to the lab as priority one."

He smiled at the detective and hesitated

before shaking his hand.

Matt said, "What are her chances?"

He glanced at his partner.

"She started fading away in the ambulance and it scared the hell out of me."

"Her pupils are dilated and her vitals are down, but stabilized."

He checked the EKG screen.

"We need to keep her overnight for observation. I'll order a room on the second floor close to ICU as a precaution."

"Intensive care?"

Matt's voice went up a notch.

"That doesn't sound too promising."

He looked at Ann. *We're going to get you through this. You'll make it.*

Kellogg studied the doctor's face.

"Can't you give her something to counteract *Rohypnol?*"

"I have to get the tox-screen back from the lab before I can give her anything."

He looked at the EKG again.

"Her pulse and BP are low, but steady and that's a good sign."

"Doctor, *Rohypnol* is the weapon of choice for the bastard who did this to Ann. However, on at least one victim, he mixed it with another similar drug. Our lab tech said a dose of it would eventually cause death."

"That's exactly why I need the tox-screen

before I can put something else in her system. Now, we need to get her up to the second floor and settled in."

"I'll stay with her. I want to be there when she wakes up."

Captain Sawyer came into the small room with Ken and Jack right behind.

Sawyer said, "How is she?"

The EKG monitor beeped. Ann's heart rate dropped, then shot up over one-hundred and went into fibrillation.

Dr. Eckles shouted, "Code blue, stat!"

* * * *

THE OLD VICTORIAN – 6:30 PM:

Michael cleaned up the mess from the shattered glass of wine and dumped it in the trash. He walked back into the dining room and poured himself another.

"What mistake did I make with that bitch, Amanda Price?"

Samantha trotted in from the living room, where she had gone to hide when Michael screamed at his dead mother. She sat at her place on the table and started in on her own house cleaning.

"Where did I screw up, Sam?"

He sipped some Merlot.

"Daddy's going down to the basement. I'll give you treats when I come up."

* * * *

He carried his glass of wine to his desk in the operating room and set it on a coaster.

"Think … think about your session with Amanda."

The memory of Amanda calling him names and fighting back was clear.

"I spent more time with her to make the bitch write her last story."

Michael yelled into the large room.

"All that fucking effort, and smart ass Kellogg didn't release it to the press."

Michael took a swallow of wine and paced behind his desk.

"What—what the hell did I do wrong?"
He remembered Amanda screaming and swearing at him while he forced her to type her story just the way he wanted it.

"The mistake wasn't in the draft. I read it over several times."

He walked around his stainless steel operating table and visualized the woman still fighting him before he dismembered her arms and legs.

"She brought all that on herself."

The refrigeration unit kicked on and drew his

attention. His mind raced through images of severed limbs.

"Maybe the answer's in there."

He went over and opened the door to the walk-in freezer. A cloud of icy vapor wafted out from the interior. He switched on the lights and stepped in.

Two rows of frozen female legs and four feet, left over from the *Oaks North* killings, hung on either side of the box. Each one wrapped in freezer paper and labeled by victim names and dates.

"I'll have to get rid of the old feet, they're freezer-burned."

When he came to Amanda's legs and arms he paused. Warm air, from the basement, caused a layer of frost to form on the hanging horror.

Something clicked in Michael's brain.

"That's it!"

He came out of the freezer and secured the door.

"Her purse. I left her damn purse with the body. There's something in it I didn't find."

* * * *

Back in the dining room, he gave Samantha a handful of homemade, dried, meat treats.

"Daddy's figured it out, Sam. My mistake is in Amanda's purse."

Another sip of wine before adding a little more to his glass he smiled.

"By now, the cops have returned the bitch's car and purse to her parents. All I have to do is get it back."

He laughed.

"I'll find out where they live and pay them an official police visit."

Chapter Fifty

Intensive Care

UNIVERSITY HOSPITAL
SAN DIEGO - 6:30 PM:

Through the large ICU window, the four officers observed the activity that would hopefully save Ann Beck's life.

Dr. Eckles jotted notes on the patient's chart and an RN adjusted Ann's oxygen tube and the IV drip.

Matt Looked at the other three cops.

"The perp got to her right under our noses and we won't know how until she can tell us."

Captain Sawyer said, "We're dealing with a clever killer here. Sooner or later he'll slip up and we'll nab him."

Jack stepped away from the glass.

"I've worked with Ann for over eighteen

months, and I can tell you she's one of the best."

He glanced back into the ICU.

"If the drug hasn't scrambled her brains, she'll be able to tell us how he got in the reception room and what he did to keep her from pulling her weapon."

"Obviously, she didn't feel threatened."

Kellogg rubbed his eyes.

"Thanks for being here. You guys can call it a day. I'm staying with her for the night."

The Captain said, "I want to hear what the doc has to say."

Dr. Eckles came out of ICU leaving Ann in the nurse's care.

"Gentlemen, Ms. Beck's condition is guarded."

He consulted his clipboard. "As you know, she was injected with *Rohypnol*, she didn't *ingest* the drug."

Matt said, "And that is a complication?"

"It puts a different spin on treatment. The tox-screen came back showing that the chemical was laced with liquor and we don't know how much."

Ken leaned on the back of a chair. "That son-of-a-bitch!"

The doctor continued.

"Alcohol accelerates the effect of the drug when it's ingested with a drink."

He hesitated.

"When *injected,* it's ten times more potent and

disables the victim instantly."

Matt shook his head.

"Bottom line, Doctor?"

"Detective, your partner has slipped into a coma."

"Good God."

He stared into the ICU.

"How bad is it?"

"There are eight levels of coma, Ann is in stage one."

"Which is what?"

"She's breathing on her own, but can't react to stimuli. Ann has no severe brain trauma and I expect her coma state to be temporary."

"You mean brief?"

"If she responds in the next twelve hours, she'll be on the way to recovery."

Kellogg drew a breath.

"If not?"

"Let's take it one hour at a time."

* * * *

THE OLD VICTORIAN
AT THAT SAME TIME:

Samantha had curled up on the bed watching her master.

Michael held up a cheap tan sports coat from *Sears.*

"What do you think?"

He tickled the cat's belly.

"I can't very well show up in one of my *Armani* suits and a two hundred dollar custom made shirt can I?"

He chuckled.

"Hell, cops don't make that kind of money."

The cat scratched her left ear with her left hind paw.

Michael hung the garment on a nearby cherry wood clothing rack and held two *Target*-bought ties against the jacket.

"You like the red stripes or the powder blue with the coat?"

Sam blinked at him.

"Okay, powder blue gets the nod."

He went back to the closet and brought out a pair of dark brown slacks and held them up to the ensemble.

"Do they work?"

Samantha scratched her right ear with her right hind paw.

"I guess that's a yes."

He hung the trousers on the rack and admired the outfit.

"Do I wear a pair of loafers or wingtips?"

He tapped his chin.

"I'll decide that in the morning."

Michael pulled on Sam's tail.

"Let's go downstairs and watch *Silence of the Lambs* again."

He left the second floor bedroom and the cat followed after.

* * * *

UNIVERSITY HOSPITAL
SAN DIEGO– ICU
TWO HOURS LATER:

With the doctor's permission, Matt sat in an uncomfortable, plastic, chair on the right side of Ann's bed. He held her cool hand to his face.

Dear God, let her get through this.

He brushed her right cheek with his warm touch and whispered, "Don't leave me, Baby … you're the only thing on this planet that really matters to me."

Kellogg kissed her hand.

"I'm right here and I'm not going away."

Ann's right index finger twitched.

Chapter Fifty One

Detective Frank Doyle

THE OLD VICTORIAN
WEDNESDAY – 8:30 AM:

In his second floor bedroom, Michael took a box down from the top shelf of the walk-in closet, set it on the neatly made bed, and opened it.

"Now, the final touch to top off my outfit."

Samantha snoozed between two decorator pillows.

Michael put a black leather clip-on holster on the bed and dropped the heavy *Colt* .45 beside it, disturbing the cat.

"Sorry, Sam, I didn't mean to wake you."

True to her feline nature, curious Sam crept to the weapon and sniffed it.

"Careful, sweetheart, it's loaded."

He took an extra clip and its holder out of the

box and hooked it on his belt.

"Armed to the teeth. That's the way they say it on TV."

Next, the gold shield and ID card in a special leather wallet.

"Look at this, Sam."

He flipped it open.

"Police, hold it right there!"

Michael laughed.

"Does it look authentic?"

He studied the ID card and smiled. The thumbnail photo showed him in his favorite salt and pepper wig and pockmarked complexion makeup.

"I love it, Detective Frank Doyle."

The cat watched him and cocked her head.

Michael clipped the holster to his belt and shoved the forty-five into it. He slipped into his sports coat and admired himself in the full length standing mirror.

"Now, there's a handsome detective."

He pulled the right side of his coat back to reveal his weapon.

"Wow! Samantha, I should have my own cop show."

He tucked a notebook and pen into the inside left pocket of his jacket.

"I'm ready and loaded for bear."

He scratched the cat under her chin.

"You be a good girl while Daddy's gone. I

should be back in time to fix us a great lunch."

* * * *

UNIVERSITY HOSPITAL–ICU
FOUR HOURS EARLIER:

The EKG monitor beeped faster and Ann started coming out of her coma.

Matt snapped up from a doze when she squeezed his hand.

"Ann …."

He stood to see the fear in her open eyes.

"I'm here … you're in the hospital."

Dr. Eckles and a different RN came into the unit. The doctor glanced at the screen and smiled.

"She'll make it, Detective. Let us have the room."

"I'll be right outside, Ann. You're going to be okay."

He grinned.

"You'll be all right."

* * * *

Fifteen long minutes passed while Kellogg watched through the window. That's all he could do. He noticed color coming back to Ann's pale cheeks, and he saw her sip water through a straw.

I promise, I'll nail the sonofabitch who did this

to you if I have to risk my badge to do it.

The nurse stepped out of the unit first. She smiled at Matt.

"Your partner's doing fine."

"Thank you."

Two minutes later the doctor came out.

"Ann's a little weak, but her strength will come back. She'll feel like hell for a while yet, but she's out of danger."

"Thank God."

He shook the doctor's hand.

"Thank you."

"I've got her on *activated charcoal* for now."

"Charcoal?"

Eckles smiled.

"It's used mostly for patients who've ingested similar drugs but in this case it will be an added plus."

Kellogg said, "Could you fill me in?"

"What it does is absorb the *Rohypnol* from the patient's system and flushes the contamination."

He hesitated.

"In Ann's case, because the poison was injected, it takes longer."

"So, she can't go home tomorrow?"

"We can move her out of ICU in the morning, but I need to keep her for at least three days."

He checked his watch.

"We'll have her in a private room by eight o'clock."

"She's going to make a fuss, guaranteed."

Kellogg glanced at Ann through the window. Her eyes were closed.

"We'll need your help, Matt. Convince her she needs the full detoxification process before I can release her back to duty."

They shook hands.

Matt said, "She's yours for the next few days, but I'll be in and out."

The doctor smiled.

"You're welcome, stay as long as you like.

Let's do lunch one of these days."

"You're on, Doc."

He went back into the unit, held Ann's hand and said, "Hi, Beautiful."

She opened her eyes and spoke in halting, slurred speech, "He … was ... dressed … as ... a … priest, Matt."

Chapter Fifty Two

Michael on a Mission

NORTH COUNTY SENTINEL
WEDNESDAY – 9:30 AM:

𝕿𝖍𝖊 𝕷𝖆𝖙𝖊 𝕬𝖒𝖆𝖓𝖉𝖆 𝕻𝖗𝖎𝖈𝖊 worked at the Vista newspaper for five years before her fatal encounter with the *Legs Collector*. She unknowingly left a clue in her purse.

* * * *

Michael walked into the Sentinel and approached the clerk at the front desk.
"Good morning."
He flashed his fake badge and ID.
"I'm Detective Frank Doyle, SDPD, *Special Victims Unit*."
When he returned the ID wallet to the inside

pocket of his sports coat he made sure the hefty .45 auto could be seen.

The young woman wasn't all that impressed.

"How can I help you?"

"I need to talk to the senior editor. It's police business."

He leaned on the counter and noticed the girl was wearing a skirt and had decent looking legs.

"Larry's in an editorial meeting. I'm the office manager. What can I do for you?"

Her mouth smiled, her eyes didn't.

"It's sensitive material, Miss, and involves Amanda Price."

Michael didn't expect resistance.

The clerk shuddered.

"What about Amanda?"

Her weak smile went away.

Michael read her name tag. "How much authority do you have, Joan?" *This little bitch is starting to piss me off.*

"There's a matter of investigation that involves her parents. I need their address and phone number."

"Don't you cops already have that information?"

He grinned.

"If I did, I wouldn't be here asking for it, now would I" *If you knew who you're really talking to you'd pee your panties.*

"Amanda's parents are mourning the brutal

murder of their daughter, Mr. Detective."

She glared at him.

"I understand that, Joan, and I hate to be the one to intrude on their grief." *Who the fuck does she think she is?* "All I need are the address and phone number, then I can go about the sad task of talking to them."

"You should've caught the killer by now instead of harassing the family. Amanda was a friend and everybody here loved her. This monster, you cops can't catch, has killed again."

"That's all the more reason we need your help." *What the hell is with this chick?* "If you don't want to help us do our job, then let me talk to someone in the human resources department."

"We don't have one. I handle personnel files."

"Excellent."

He took out his note book and started writing. *I'll give this sassy bitch a little scare.*

"What are you doing?"

"I'm noting your resistant comments, the date and time. Then, I call downtown and have a warrant here within the hour."

He put the notebook away and smiled.

"A warrant for what?"

"For the information I've asked for. I'd hoped we could do this without a problem, but I guess not."

An older woman entered the lobby. She nodded at Joan and started down the hall.

Joan said, "Betty, this detective wants personal information on Amanda's parents."

The richly dressed, heavyset, lady looked at Michael.

"And you are?"

Michael gave her one of his best movie star smiles and offered his hand.

"Detective Frank Doyle with Special Victims. All I want is an address and phone number for the Price family."

"Pleased to meet you, Detective, I'm Mrs. Hammond. My husband and I are the publishers of the Sentinel. Is there anything new with the investigation?"

"We're following a lead that Amanda's parents can help us with and I need to ask them a few questions."

"Amanda's mother has been on medication since this horrible nightmare struck the family."

"I assure you, Mrs. Hammond, I will not cause further stress to the parents."

The woman looked at Joan.

"Give the detective what he needs. We all want that bastard caught and punished."

"Thank you, Ma'am." *Now there's a woman I could like.*

* * * *

UNIVERSITY HOSPITAL
ROOM 205 – AT THAT SAME TIME:

Two orderlies in green scrubs helped Ann get settled in. She was a little pale and weak, but managed a smile.

"Thank you guys, I enjoyed the ride."

One of them said, "Our pleasure. It's still breakfast time and someone will bring a tray in a few minutes."

"I don't really have much of an appetite, but I'll try to eat something."

She grinned at Matt sitting in the corner by the window.

"He'll finish what I can't"

Kellogg laughed.

"You can bet on that."

He dragged his chair over by Ann's bed and took her hand.

"I knew you'd make it. I didn't doubt it for a minute."

"Yes you did, I saw the fear on your face before I zonked out in the ambulance."

She kissed him.

"You know, Matt Kellogg, you're the best there is, ever."

"Well, I guess that makes two of us."

He squeezed her hand.

Ann's expression became stiff.

"His eyes Matt, they were piercing … there

wasn't anything in them but evil."

He stood, leaned forward and hugged her.

"Not now, we won't go there until you're feeling better, okay?"

"Okay … I love you."

* * * *

NORTH SAN DIEGO COUNTY
THE TOWN OF VISTA – 10:15 AM
SAME DAY:

Michael climbed into his Benz and dialed the number for the Price household. *That snotty clerk has just marked her pretty little ass.*

After four rings Amanda's father answered.

"Hello."

Michael grinned.

It's going like clockwork. "Is this the Price residence?"

"Yes."

Bill's voice sounded strained and tired.

"Good morning, sir. I'm Detective Frank Doyle with the Special Victims Unit of SDPD. Our investigation has taken a positive turn."

"Well, I'm glad to hear that, but why are you calling us?"

He put on his sympathetic tone.

"It seems our lab techs overlooked something in your daughter's shoulder bag and we need to get it back for further examination. I know this is a tough time for you, but it's important. Do you still have it?"

He checked the Price's home address.

"Yes, I do and we don't want to lose it."

The man's voice cracked.

"I understand, sir. We just need it for a couple of days. I'll see to it you get it back with all contents intact."

Michael grinned. *Don't hold your breath, Price.*

"Are you at 342 Willow Avenue?"

"Yes, do you know how to get here?"

"I'm familiar with Vista. I'll be there in fifteen minutes."

"That'll be fine, Detective, but you won't be able to talk to my wife about this."

"I understand, sir. I just need to pick up the bag."

"All right, I'll be waiting."

"Thank you. See you in a few."

Clockwork, tick, tick, tick-tock.

Chapter Fifty Three

Detoxification Begins

UNIVERSITY HOSPITAL
WEDNESDAY - ROOM 205 - 11:00 AM:

Dr. Eckles joined Kellogg and Beck in her room.

"Good morning, how's my patient?"

"I'm feeling a lot better than I did last night. At least I can talk straight and breakfast chased the headache away."

She smiled.

"It was like a kettledrum earlier."

The doctor made a note on Ann's chart.

"I had a look at the results of your latest blood work and the toxins have decreased by fifteen percent."

He glanced at the EKG monitor. "Do you feel any dizziness?"

"I did a while ago, but it passed."

She looked at her partner.

"During breakfast, we were talking about the effects of the drug. What puzzles me is the fact that I have a fuzzy memory of the entire, frightening ordeal. *Rohypnol* is supposed to cause partial or total memory loss of the event."

Eckles jotted another entry on Ann's chart.

"You're right, it's called, *anterograde* amnesia."

He looked over at both of them. "Whoever did this to you knows what he's doing."

Matt got up off the chair and held Ann's hand.

"He wanted her to remember, and made sure the dose wouldn't kill her."

"Exactly."

The doctor put the chart back in place at the foot of the bed.

"He diluted the *Rohypnol* and mixed it with just enough alcohol to accelerate the effect and counter most of the memory loss."

Ann squeezed Matt's hand.

"So where am I with the side effects of detox?"

"Your healthy liver is your best friend for now. It's processing the junk in your system and the activated charcoal is working faster than I expected."

An RN came in with a different IV bag.

"Are we ready?"

"Yes, go ahead. Ms. Stewart is going to start a new drip that will help your liver flush the contamination."

He grinned.

"If this medication works, as I believe it will, I may be able to release you tomorrow afternoon."

"Thank you, Doctor, I'm all for that."

"No promise, we'll see how it goes."

The nurse hooked up the new IV and adjusted the drip.

Matt said, "You're on your way back to the job, Sergeant."

"Yeah, I am, and we're going to nail that sonofabitch to the courthouse wall."

"I don't think it will be the courthouse wall."

Matt kissed her on the cheek.

* * * *

THE NORTH COUNTY - VISTA –
342 WILLOW AVE
AT THAT SAME TIME:

Michael parked a block away and walked by six fifties-style homes to the Price residence.

This looks nice and cozy.

He climbed the few steps to the porch and rang the bell.

Play it cool and try to show some sympathy for the dearly departed. At least fake it.

He chuckled.

A black wreath on the front door. Of course they'd have that in place.

Bill Price looked through the lace curtain and opened the door.

"Detective Doyle?"

"Yes, sir."

He flashed his phony badge and ID.

Mr. Price stepped back.

"Please, come in."

Michael walked into an inexpensive, but nicely furnished living room.

"I'm sorry to have to intrude at such a difficult time."

"I understand, you have to do your job."

He gestured toward an overstuffed green sofa with neatly placed throw-pillows stacked against each arm. Gold framed eight by ten photographs of Amanda were displayed on both end tables.

"Please, make yourself comfortable."

He went into the small dining room and picked up Amanda's shoulder bag off the dark walnut table.

Michael sat and held back an urge to grin.

Make it snappy, old man, so I can get the hell out of here.

Mr. Price carried the purse into the living room and hesitated.

"You need to know, Detective, this means a lot to us. I hope it helps your investigation, but we want it back as soon as possible."

"I give you my word, the minute the lab is finished with it, I'll carry it back here myself."

He smiled.

Give me the fucking bag and kiss it goodbye.

He took an official-looking pad out of his side pocket and started writing.

"This is a receipt for the purse and contents, which have already been accounted for by SVU, so you're double covered."

The *phony detective* stood, towering over Mr. Price, and took possession of the purse.

Bill looked up at him.

"I hope you catch the killer soon."

"You can count on it, sir. Thank you for your cooperation."

The day they catch me, demons will be snow-boarding in hell.

He started for the front door and turned back.

"I need you to know, I'm sincerely sorry for your loss."

"Thank you, Detective. It's been an emotional drain on the family."

"I'm sure it has."

If your bitch daughter hadn't fought me, I would've been easier on her.

"Give my heartfelt condolence to your wife, and thank you again."

"You're welcome."

* * * *

UNIVERSITY HOSPITAL
ROOM 205 – ONE HOUR LATER:

Ann dozed and appeared at ease. Kellogg watched her and shivered at the IV drip and the oxygen tubes in her nose.

I love you Ann Beck. We'll get this bastard, that's a promise.

He stood by the window staring out at the bright, sunny day. People were coming and going in and out of the parking lot. Each one had their own crises to fight.

Matt's cell rang.

"Kellogg. Hi Cap … Ann's doing great. What've you got?"

"Bill Price called and he wants you to get back to him."

"What's the number?"

He wrote it on a napkin.

"Any message?"

"He just said it was important."

"I'll get in touch right away."

He noticed Beck was awake.

"Thanks for the call."

Ann said, "What is it?" She reached out to take Matt's hand.

"Amanda's father wants me to call him. He has something he thinks is important."

"Those poor parents have got to be in serious grief."

"Yeah, that's a fact."
He dialed the Price's number.

* * * *

Bill Price picked up on the third ring.
"Hello."
"Mr. Price, Matt Kellogg here, you wanted me to call."
"Yes, thank you. One of your team members came here this afternoon to get Amanda's purse for further lab tests."
"That shouldn't be necessary."
Something's wrong with this.
"Who was it?"
"He identified himself as, Detective Frank Doyle. I gave him the bag, but I forgot that I had taken a note that Mandy wrote out of the purse. You might need it for the investigation. It may be important."
Matt sat in the chair and pinched the bridge of his nose.
I can't tell him he just met the killer.
"Mr. Price, what is written on the note?"
"I found it under a flap at the bottom of the bag. I wanted to keep it because Mandy always doodled on her notes since she was in grade school."
His voice wavered.
"She drew pretty flowers and unicorns. She

did that on all of the letters she sent while she was in college."

The man's voice was on the edge of breaking.

"I wanted to keep this last note from our little girl."

Matt said, "Why would your daughter's doodles be useful in our investigation?"

He drew a breath and nodded at Ann. He covered the mouthpiece of his cell and whispered, "We may have something."

Bill Price continued.

"Most of it is gibberish to me, but Amanda wrote, *Old man with cane.* Then she scribbled, *ill.* That doesn't seem right. Did she mean the old man was sick?"

"What else is on the note?"

"Well, below that she wrote, *Prank call – 7:30 PM.*"

Kellogg thought, *That was about the time of Amanda's abduction.*

He said, "Anything more?"

"She has the words, *Crime scene location* underlined."

"Read the rest. This is all important."

"Okay, she noted, *Old man with cane* again. Above that she wrote, *Old Vic.* I don't know what that means."

Matt shook his fist in the air.

"Mr. Price, you have no idea how helpful you've been."

"I hope so."

"Can you FAX that note to my office?"

"Yes, I have a FAX program on my computer."

"Great, here's the number, 858-777-2943. Send it. I'm on my way to the station now."

"Detective, is it customary for plain clothes cops to wear skin-tight leather gloves?"

"Not usually, why?"

"Mr. Doyle had on a pair and didn't take them off."

"Thank you, I'll look into that. I apologize for all this stress on your family."

"Not a problem, I'm glad we could help. Get the bastard anyway you can."

Chapter Fifty Four

Amanda's Shoulder Bag

THE OLD VICTORIAN
THIRTY MINUTES EARLIER:

𝔖amantha heard her master come into the kitchen from the garage and ran in to greet him.

Michael swaggered in swinging the bag by its straps and humming the theme from the old TV show *Kojack.*

"Daddy's home, my lovely."

He set the purse on the table, took off his jacket and then the wig.

"Well, Dearest, I had a productive morning and afternoon."

He tossed the wig next to the bag.

"All parties bought me as a detective."

He laughed.

"That's because they're easy to fool."

The cat jumped up on the table, sniffed at the purse, and investigated the salt and pepper hair as if it were alive.

"Let's see what I missed the first time."

He dumped the contents of Amanda's purse on the table, looked inside, turned it over and shook it.

"There's nothing I didn't see before, Sam."

He picked up the cell phone and clicked *on*.

"The battery's dead."

Michael looked into the bag again and spotted a flap on the bottom.

"Ah-ha, a secret compartment."

He pulled it open.

"Shit, there's nothing there."

Of course there isn't, you moron.

His dead mother's visage stood at the far end of the table behind Samantha.

The room became freezing.

"Get out of here, Witch."

The cat jumped off the table and ran for a place to hide.

Whatever's missing is now in the hands of the police, Mickey, idiot, Mickey.

"Shut your dead mouth and go back to hell."

He threw the cell phone at the image. It landed on the counter and bounced onto the floor.

Elizabeth Moran now reappeared in the dining room doorway.

They're coming after you, Mickey. If I had known the evil I carried in my belly, I would've aborted it and kept it from this world. Your overdue punishment is on the way, Mickey.

He drew his gun, jacked a shell into the chamber, and fired two rounds. Glass in the hutch exploded and pieces of hand painted china plates shattered inside the cabinet.

The kitchen filled with the smell of cordite. Michael's ears rang with the thunder of the .45.

Samantha darted through the doorway to get away from flying glass.

Michael fired at the blurred image.

The cat slammed against the hutch and landed on the carpet.

"Sam--"

He stood. His chair toppled over.

"Samantha!"

Michael dropped the weapon on the kitchen floor, went into the dining room, and fell to his knees in front of the dying animal.

The cat's legs shuddered. She turned her head to see her master for the last time.

He picked her up and held her. Blood ran down over his powder blue tie and his dark blue shirt.

"My beautiful Samantha, what have I done?"

He rocked Sam's body in his arms.

"I've killed the only thing I ever really loved."

* * * *

UNIVERSITY HOSPITAL
WEDNESDAY - ROOM 205 - 1:15 PM:

Ann sat up and grabbed the rail on her bed.

"What the hell have you got, Matt?"

"Just what I thought days ago. The killer *is* Michael Moran!"

"How do you know?"

"Amanda's father found a note in her purse and on it she had written, *Old Vic* in La Mesa and *crime scene.*

He dialed Captain Sawyer's number.

"Mr. Price had a visit from our perp this afternoon. He posed as a detective and picked up the shoulder bag."

"How could the perp know about the note?"

She rested back against her pillow.

"This is craziness."

"It is for sure, but he made a move and it's in our favor."

"We have to have more to go on, Matt."

She shook her head.

"I want out of here and on the job."

He gripped her hand.

"You'll stay put until Eckles releases you."

Captain Sawyer answered.

"What's up, Matt?"

"The killer is Michael Moran as I told you earlier."

"And you know this, how?"

"I'll cut to the chase."

"Please do."

"The call to Amanda's father had the answer."

He drew a short breath.

"The victim left a note in her purse that her dad found. Here are the key words."

"I'm listening."

"Amanda wrote, *Old Vic, crime scene, La Mesa.* Moran lives in an old Victorian in La Mesa, Ken and I were there, remember?"

He gripped Ann's hand.

"It's enough for a warrant."

He thought a second. "Price FAXED the note to SVU under my name. Run the sonofabitch through DMV, like we should've done earlier."

"Then what, Matt?"

"We hit the Victorian with a SWAT team."

Chapter Fifty Five

Farewell Samantha

THE OLD VICTORIAN
AT THAT SAME TIME:

𝕾𝖙𝖎𝖑𝖑 𝖎𝖓 𝖍𝖎𝖘 𝖇𝖑𝖔𝖔𝖉𝖞 𝖈𝖑𝖔𝖙𝖍𝖊𝖘, Michael carried his beloved Sam to the upstairs bedroom.

"I'm so sorry … I didn't mean to hurt you … I'm so ashamed of what I've done."

He picked up her cat-bed, put it on his own, and laid her in it.

"Daddy will always love you."

His voice fluttered. "I'll never forget all the fun we had together."

Michael wept while he wrapped Sam's body in her favorite blanket. Just before he covered her head, he scratched her chin one last time.

"I'm sure you're in a good place now."

She's in a better place than you'll soon be,

The presence of Elizabeth Moran appeared in the hall outside the room.

Samantha's free of you, Mickey, and when this day ends, the world will be too.

"Shut up, you horrible witch. You caused the death of the only love I've ever had—are you happy now?"

The vision dissipated, formed again in the large mirror above the oak dresser, and laughed at him.

Mickey Moran, the idiot moron. Look at yourself, you're pathetic. You cry for a dead cat and collect the legs of young women. You're a demon, Mickey, a malignancy on the face of the earth.

Michael grabbed a water glass off the nightstand and threw it. The mirror shattered his image into hundreds of distorted reflections.

The ghost disappeared.

He sat on the edge of the bed and patted the blanket covering Samantha.

"I'm so sorry ... Daddy's so sorry. Wherever you are, please forgive me."

* * * *

UNIVERSITY HOSPITAL- ROOM 205
AT THAT SAME TIME:

The security guard Kellogg had asked for tapped on the open door.

"Hi, I'm Weaver."

The officer nodded at Matt and Beck.

"I have the lady's back."

He smiled.

Matt said, "What's your first name?"

"Jim, sir."

"Okay, Jim."

They shook hands.

"Park yourself outside Sergeant Beck's door. Nobody but a female nurse or Doctor Eckles gets in, savvy?"

"You got it."

He tipped his hat at Ann.

"Do you know what the doctor looks like?"

Matt studied the young man's face.

"I've seen the doc at least a hundred times."

"Great. I said *female* nurse for a reason. No other male gets in this room no matter if he's in scrubs or running shorts or whatever he tells you."

He hesitated.

"Are we clear?"

"Understood, sir."

He grinned.

"Why the tight security?"

Kellogg pointed to Ann.

"That young lady is a police officer and she's a target of the *Legs Collector*. Have you seen the news lately?"

"My Sergeant just sent me up here, to guard a patient. I didn't know why."

"Now you do."

Matt gave the guard a stern look.

"If a six foot, three or four, man, built like a brick shithouse, approaches this room you'll be faced with the killer. Get my drift?"

"Yes, sir, I'll be on alert."

"You damn well better be."

He checked his watch.

"I have a uniformed cop on the way up here. You're glued to that doorway until he arrives."

"Not a problem, I'll be on the door until relieved."

"Speaking of that, you have to pee?"

"Sir?"

"If you need to go to the men's room, do it before I leave."

Ann laughed.

"Matt, you're embarrassing him."

"Just needed to make a point."

He smiled at Weaver.

"You okay?"

"I'm fine."

He left the room and stood tall by the door.

Kellogg walked over to Ann's bed and gave her a kiss.

"I have to go back to the unit. We need to move on Moran ASAP. I'm pretty sure he's at his house with Amanda's purse and we have to nail him before he makes another move."

"I want to be in on it. I want to see him cuffed and brought down."

"I understand that. I wish you could, but you can't. I need to know you're safe here."

"Dammit, Matt—"

"I'm sorry, but that's the way it is."

He kissed her again.

"A few more legal steps and the house of Michael Moran comes crashing down."

"And you're sure it's him?"

She squeezed his hand.

"I'm betting my pension on it."

He put on his jacket.

"I haven't had a shower or shave since yesterday morning."

"I love you even if you stink."

She laughed.

"You be careful with that animal."

"Count on it. The days of the *Legs Collector* have come to an end."

He left the room.

Ann looked out the window and remembered seeing Amanda's maimed remains.

Dear, God, I pray Matt's right.

Chapter Fifty Six

Tactical Plans

SDPD CONFERENCE ROOM
SIXTY MINUTES LATER:

Captain Sawyer introduced the S.W.A.T commander to the SVU team.

"Gentlemen, meet Lieutenant Alan Slater. His men are gearing up as we speak. He has a few questions."

"Thanks, Roy. Kellogg, you and Black have been to the target location. What are we up against?"

Matt consulted his notes.

"The place is like Fort Knox. There's a fifteen foot wrought iron gate and surveillance camera. The gate is electronically controlled, and iron fencing circles the property. It's not an easy entry."

He looked at Ken.

"We talked our way in last week."

Detective Black added, "The house sets way back from the entrance. It's big and solid, and can't be seen from the gate."

Kellogg said, "The front door is heavy oak and I'd guess there are at least fourteen rooms in the three story structure."

Slater said, "Anything else?"

"There's a basement."

Ken took a sip of coffee.

"The guy said he was down there when we spoke to him on the intercom."

"Okay, there are two ways to get in there."

He went to the white board and used a red dry marker. He drew a crude house and circled it with a black pen.

"How much space is there around the building?"

Kellogg said, "There are trees close to the house, but a lot of open area in the front yard."

"Clear enough for a chopper?"

"I'd guess yes, there is."

"I don't like guesses, Detective."

He drew a circle with an X in it.

"I need room to put four of my men on the ground in the front yard."

He tapped the black marker to the area that would be the rear of the house.

"Do we have space back here?"

Matt said, "We didn't see the rear yard area, but I didn't notice any trees in the way."

He stood and went to the coffee machine.

"We're eating up time here."

Slater dropped the marker in the tray.

"I have eight of my men and you four to be concerned about. We need to go in hot and safe or it's no go."

Captain Sawyer held up his hand.

"Everybody take a breath."

He stood and walked to the board.

"What if we do this?"

He drew an arrow to where the iron gate might be.

"Commander, your guys pull in with a truck, wrap a chain around the damn thing and pull it down."

Sergeant Towne went to the board and drew a red circle around all the images.

"This asshole has fortified himself in."

He smiled.

"Think about it. He's made himself a fish in a barrel. It doesn't matter how we get in there, we got him."

Matt grinned.

"A big barrel, with lots of walls to hide behind."

Commander Slater leaned on the table.

"A frontal hit on the gate won't work, now that I see the picture. It would take my men too long to get to the house and the target would be alerted.

If he's armed, my point man could be hit."

Kellogg said, "I have every reason to believe the perp is armed. He posed as a detective earlier today, and my guess is, he packed a firearm."

Slater smiled.

"You do a lot of guessing, Detective."

Matt sat down with his fresh coffee.

"Yes, I do, Commander, and I'm usually right."

He glared at Slater.

"Based on what I know about this nutcase we're after, I'm *guessing* he's in that house right now going crazier because he didn't find anything in Amanda's purse."

He sipped some coffee.

"Are we going to sit here and play war games or go get him?"

Captain Sawyer said, "We have the warrant, we know Michael Moran is not a cripple. He lied to the police He's six four and weighs two hundred fifteen pounds, and he's thirty-six years old. His house, the *Old Vic,* was written on a note by his victim, Amanda Price. Let's nail him."

Slater said, "We'll go in with two choppers on silent mode. I'll drop four men in the front yard and four in the back. The two teams bust in simultaneously and clear the rooms. My teams lead."

Kellogg smiled and held up his hand.

"I lead the front door team and that's a given."

"It's your ass, Detective."

"Yes, it is, Commander."

* * * *

THE OLD VICTORIAN
THIRTY MINUTES EARLIER:

Michael had taken the body of Samantha to the basement and gently laid it on his desk.

"They made me kill you. My witch mother, and that bitch, Amanda Price, they caused your death."

He stroked the blanket.

The heat of fury filled his head. He screamed at the cold walls of the cellar,

"You fucking bitches!"

He went to the walk-in freezer, yanked open the door, and flipped on the lights. Icy vapor drifted out from the interior.

"I'll finish killing the fucking bitch."

He grabbed Amanda's frozen legs, pulled them down from their hooks, and carried them to the stainless steel table. He slammed them down and went back to get her arms.

"I'll kill you again."

Michael dropped the dead limbs next to the legs and ripped off the freezer paper.

"I want you to feel pain, lots of pain."

He grabbed a meat cleaver from a rack near his operating table and began hacking at the frozen limbs with an insane fury.

"Can you feel that, Bitch? I hope so."

He chopped the hand off the right arm.

"Can't write much now can you, Ms. Reporter."

Chapter Fifty Seven

S.W.A.T. Operation

LEAD POLICE CHOPPER
AT THAT SAME TIME:

𝕶𝖊𝖑𝖑𝖔𝖌𝖌 𝖆𝖓𝖉 𝕮𝖆𝖕𝖙𝖆𝖎𝖓 𝕾𝖆𝖜𝖞𝖊𝖗 sat behind four S.W.A.T. officers and listened as the operation unfolded. It worked like the movement of a *Swiss* watch.

"Cobra two, this is Cobra one. We have target in sight. Descend to five hundred and go silent."

Copy that, we're right behind you. Cobra two, on descent.

Ken and Towne sat apprehensive and tense in the rear of the second helicopter. They heard the same communications. Ken looked out and nodded when he saw the roof of the Victorian.

S.W.A.T. Commander Slater had the right front seat in the lead chopper. He clicked on his mike and spoke to Sawyer and Kellogg.

"When we hit the ground, team one has the front of the house. Captain, Detective, you two stay behind my point man until we clear the entrance."

He turned back and saw them agree.

He clicked off.

The pilot reached up and flipped two toggles.

"Cobra two, we're at five hundred and silent."

The interior vibrations eased. The rotor blades changed pitch and appeared to shift into slow motion.

The second chopper responded, *Affirmative, Cobra one. We'll vector north and take the rear yard.*

"Okay, Cobra two, let's put our guys on the ground."

* * * *

THE OLD VICTORIAN
TEN MINUTES EARLIER:

Michael swung the cleaver again, dismembering the foot from Amanda's frozen right leg. Pieces of thawing flesh clung to his blood-soaked shirt and tie.

A splinter of bone flew up and nicked his face.

"Still trying to fight me, Bitch?"

His screaming voice echoed off the cement walls of the basement.

"Samantha's dead because of you and my witch mother."

He hacked at what was left of the leg. The cleaver stuck deep in the thigh bone. Michael lifted the leg and slammed it against the edge of the steel table. The bone cracked; he pulled the cleaver free and began chopping at the left leg.

"Suffer, you fucking whore."

* * * *

The battering ram smashed in the front door on the third hit.

The back door went easier.

* * * *

In his screaming rage, Michael didn't hear anything but his own raving and the sound of the cleaver hitting bone on the steel table.

They're here, Mickey—they've got you.

"Shut up, Mother."

He chopped at the leg twice more.

Stupid, Mickey, I told you, they'd come for you—idiot.

He turned to see Kellogg and five S.W.A.T. officers rush down the stairs and into the basement.

Matt shouted, "Drop the weapon, Moran—it's over."

Michael saw the specter of his mother sitting on his desk beside the departed Samantha. He shrieked with the sound of a cornered, wild animal and raised the cleaver.

Kellogg fired twice.

Chapter Fifty Eight

The Crime Scene

THE OLD VICTORIAN
GAME OVER:

𝕶𝖊𝖑𝖑𝖔𝖌𝖌'𝖘 357 𝖙𝖍𝖚𝖓𝖉𝖊𝖗𝖊𝖉.

Michael's right and left knees exploded, in that order. He landed on his right side screaming in pain. The meat cleaver slid out of reach on the cement floor.

Matt holstered his weapon.

"You'll need your wheelchair from now on, you piece of garbage."

"Fuck you, Kellogg, and your bitch partner."

He pushed himself up, leaned on his right elbow and laughed.

Matt grinned.

"Looks to me like you're the one who's screwed."

He went to the open freezer door.

"God in heaven."

He closed it.

"Ken, get CSI in here. They were bitching about no crime scene, now they have one."

"I'm on it." He dialed the lab.

For the first time, Kellogg got a clear look at the carnage on the steel table.

"Moran, you're one sick puppy."

He spotted a surgical gown folded on a nearby counter, grabbed it and covered the chopped limbs.

To Sergeant Towne he said, "Read that animal his rights."

Jack reached down and yanked Michael's right arm forcing him to roll onto his back and cuffed his hands in front.

"You have the right to remain silent. Anything you say, can and will be used against you in a court of law. If you can't afford an attorney, one will be appointed for you at no charge. Do you understand these rights?"

"What's to understand, Asshole? I can buy a dozen lawyers."

Captain Sawyer closed his phone. "EMS is three minutes out."

He looked at Commander Slater.

"Did you find the controls for the gate?"

"Right over there."

He pointed toward the desk. "Hit the button

and it opens. There's one in every room of this place."

Sawyer activated the control and watched the gate swing inward on the small monitor.

The commander said, "The house is clear. We're done here."

The captain shook Slater's hand.

"Thanks, your guys did a great job."

"That's what we're trained for. Your men need a ride?"

"We're covered."

Slater glanced at Michael and shook his head.

"Put that dirt bag where he belongs."

"That would be in hell, and I believe he's on his way."

Sawyer examined the cat-bed on the desk.

"What's this?"

Michael saw the captain tug at the blanket and he screamed.

"Leave her alone—don't touch Samantha."

He tried to move his legs and yelled in pain.

Sawyer pulled the blanket back from Sam's head.

"It's a dead cat."

"They killed my Sam."

He tried to sit up and couldn't.

"My mother and that fucking bitch reporter, Amanda Price."

He glared at Matt.

"That's what's left of her on the table, I killed

the rotten bitch again."

Kellogg shuddered.

"What?"

He removed the cover, looked at the mutilated body parts and it hit him.

"You filthy, raving, lunatic."

He drew his weapon, bent down, jammed the muzzle against the left side of Michael's head and cocked the gun.

"I'll send you straight to hell right now."

Michael grinned.

"Do it, Kellogg an' we'll be there together."

Jack stepped away.

"Don't do it, Matt."

Captain Sawyer yelled, "Kellogg—back off."

Michael laughed.

"C'mon, Detective, squeeze that trigger."

Silence.

Matt released the hammer and put the weapon away.

"Blowing your diseased brains out would be a pleasure, but sudden death is too easy for you."

He stood and re-covered Amanda's desecrated limbs.

Michael looked up from the floor to see the phantom of his mother sitting on the desk holding an apparition of his beloved Samantha.

He shrieked in agony and pain, "Put her down, you witch. Don't touch my Sam."

The ghost grinned and stroked the image of

the cat and scratched Sam under the chin.

It's all over for you, Mickey, your time has come.

"Take your dead hands off my Samantha, Mother—get your vile hands off her!"

Sam's with me now, Mickey, stupid, Mickey. She won't be in hell with you, evil, Mickey.

Michael held his cuffed hands to his face and sobbed, "I'm so sorry, Samantha … I'm so sorry."

Epilogue

The beating heart of evil
cannot be stilled.

Two Months Later

* * * *

𝕸𝖎𝖈𝖍𝖆𝖊𝖑 𝕸𝖔𝖗𝖆𝖓 spent a full four weeks under armed guard in University Hospital before he could stand trial. He had been charged with seven counts of murder and dismemberment in the first degree. Two Kidnap charges were dropped for lack of evidence.

DNA from two of the remaining feet in Michael's freezer, matched two of the severed legs recovered from the Oaks North cases. The others could not be found.

The San Diego County DA's office went for the death penalty. The two local prosecutors had been defeated, hands down.

Three, high powered defense attorneys, from one of the top firms in Los Angeles, dominated the proceedings. They pleaded to a jury of five men and seven women. The trial lasted six weeks.

In his closing argument, the lead defense attorney paced before the jury box with disarming confidence.

"There is no question that my client, Michael Moran, brutally murdered and mutilated seven young women."

He turned and pointed at the defendant.

"It sickens me, and my colleagues, that such a beast could roam the streets of this fine city."

He leaned on the railing, for effect, and studied the faces of the seven female jurors.

"However, the letter of the law is clear. Every criminal has the right to a fair trial. Michael Moran must be removed from our society for the rest of his life."

A young, attractive, female juror caught Michael's stare and grin. She shuddered.

The lawyer continued.

"It is your duty, each and every one of you, to return a verdict of not guilty by reason of insanity."

He smiled.

"Thank you ladies and gentlemen."

* * * *

TWO WEEKS LATER:
SAN DIEGO SUPERIOR COURT
DEPARTMENT FOUR – 8:45 AM:

Detective Kellogg and Sergeant Beck had jostled their way through a pack of reporters and stopped outside the open courtroom doors.

Ann said, "Can't you keep your tie straight?"

She reached up and fixed it.

"There, you look dapper."

"For the sentencing of Michael Moran I should be in a Tee shirt and jeans."

"You'll be on camera in this media circus and you need to look good. A Tee and jeans would've been appropriate for his execution, but that isn't going to happen."

"No, not now, but I had a chance to be the executioner over two months ago."

He looked around the crowded hall.

"I don't see the rest of our people."

"Except for the captain, I think Jack and Ken are inside."

She thought a moment.

"Matt, I believe if I had been there, I would've killed him."

Kellogg looked at her. "Yeah … I'm glad you weren't."

* * * *

Michael was seated in, his wheelchair, at the defense table alongside his three high-priced attorneys. He looked over at Matt and Ann who were in the front row, as they had been when they appeared to testify against him.

He grinned and mouthed the words, *Fuck you.*

* * * *

A female Superior Court Judge entered from her chambers.

The bailiff said, "All rise. Judge Karen Emerson is presiding in the sentencing of Michael Moran."

She took her seat and slammed the gavel.

"This court is in session, be seated."

Matt whispered, "What irony, the sonofabitch is being sentenced by a woman."

Beck gripped his arm.

"I love it."

Judge Emerson glared at Michael.

"Before I pronounce sentence on you, Mr. Moran, I'm compelled, by law, to tell you that punishment, in the State of California, capital crimes, is determined by the jury. Do you understand that?"

Michael grinned.

"Yeah, the seven bitches in the jury box wanted me to get the needle, but I don't think that's going to work out."

"You will refrain from foul language in my courtroom, understood?"

One of his lawyers spoke in Michael's ear.

"I understand, your Honor."

Kellogg whispered, "I'd like to shoot that bastard right now."

Ann nudged him.

"So would I."

The Judge continued.

"In twenty years on the bench, I have never encountered a more appalling defendant than you are, Mr. Moran."

Michael chuckled.

"Thank you for saying that."

"Counselor, instruct your client to keep his mouth shut."

She took a breath.

"Michael Moran, You have been found not guilty, by a jury of your peers, on seven counts of murder in the first degree by reason of depraved mental disorder. I hereby sentence you to the rest of your natural life at Patton State Hospital, for the criminally insane, in San Bernardino, California."

Applause, and some cheering, erupted in the courtroom. Judge Emerson called for order and continued.

"Michael Moran, your estate and all existing possessions will be confiscated by the County of San Diego, California and shall be liquidated. The proceeds will be divided equally among any known survivors of the five women you brutally murdered. Unfortunately, the remains of two additional victims could not be found."

When the judge slammed her gavel down, Michael saw her become his dead mother. The phantom held an image of Samantha in front of her and stroked the cat's neck.

You've gotten what you deserve, Mickey, I knew there would be due punishment for you, stupid, Mickey, and now you have it. Rot in the asylum, Mickey, that's where you belong.

Michael screamed at the vision, "You whore, you bitch, leave Samantha alone—get away from her!"

The specter of his mother laughed.

How does it feel, Mickey, to be like the women you murdered?

Kellogg stood.

"He's raving at his dead mother again. He did that after I shot him."

Two court deputies restrained Michael in his wheelchair.

One said, "Easy, you're not going anywhere."

Michael looked down and gripped the stumps of his legs.

The damage done by Matt's three fifty-seven Mag was irreparable. Michael's legs were amputated two inches above the knees.

Kellogg stepped around the three lawyers, tapped Michael on the shoulder and whispered,

"Not so tall now are you, Dr. Moran?"

Afterword

During the course of writing this novel, I became involved with my two main characters, Detective Matt Kellogg and Sergeant Ann Beck.

It was apparent they had earned continued employment.

I hope you enjoyed *The Legs Collector.* Kellogg and Beck will be back soon to catch more bad guys.

Ted Tillotson
01/09/2014

* * * *

About the Author

Ted Tillotson lives with his family in Central California and their six rescued feline guests. *Samantha* is a celebrity, alive and well among them.

* * * *

Please visit our Website:

http://www.tedtillotsondragonlairbooks.com

Comments and questions are most welcome.